PENGUIN MODERN CLASSICS

The Great Gatsby

'One of the best novels to have come out of America: concisely expressed, rich in imagination, lyrical in style'
Anthony Powell, *Daily Telegraph*, Books of the Century

'Fitzgerald confronts no less a problem than what might be involved, what might be at stake, in trying to see, and *write*, America itself. *The Great Gatsby* is, I believe, the most perfectly crafted work of fiction to have come out of America' Tony Tanner, in the Introduction

'A modern classic, a key American novel ... For once, Fitzgerald really had won what he wanted: to create, amid the glitter and the gold, "a conscious artistic achievement"'
Malcolm Bradbury, *Mail on Sunday*

'It must be one of the most perfect novels ever written. Technique and tact and moral sensibility are as finely tuned as in any of Turgeniev's great novels, and yet it is as American as Hollywood'
John McGahern, *Irish Times*

'A prose that has the tough delicacy of a garnet'
Brad Leithauser, *The New York Review of Books*

'Lost time and the irretrievability of the past are themes which filter through almost every page of this exquisite novel'
Jason Cowley, *Sunday Times*

F. Scott Fitzgerald was born in 1896 in St Paul, Minnesota, and went to Princeton University, which he left in 1917 to join the army. He was said to have epitomized the Jazz Age, which he himself denied as 'a generation grown up to find all Gods dead, all wars fought, all faiths in man shaken'. In 1920 he married Zelda Sayre. Their traumatic marriage and her subsequent breakdowns became the leading influence in his writing. Among his publications were five novels, *This Side of Paradise*, *The Great Gatsby*, *The Beautiful and Damned*, *Tender is the Night* and *The Last Tycoon* (his last and unfinished work); six volumes of short stories and *The Crack-Up*, a selection of autobiographical pieces. Fitzgerald died suddenly in 1940. After his death *The New York Times* said of him that 'He was better than he knew, for in fact and in the literary sense he invented a "generation" ... he might have interpreted and even guided them, as in their middle years they saw a different and nobler freedom threatened with destruction.'

Tony Tanner was a Fellow of King's College, Cambridge, and Professor of English and American Literature. He taught and travelled extensively in America and Europe. Alongside books on Conrad and Saul Bellow, he published *The Reign of Wonder* (1965), a study of American literature; *City of Words* (1970); *Contract and Transgression: Adultery and the Novel* (1980); *Jane Austen* (1986); *Scenes of Nature, Signs of Men* (1987); *Venice Desired* (1992); and *Henry James and the Art of Non-Fiction* (1995). Tony Tanner died in December 1998.

F. SCOTT FITZGERALD

The Great Gatsby

PENGUIN BOOKS

PENGUIN CLASSICS

Published by the Penguin Group

Penguin Books Ltd, 80 Strand, London WC2R ORL, England

Penguin Group (USA) Inc., 375 Hudson Street, New York, New York 10014, USA

Penguin Group (Canada), 90 Eglinton Avenue East, Suite 700, Toronto, Ontario, Canada M4P 2Y3
(a division of Pearson Penguin Canada Inc.)

Penguin Ireland, 25 St Stephen's Green, Dublin 2, Ireland (a division of Penguin Books Ltd)

Penguin Group (Australia), 250 Camberwell Road, Camberwell, Victoria 3124, Australia
(a division of Pearson Australia Group Pty Ltd)

Penguin Books India Pvt Ltd, 11 Community Centre, Panchsheel Park, New Delhi – 110 017, India

Penguin Group (NZ), 67 Apollo Drive, Rosedale, North Shore 0632, New Zealand
(a division of Pearson New Zealand Ltd)

Penguin Books (South Africa) (Pty) Ltd, 24 Sturdee Avenue,
Rosebank, Johannesburg 2196, South Africa

Penguin Books Ltd, Registered Offices: 80 Strand, London WC2R ORL, England

www.penguin.com

First published 1926
Published in Penguin Books 1950
Reprinted with an Introduction and Notes 1990
Reprinted in Penguin Classics 2000

41

Introduction and Notes copyright © Tony Tanner, 1990
All rights reserved

Printed in England by Clays Ltd, St Ives plc
Set in Monophoto Baskerville

978-0-141-18263-6

www.greenpenguin.co.uk

Penguin Books is committed to a sustainable future
for our business, our readers and our planet.
The book in your hands is made from paper
certified by the Forest Stewardship Council.

Contents

*

Introduction

IT was not always to be called *The Great Gatsby*. In a letter to Maxwell Perkins Fitzgerald wrote: 'I have now decided to stick to the title I put on the book. *Trimalchio in West Egg*' (*circa* 7 November 1924). Trimalchio is, of course, the vulgar social upstart of immense wealth in the *Satyricon* of Petronius – a master of sexual and gastronomic revels who gives a banquet of unimaginable luxury in which, unlike Gatsby who is a non-drinking, self-isolating spectator at his own parties, he most decidedly participates. He is a most literal glutton, while Gatsby stands at a curious distance from all he owns and displays, just as at times he seems to stand back from his own words and consider them appraisingly, as he would the words of another, just as he will display shirts he has never worn, books he has never read, and extend invitations to swim in the pool he has never used.

If Fitzgerald thought of Gatsby as some sort of American Trimalchio thrown up by the riotous licence of the Twenties, he certainly subjected him to some remarkable metamorphoses. (He is called Trimalchio just once in the novel.) But there are some distinct genealogical traces of Gatsby's ancient ancestor. In the *Satyricon* Trimalchio is first mentioned in the conversation of two friends discussing where that night's feast is to be held: 'Do you not know at whose house it is today? Trimalchio, a very rich man, who has a clock and a uniformed trumpeter in his dining-room, to keep telling him how much of his life is lost and gone.' Gatsby's concern with time – its arrestability, recuperability, repeatability – is equally obsessive (as was Fitzgerald's – he seemed to write surrounded by clocks and calendars, said Malcolm Cowley). One of the 'punctilious' Gatsby's few clumsy physical movements nearly results in the breaking of a clock. No doubt in some corner of his being he would like to break them all. The obsession is partly the Trimalchian fear of transience – there is always too little time left: more grandly (if more foolishly), it comes from some deep refusal to accept the linear irreversibility of history. 'Banish the uniformed trumpeter!' would be Gatsby's cry: 'I will not hear his flourish.'

When Gatsby's illustrious forebear Trimalchio is first seen he is 'busily engaged with a green ball. He never picked it up if it touched the ground.' Gatsby comes to orient his life in relation to not a green ball but a green light. 'You always have a green light that burns all night at the end of your dock,' he says to Daisy. Seen from across the water – and everything else – that separates him from Daisy, the green light offers Gatsby a suitably inaccessible focus for his yearning, something to give definition to desire while indefinitely deferring consummation, something to stretch his arms towards, as he does, rather than circle his arms around, as he tries to. The fragile magic of the game depends on keeping the green light at a distance or, we might say, on keeping the green ball in the air. The green ball fallen to the ground would be too much of a reminder of that ineluctable gravity that pulls all things back to the earth, balls and dreams alike. Likewise with the annulment of distance: lights too closely approached may well lose their supernal lustre and revert to unarousing ordinariness. You can wish only on the star you can't reach.

Daisy put her arm through his abruptly, but he seemed absorbed in what he had just said. Possibly it had occurred to him that the colossal significance of that light had now vanished forever. Compared to the great distance that had separated him from Daisy it had seemed as close as a star to the moon. Now it was again a green light on a dock. His count of enchanted objects had diminished by one.

Possibly – and possibly not. Or possibly something different. Certainly in this book there is abroad a hunger for 'enchanted objects', a taste for the 'colossal' and a concern to try to establish and differentiate those times – moments, configurations – when a light might be a star of 'colossal significance' as opposed to just another dock light. This is Nick Carraway's version, and we may wonder whether, in retrospect, the green light didn't shine more brightly for him even than, possibly, for Gatsby.

Of the many exotic courses served at Trimalchio's banquet I want to single out one:

a tray was brought in with a basket on it, in which there was a hen made of wood, spreading out her wings as they do when they are sitting. The music grew loud: two slaves came up and at once began to hunt in the straw . . . Peahen's eggs were pulled out and handed to the guests . . . we took our spoons and hammered at the eggs, which were balls of fine meal. I was on the point of throwing away my portion. I thought a peachick had already formed. But hearing a practised diner say, 'What treasure have we here?' I poked through the shell with my finger and found a fat baccafacio rolled up in spiced yoke of egg.

In October 1922 the Fitzgeralds moved to a house in Great Neck, Long Island, on a peninsula at the foot of Manhasset Bay. Their house was a relatively modest one compared with the opulent summer homes of the seriously rich old American families – the Guggenheims, the Astors, the Van Nostrands, the Pulitzers – on another peninsular across the bay. This, of course, provided Fitzgerald with the basic topography for his novel: new-money Gatsby and no-money Nick on one side of the bay and 'old-money' (but what is 'old' money in America?) Buchanans on the other. In the course of being transposed into the novel the 'Necks' became 'Eggs'.

Twenty miles from the city a pair of enormous eggs, identical in contour and separated only by a courtesy bay, jut out into the most domesticated body of salt water in the Western hemisphere, the great wet barnyard of Long Island Sound. They are not perfect ovals – like the egg in the Columbus story, they are both crushed flat at the contact end – but their physical resemblance must be a source of perpetual wonder to the gulls that fly overhead. To the wingless a more interesting phenomenon is their dissimilarity in every particular except shape and size.

A deep, generating question behind the whole book is just this. As a result of the 'domestication' of the great wild continent discovered by Columbus, what has been hatched from it? What will you find if you take your spoon to the great egg – or is it eggs? – of America? A disgusting, aborted, stunted and still-born thing, fit only to be thrown away? Or a treasure, something special (baccafacio, a small bird, was considered a great delicacy) and marvellous and rare? Are the true products of America as 'dissimilar' as the two Eggs might suggest, with the East Egg Buchanans representing and embodying the sort of devouring, self-pleasuring and hypocritical materialism that the stupendous and ruthless success of nineteenth-century capitalism fostered and enabled, and the West Egg alliance of Nick and Gatsby holding out for the possibility, the necessity, of that something else, something more, which materialism can never satisfy – a nostalgic yearning for some sort of ideal that refuses to concede any absolute dominion to the merely accidental triumphs of the matter and matters of the day? From this point of view, if you went back far enough into American history, then, archetypally, Benjamin Franklin was the driving genius of East Egg, while Jonathan Edwards would be the tutelary spirit of West Egg. This is a comprehensible and justifiable reading of the striking 'dissimilarity' of two of the more striking types hatched by America – Nick himself speaks of 'the bizarre and not a little sinister contrast' between the two Eggs. But, in his own terms, this is the perspective of the 'wingless'. Seen from a sufficiently soaring height, it is their 'resemblance' that is a source of 'perpetual wonder'. This novel will indeed concern itself with dissimilarities and resemblances, and there is no disputing the differing aspirations and fates of the necessarily wingless protagonists. But near the end Nick makes a summarizing statement: 'I see now that this has been a story of the West, after all – Tom and Gatsby, Daisy and Jordan and I, were all Westerners, and perhaps we possessed some deficiency in common which made us subtly unadaptable to Eastern life.' Is there a Buchanan egg and a Gatsby egg? This one an abortion, that one a treasure? Or, allowing for mutations and variations, does the barnyard produce only one animal? It depends, perhaps, on how high you fly, how far away you stand – which points to a crucial matter raised by the book: what is and is not 'distorted' vision? What mixture of proximity and distance affords the best, the most appropriate, perception? How should Nick look at what he has seen?

In 'Winter Dreams', a story Fitzgerald wrote in 1922, Dexter Green is the son of a grocery-store owner in Minnesota, a quick, alert Midwestern lad who is 'unconsciously dictated to by his winter dreams'. The winters are characteristically 'dismal'; the dreams, reactively, turn towards intimations of the 'gorgeous'.

But do not get the impression, because his winter dreams happened to be concerned at first with musings on the rich, that there was anything merely snobbish in the boy. He wanted not association with glittering things and glittering people – he wanted the glittering things themselves. Often he reached out for the best without knowing why he wanted it – and sometimes he ran up against the mysterious denials and prohibitions in which life indulges . . . He made money. It was rather amazing.

Dexter Green is an embryonic Gatsby, and we may note a rather curious distinction on which the narrator insists – 'not association with glittering things and glittering people [but] the glittering things themselves': not association but *possession*. But what would, or could, or might it be to possess a glittering thing or a glittering person? Can the attempt to go beyond association into appropriation ever *not* encounter 'denials and prohibitions'? These are tacit questions that will haunt the later novel.

Like many aspiring children of immigrant parents, Dexter cannot afford to be natural and spontaneous, for that might betray something of his 'peasant' origin. He assembles himself, as he assembles his wardrobe, with care. 'He recognized the value to him of such a mannerism and he had adopted it . . .' This is to build the self from the outside, as it were. The result is successful – 'He made money. It was amazing' – but vulnerable and precarious. The more he gets, the less he has. On one level he simply allows himself to be ensnared and enthralled – and used and abandoned – by a heedless, capricious, whimsical, dizzy, shallow rich girl, Judy Jones, who announces and reveals herself in her smile, 'radiant, blatantly artificial – convincing' (like Gatsby's smile). But she is perhaps no more artificial, self-constructed, than Dexter himself, and we might think of it as a matter of artifice reaching out and responding to artifice. We might, a little, think of Gatsby and Daisy that way too. For Dexter it is simply immaterial whether Judy is sincere or acting when she again takes him up before she again lets him down: 'No illusion as to the world in which she had grown up could cure his illusion as to her desirability.' It might seem as though Judy is the glittering thing-person of his winter dreams, but in a curious way she is a rather incidental figure, almost a function around which he can assemble and indulge a personal lexicon of ineffable glitteringness – 'beautiful', 'romantic', 'gorgeous', 'ecstasy', 'magic of nights', 'fire and loveliness'. His relationship is with these words more than with her. Early in their relationship he says to her: 'I'm nobody . . . My career is largely a matter of futures.' But – and this is the other, more important, level of his relationship with her – his future is largely a matter of pasts.

As a boy Dexter was a caddy. Now a wealthy young man, he can afford caddies of his own when he goes golfing. But he keeps glancing at them, 'trying to catch a gleam or gesture that would remind him of himself, that would lessen the gap which lay between his present and his past'. The greatest intensity of feeling comes not from possession but from intimation of imminent or actual loss. Fairer through fading, writes Emily Dickinson: glittering because going, Fitzgerald implies ('It was a mood of intense appreciation, a sense that, for once, he was magnificently attuned to life and that everything about him was radiating a brightness and a glamour he might never know again'), glittering because the radiance is about to dim. And when it has dimmed and the world seems definitively deglamorized, then emotionally the only future that matters really *is* the past.

The story concludes with an incident that occurs many years after Dexter has resigned himself to the fact that Judy has disappeared from his life. From a chance encounter

Dexter learns that Judy has married a boor who 'drinks and runs around' – shades, or rather intimations, of Tom Buchanan – that she probably loves him and that her looks have gone: squalor and degradation all round, in other words. And now Dexter feels a further loss:

The dream was gone. Something had been taken from him. In a sort of panic he pushed the palms of his hands into his eyes and tried to bring up a picture of the waters lapping on Sherry Island and the moonlit veranda, and gingham on the golf-links and the dry sun and the gold color of her neck's soft down. And her mouth damp to his kisses and her eyes plaintive with melancholy and her freshness like new fine linen in the morning. Why, these things were no longer in the world! They had existed and they existed no longer.

For the first time in years the tears were streaming down his face. But they were for himself now. He did not care about mouth and eyes and moving hands. He wanted to care, and he could not care. For he had gone away and he could never go back any more. The gates were closed, the sun was gone down, and there was no beauty but the grey beauty of steel that withstands all time. Even the grief he could have borne was left behind in the country of illusion, of youth, of the richness of life, where his winter dreams had flourished.

'Long ago,' he said, 'long ago, there was something in me, but now that thing is gone. Now that thing is gone, that thing is gone. I cannot cry. I cannot care. That thing will come back no more.'

This is a very young man's prose, and such a plangent lament for not only loss but also the loss of the sense of loss comes across as barely post-adolescent. I quote the passage at length partly to suggest how much Fitzgerald had to excise or, let us say, otherwisely to absorb before he could achieve the perfect tonal command of *The Great Gatsby*. One feels here, as so often with Fitzgerald's earlier writing, that the author has very imperfectly distanced himself from the emotional turbulence of his own autobiography. He needed to put something, someone, between himself and his writing if he was to avoid ending up in a sentimental cul-de-sac. The passage also reveals, in inchoate form, an insight that I believe is absolutely central to Fitzgerald's work; namely, that the American Dream – whatever one takes that phrase to mean – is not an index of aspiration but a function of deprivation. But, as Gatsby shows, there can be another turn to the screw. Dexter sinks rather wallowingly into his sense that his future is largely a matter of the past. Gatsby too recognizes this, but he will not let the issue rest there, for he insists that the past can be turned into the matter of the future by someone who has made so much, including himself. And begone the uniformed trumpeter!

'It might interest you to know that a story of mine, called "Absolution" . . . was intended to be a picture of Gatsby's early life, but that I cut it because I preferred to preserve the sense of mystery' (to John Jamieson, 15 April 1934). How much the stature of *The Great Gatsby* depends on what Fitzgerald cut out is a matter to which I will return. Here we might consider what he had initially decided to write in as a crucial episode in Gatsby's childhood.

Eleven-year-old Rudolph Miller – young Gatsby – has rebelled against his 'ineffectual' father and been forced to attend confession, during the course of which he lies. He has come to tell his story to Father Schwartz, to whom he admits that he is guilty of 'not believing I was the son of my parents' (a fantasy Fitzgerald himself owned to – 'that I wasn't the son of my parents, but a son of a king, a king who ruled the whole world' – exactly Freud's 'Family Romance'). For the dismalness of being Rudolph Miller he substitutes the gorgeousness of imagining himself to be Blatchford Sarmenington. 'When he became Blatchford Sarmenington a suave nobility flowed from him. Blatchford Sarmenington lived in great sweeping triumphs.' But he keeps the lie in the confessional to himself; indeed, the secret lie, like the secret fantasy, comes to constitute his essential self.

An invisible line had been crossed, and he had become aware of his isolation – aware that it applied not only to those moments when he was Blatchford Sarmenington but that it applied to all his inner life. Hitherto such phenomena as 'crazy' ambitions and petty shames and fears had been but private reservations, unacknowledged before the throne of his official soul. Now he realized unconsciously that his private reservations were himself – and all the rest a garnished front and a conventional flag. The pressure of his environment had driven him into the lonely secret world of adolescence.

Effectively, the boy is rejecting his biological father and rebelling against his spiritual father, as if to say: most importantly, essentially, I *am* my 'private reservations' – my refusals, my repudiations, my fantasies, and, yes, my guilty lies. If you want *me*, don't ask for Rudolph Miller. Ask for Blatchford Sarmenington. Ask for Jay Gatsby.

But the most interesting aspect of the story is the curiously disturbed state of Father Schwartz. (I am not concerned here speculatively to relate this figure to such people as Father Sigourney Webster Fay, who undoubtedly had an important influence on Catholic Fitzgerald. André le Vot has done this well in his biography, *F. Scott Fitzgerald*, Penguin, 1983.) At the start the Father is clearly disturbed by 'the hot madness of four o'clock' – a 'terrible dissonance' made up of the rustle of Swedish girls, yellow lights, sweet smells and the Dakota wheat that is 'terrible to look on'. After he has listened to the boy's story the Father breaks into a trembling, monologue, which is distracted, if not deranged.

'When a lot of people get together in the best places things go glimmering . . . The thing is to have a lot of people in the centre of the world, wherever that happens to be. Then . . . things go glimmering . . . my theory is that when a whole lot of people get together in the best places things go glimmering all the time . . . Did you ever see an amusement park? . . . It's a thing like a fair, only much more glittering. Go to one at night and stand a little way off from it in a dark place – under dark trees. You'll see a big wheel made of lights turning in the air, and a long slide shooting boats down into the water. A band playing somewhere, and a smell of peanuts – and everything will twinkle. But it won't remind you of anything, you see. It will all just hang out there in the night like a colored balloon – like a big yellow lantern on a pole . . . But don't get up close . . . because if you do you'll only feel the heat and the sweat and the life.'

These are, in fact, the dying words of the Father, and we may take them as expressing his delirious regret for all the sexuality and glamour, the heat and light, that, as a celibate priest, he has repressed and kept his distance from. But as the expression of an eager, tremulous excitement aroused by the thought, the sense, the apprehension, of some kind of glittering glimmeringness – sexual and immaterial, incandescent and transcendent – generated by a forgathering of the beautiful and the blessed (or damned), the glamorous and the gorgeous, at a mythical, unreachable 'centre' – a heavenly amusement park – these words testify to a confused and inarticulate longing – for what? The light that never was on land or sea? – that is somewhere at the heart of Fitzgerald's work, to be indulged or dealt with as the case may be. It is a sort of uninstructed neo-Platonism gone somewhat berserk amid the endless wheat, the untouchable girls and the occasional brilliances of an otherwise dreary and dismal Middle West.

But there is a crucial difference between Dexter Green's

desire to possess the glittering things and Father Schwartz's advice to stand back from the glimmering light, and it lies precisely in the latter's apprehension that getting too close might be dangerous, ruinous to the vision of earthly (and heavenly?) delights. Rudolph Sarmenington Gatsby is partly Green and partly Schwartz (and André le Vot has shown how careful Fitzgerald was with his colour ascriptions – of which more later). He thinks he can possess – repossess – the glittering girl. Indeed, he attempts to make his house into a glimmering, glamorous centre to attract her: 'Your place looks like the World's Fair,' says Nick to him, seeing his house 'lit from tower to cellar'. We know that as a boy Fitzgerald was very struck by the brilliance of the Pan-American Exposition in Buffalo in 1901, where there was 'a Goddess of Light whose glow could be seen as far away as Niagara Fall' (le Vot, p. 27), and Gatsby also uses the magic of electricity (he is after all a dedicated reader of Benjamin Franklin) to signal what he hopes and believes is a more than electrical glimmering. But for all the dedication of his quest for repossession, re-enactment, he can enjoy, indeed experience, his desire and his dreams better at a distance. He is not really at home in the light he has himself turned on and is more usually to be found, as the good Father advised, standing 'a little way off from it in a dark place'. When he does 'get up close' and encounters 'the heat and the sweat and the life' – particularly in the form of Tom Buchanan, the crude but confident snobbery of his discourse, the class-supported brashness of his hypocrisy, the brutality of his 'cruel body' – Gatsby is indeed destroyed. The Green is gone: all is Schwar(t)z.

Fitzgerald planned *The Great Gatsby* during the summer of 1922 but wrote it during the summer of 1924 while living on the Riviera (he – crucially – revised the proofs in Rome during January and February of the following year). This is just when Nick Carraway is writing *his* book about his summer with Gatsby of two years earlier – but he is back in the Midwest. Fitzgerald has introduced a narrator between himself and his omniscient indulgences. Fitzgerald's book is Nick's book, but Nick is not Fitzgerald, however many refracted biographical fragments we may imagine we can discern. Nick is a character, of confessedly limited literary abilities (he has written only 'a series of very solemn and obvious editorials for the Yale News'), and while Nick is trying to write Gatsby, we are also reading Nick.

Among writers he admired Fitzgerald had plenty of precedents for the introduction of a narrator. Henry James, discussing how a writer can extract maximum significance from his material, stresses the value of sometimes choosing a particular kind of narrator: 'By so much as the affair matters *for* some such individual, by so much do we get the best there is of it.' He points out the need for 'a reflecting and colouring medium' and adds:

We want it clear, goodness knows, but we also want it thick, and we get the thickness in the human consciousness that entertains and records, that amplifies and interprets it . . . prodigies, when they come straight, come with an effect imperilled; they keep all their character, on the other hand, by looming through some other history – the indispensable history of somebody's *normal* relation to something.

Gatsby is a self-styled, self-styling 'prodigy' of some sort – prodigiously criminal, prodigiously romantic – and Nick is, or so he would insist, nothing if not 'normal', though he would add, 'abnormally honest'. Gatsby certainly looms – looms and fades, looms and fades – through Nick's 'history', and Nick certainly 'amplifies and interprets' – amplifies, we might come to think, quite inordinately.

Joseph Conrad made some of his most important innovations in the art of fiction through the introduction and deployment of his sailor-narrator Marlow, particularly as Marlow tries to put together a narrative that will somehow make sense of Lord Jim. Was Jim a coward or an idealist? Coward *and* idealist? What is the significance, what are the implications, for 'us' – us sailors, us British, us decent and reliable white Westerners – of his aspirations and failures, his dreams and defections? Marlow has a lot invested in Jim, and in his attempts at narrative recuperation and evaluation. For surely Jim was 'one of us'. And yet . . . *Mutatis mutandis*, much of this is paralleled in the relationship of the bondsman-narrator Nick with the enigmatic Gatsby. Is Gatsby criminal or romantic? Criminal *and* romantic? What are the implications for us Americans of his grandiose plans and their dubious grounding? Of his glamorous dreams and the 'foul dust' that, inevitably, 'floated in the wake of his dreams' and in his wretched waking from them? Nick has a lot – a *lot* – invested in Gatsby and in his own written attempt at the retrieval and, indeed, elegiac celebration of the man. 'They're a rotten crowd . . . You're worth the whole damn bunch put together.' So they are, and so – Nick can make us feel – he is. For surely America can produce something better than Buchanans, more splendid than Carraways. And yet . . .

The extent to which the book *is* Nick's version can hardly be overstressed. To be sure, he assembles his material from different sources. In addition to his own memory, there are documents, like the youthful Gatsby's copy of *Hopalong Cassidy* with its Franklinesque 'SCHEDULE' on the flyleaf and Nick's own infinitely suggestive list of Gatsby's guests of the summer of 1922, which is now 'disintegrating at its folds', suggesting perhaps the inevitable disintegration of other depositories of time – including the memory of the narrator. Then there is the long oral account of the first phase of the relationship between Gatsby and Daisy, given to him by Jordan Baker, and the accounts of Gatsby's early life, Dan Cody and the war years given to him by Gatsby himself during the doomed and hopeless vigil after the night of the fatal road accident. But it is Nick who transcribes these accounts; how much he may be requoting his sources and how much translating them – transforming, embellishing, amplifying, *re*wording – we can never know. By the conventions of fictional narrative, if a narrator gives the words of another character in quotation marks, then these were indeed the very words: he is allowed a (slightly implausible) perfect recall. Now, by my admittedly rough count, about 4 per cent of the book is in Gatsby's own words, and it is revealing to discover that Fitzgerald considerably *reduced* the amount of direct speech given to Gatsby in the draft of the novel. For example: ' "Jay Gatsby!" he cried suddenly in a ringing voice. "There goes the great Jay Gatsby. That's what people are going to say – wait and see." ' With such outbursts Gatsby would too crudely and unequivocally have announced and revealed himself. By systematic deletion Fitzgerald makes Gatsby a far more shadowy, less knowable, more ultimately elusive figure. Instead we get more of Nick's hypothesizing, speculating, imagining – and perhaps suppressing, recasting, fantasizing.

His account is constantly marked by such words and phrases as the following: 'I suppose', 'I suspect', 'I think'; 'possibly', 'probably', 'perhaps'; 'I've heard it said', 'he seemed to say', 'there must have been', 'I have an idea that', 'I always had the impression'. 'As though' and 'as if' (used over sixty times) constantly introduce his own transforming similies and metamorphosing metaphors into the account. 'Possibly it occurred to him . . .' – and possibly it didn't. We can never know. What we do know is that it occurs to Nick. However we assess or respond to 'Gatsby' – 'the man who gives his name to this book', as Nick rather interestingly scruples to spell out – we should always remember that we are responding to what Nick has made of him. From Gatsby's first appearance ('a man of about my own age') to the moment after Gatsby's death, when Nick is mistaken for Gatsby by a telephone caller and he subsequently experiences 'a feeling of defiance, of scornful solidarity between Gatsby and me against them all', we are aware of a strong tendency on Nick's part to identify with Gatsby as well as to make him a hero. This is why it is so important for him to be able to feel that the account Gatsby gives of his life is 'all true', why he is glad to have 'one of those renewals of complete faith in him that I'd experienced before'. Outside business hours, when he is mainly moving around the money that money makes, Nick invests everything in Gatsby – *his* Gatsby.

Nick reveals, or portrays, himself as the very antithesis of Gatsby, as one of Fitzgerald's 'Sad Young Men'. (There is some resemblance here to the emotionally timid Lockwood putting together his narrative account of the passionate Heathcliff in *Wuthering Heights*.)

I knew the other clerks and young bond-salesmen by their first names, and lunched with them in dark, crowded restaurants on little pig sausages and mashed potatoes and coffee. I even had a short affair with a girl who lived in Jersey City and worked in the accounting department, but her brother began throwing mean looks in my direction, so when she went on her vacation in July I let it blow quietly away.

When it comes to emotional or sexual involvements, what he doesn't let blow quietly away he blows away himself – as he did an earlier 'engagement', as he does Jordan Baker. He is a self-isolating voyeur (characteristically, at one point: 'I was conscious of wanting to look squarely at everyone, and yet to avoid all eyes'. In this he is like the sexually anxious Isabel Archer in Henry James's *Portrait of a Lady*, who wants 'to see but not to feel'.). When it comes to the erotic, life in fantasy is safer than real life.

I liked to walk up Fifth Avenue and pick out romantic women from the crowd and imagine that in a few minutes I was going to enter into their lives, and no one would ever know or disapprove. Sometimes, in my mind, I followed them to their apartments on the corners of hidden streets, and they turned and smiled back at me before they faded through a door into warm darkness. At the enchanted metropolitan twilight I felt a haunting loneliness sometimes, and felt it in others – poor young clerks who loitered in front of windows waiting until it was time for a solitary restaurant dinner – young clerks in the dusk, wasting the most poignant moments of night and life.

As against this – and this is surely 'dismal' – it is perhaps not surprising that Nick looks hungrily for signs of the 'gorgeous' – one of his favoured words – in the life and style of Jay Gatsby. He, he implies, is everything that Gatsby is not. 'Thirty – the promise of a decade of loneliness, a thinning list of single men to know, a thinning brief-case of enthusiasm, thinning hair' – thinning everything. As opposed to, and perhaps to compensate for, these gathering attenuations and impoverishments, Gatsby surely embodies more flourishing and fecund, less emotionally etiolated and self-retractive, possibilities and potentialities.

Nick is a spectator in search of a performer. He sees Gatsby in gestural terms: 'If personality is an unbroken series of successful gestures, then there was something gorgeous about him, some heightened sensitivity to the promises of life . . .' No little pig sausages and mashed potatoes for Gatsby, not anyway in Nick's version. His own preferred position, on the other hand, observational and non-gestural, is at the margins. At the first party in New York his instinct is to 'get out', but he keeps getting 'entangled' and 'pulled back'. 'Yet high over the city our line of yellow windows must have contributed their share of human secrecy to the casual watcher in the darkening streets, and I saw him too, looking up and wondering. I was within and without, simultaneously enchanted and repelled by the inexhaustible variety of life.' Whether he knows it or not, he is quoting Whitman almost verbatim ('in and out of the game, watching and wondering at it'), and 'wonder' – the instinct, the need, the capacity for it – is as important for Nick as it has been for so many American writers. Wondering *at* often involves and requires distance and betokens a disinclination, if not an incapacity, for participation – a distaste for, if not a fear of, all that sweat and heat and life, and one senses that Nick, for all his regrets, somehow prefers the role of 'casual watcher in the darkening streets'. A difference from Whitman is his almost equal capacity for 'repulsion'. When Nick is not enchanted, he is likely to be starting to feel disgusted. For all the seeming reasonableness and the proffered impartiality of his tone, his Gatsby book is generated by a tendency to move between these extremes. It is a very American oscillation.

At the start Nick puts himself forward, fairly explicitly, as someone with an above-average 'sense of the fundamental decencies' which now manifests itself as a wish for 'the world to be in uniform and at a sort of moral attention forever'. Could it be that he is briefly attracted to Jordan Baker because, with her male-like ('slender and small-breasted') body and 'erect carriage', she looks like 'a young cadet'? Be that as it may, he clearly has something of an authoritarian character with a developed instinct for discipline, hygiene and tidiness, as he readily admits (it is part of his engagingness as a narrator). At times he is, I won't say priggish, but a touch prim. He prefers life in some sort of uniform. Indeed, on one occasion, at a peculiarly embarrassing moment at the Buchanans', he admits, 'my own instinct was to phone immediately for the police'. When he decides to make a clean break with Jordan Baker, he explains in housekeeping terms: 'I wanted to leave things in order and not just trust that obliging and indifferent sea to sweep my refuse away.' (We may note, however, that he didn't mind some unidentified element blowing an earlier involvement away.) Nick's manifest dislike of 'refuse', a slightly obsessive compulsion to clean things up, reveals itself on a number of occasions, of which I will mention two.

At the first, drunken, party in New York, as things are disintegrating into increasingly messy incoherence, even though this is one of the two times in his life Nick has allowed himself to get drunk, his fastidious instincts do not fail him: 'Mr McKee was asleep on a chair with his fists clenched in his lap, like a photograph of a man of action. Taking out my handkerchief I wiped from his cheek the spot of dried lather that had worried me all the afternoon.' Shortly after this Tom Buchanan breaks Myrtle's nose, and the party collapses into terminal chaos. But that's the Buchanans for you. 'They were careless people . . . they smashed up things and creatures and then retreated back into their money or their vast carelessness, or whatever it was that kept them together, and let other people clear up the mess they had made . . .' Tom brutally spills blood; Nick meticulously wipes off a speck of shaving lather, a tiny fragment of that matter-out-of-place which we call dirt. As well as having a politely controlled instinct to be society's moral policeman, Nick also has it in him to be one of its janitors.

The most graphic example of this is what is effectively the last gesture he makes before leaving the East for good. He returns for one more look at Gatsby's 'huge incoherent failure of a house': 'On the white steps an obscene word, scrawled by some boy with a piece of brick, stood out clearly in the moonlight, and I erased it, drawing my shoe raspingly along the stone.' Part of his 'fundamental decency' no doubt, and one can readily share and approve of his instinctive distaste for disrespectful defacement and profanation. But this gesture of 'erasure' has a farther-reaching aptness and suggestiveness. While it might be too much to say that Gatsby's actual career (we'll set aside his dreams for the moment) is itself an 'obscenity', his career, money and identity are clearly grounded in a series of more or less dirty, more or less criminal activities. There are signs that he more than once tries to signal as much to Nick and make him confront and recognize this fact. Nick always refuses: he prefers to 'erase' whatever might be the 'dirty' side of the story, either by omission, denial, over-writing, reinterpretation, or by transformation, though, of course – it is part of the brilliance of the book – we keep getting glimpses and intimations of what he is trying to keep, and write, out. (For instance, he makes of the early relationship of Gatsby and Daisy a romantic, poetic affair, and it is only subsequently he learns that he took her 'ravenously and unscrupulously'.) For the purposes of his book, Nick prefers to concentrate on the figure of the hopeful, hapless dreamer in the pink suit. At one point he informs us that he is putting down what he has subsequently learned about Gatsby's early life – Dan Cody and so on – 'to clear this set of misconceptions away', these being the wild and silly rumours that circulated around the enigmatic Gatsby. He certainly clears these away, but it is possible that he clears away – cleans up – much more as well. We take what he tells us about Dan Cody as faithfully transcribed. But what about this as a compressed account of Gatsby's adolescence?

But his heart was in a constant, turbulent riot. The most grotesque and fantastic conceits haunted him in his bed at night. A universe of ineffable gaudiness spun itself out in his brain while the clock ticked on the washstand and the moon soaked with wet light his tangled clothes upon the floor. Each night he added to his fancies . . . these reveries provided an outlet for his imagination; they were a satisfactory hint of the unreality of reality, a promise that the rock of the world was founded on a fairy's wing.

Who is this? Gatsby? Or Nick? Or should we by now simply say Nick Gatsby? Gatsby tries to use the light of the moon (dream, imagination) to defeat the tick of the clock (history, irreversibility), but Nick also favours moonlight, and he tries to prevent its being fouled and contaminated by the inscribed obscenities of the real. Gatsby provides Nick with an outlet for *his* imagination – he is Nick's reverie of 'gaudiness' – and seems to offer him a satisfactory, or almost satisfactory, hint of 'the unreality of reality'. The 'rock of the world' is hard and breaks fragile, vulnerable things, as do Tom Buchanan's fists and words; Nick prefers to imagine Gatsby imagining the world's rock impossibly taking second place to the fairy's wing – as if anything could be *founded* on fairy, grounded in gossamer, as we might say. The more general point is that it is invariably impossible to know when Nick is adding or subtracting, to establish when he is amplifying or erasing, to guess when he is simply fantasizing or, more imaginatively, empathetically eliding. On page one he tells us that, perhaps because of his perceived inclination to 'reserve all judgements' (he unreserves them in this book), he has often been the recipient of 'intimate revelations of young men' and that he has noted that the terms in which they express these 'are usually plagiaristic and marred by obvious suppressions'. We may thus be alerted early to the possibility that his own 'intimate revelations' – perhaps *all* such revelations – will also and inevitably be marked by these characteristics as well. Nick may be one of the few honest people he has ever known, but Jordan Baker may not be all wrong when, by way of farewell, she tells him that, in his way, he is 'another bad driver'.

Let me put it another way. When Nick first drives out to Wilson's garage in the valley of ashes, this is his response: 'The interior was unprosperous and bare; the only car visible was the dust-covered wreck of a Ford which crouched in a dim garage. It had occurred to me that this shadow of a garage must be a blind, and that sumptuous and romantic apartments were concealed overhead . . .' Nick cannot tolerate the thought of confronting a reality that is *merely* poor and bare, dust-covered and wrecked. There *must* be more than that, a whole hidden dimension of sumptuousness and romance for which the manifest impoverishment and degradation of the apparitional, the given, are simply a misleading 'blind', a deceptive mask. But the untranscended bareness of the garage in the valley of ashes is real enough and conceals nothing except a squalid affair. In the valley of ashes what you see is what you get. The phantasmal 'sumptuous and romantic apartments' are provided by the more generous architecture of his imagination, a function at once of his deprivation and desire. So that rather than thinking of repression and plagiarism, we might more accurately speak of erasure and supplementation provided by his imagination, and of course his writing.

I want to focus on three examples of the 'supplementation' evident in some of the key lines and passages of the book. One of the many master-strokes in Fitzgerald's almost uncannily sure-handed, almost inspired, deletions and additions to the galley proofs of the novel was the insertion of Gatsby's famous comment, 'Her voice is full of money.' Nick's comment and gloss are remarkable and remarkably revealing: 'That was it. I'd never understood before. It was full of money – that was the inexhaustible charm that rose and fell in it, the jingle of it, the cymbal's song of it . . . High in a white palace the king's daughter, the golden girl . . .' Nick is off on a reverie of unsyntactical free association. But one might legitimately feel that that is not it at all, and jingles and symbols and king's daughters are not at all to the point. Gatsby is more probably intimating that Daisy is a very expensive product, that it takes a great deal of money to make and maintain such a product, that she veritably *breathes* money, and signalling his awareness of this. Nick prefers to pass over the material base, 'the rock of the world', and take wing into fairyland. Whatever Gatsby meant by his fine, enigmatic statement, it is Nick who, confessedly, from the first finds Daisy's voice 'thrilling', full of not money but 'excitement' and 'promise'. When he speculates – 'I think that voice held him most, with its fluctuating, feverish warmth, because it couldn't be over-dreamed' – we may perhaps be more certain that it was the voice that held *Nick* most because it certainly can be over-dreamed, as he later shows (in the passage quoted above). As well as being something of a disenchanted moralist, Nick reveals himself to be quite a committed 'over-dreamer'. It is by no means a wholly unsympathetic characteristic.

At one point, when Nick has entirely taken over Gatsby's story, which he is telling in confident third-person indirect discourse, he indulges himself with this lyrical account:

Out of the corner of his eye Gatsby saw that the blocks of the sidewalks really formed a ladder and mounted to a secret place above the trees – he could climb to it *if he climbed alone*, and once there he could suck on the pap of life, gulp down the incomparable milk of wonder.

His heart beat faster as Daisy's white face came up to his own. He knew that when he kissed this girl, and forever wed his unutterable visions to her perishable breath, his mind would never *romp again like the mind of God*. So he waited, listening for a moment longer to *the tuning fork that had been struck upon a star*. Then he kissed her. At his lips' touch she blossomed for him like a flower and the incarnation was complete.

Through all he said, even through his appalling sentimentality, I was reminded of something – an elusive rhythm, a fragment of lost words, that I had heard somewhere a long time ago. For a moment a phrase tried to take shape in my mouth and my lips parted like a dumb man's, as though there was more struggling upon them than a wisp of startled air. But they made no sound, and what I had almost remembered was uncommunicable forever. [My italics.]

Perhaps the first question to ask is: *whose* appalling sentimentality? Gatsby, we learn, took Daisy 'unscrupulously and ravenously' and perhaps did not have much about 'unutterable visions' and 'perishable breath' on his mind. Tuning forks on stars are the stuff of a hundred popular songs, and not the best ones at that, and they must be humming in Nick's mind. It is surely the confirmed bachelor Nick who feels that for maximum gratification it is better to climb alone, just as there is surely something regressive about the thought of climbing to a secret place to suck wondermilk from the pap of life. (There will be more to say about paps of life and milk of wonder.) This hint of nostalgia for the pleasures of childhood is extended by the use of the word 'romp', and to compare the anarchic and egotistical freedoms and indulgences of the nursery with the mind of God is an audacious attempt to give a religious slant to these regressive yearnings. Whatever Gatsby was thinking when he was courting Daisy, he surely wasn't thinking all this, was he?

The question gains force once we discover that at one stage Fitzgerald added to the galley proofs six pages that made it very clear that the 'appalling sentimentality' *was* centrally Gatsby's. There is a dialogue between the two men in which, for instance, when Nick sympathetically says that Daisy is 'a pretty satisfactory incarnation of anything', Gatsby says, with far too much clear-eyed resignation: 'She is . . . but it's a little like loving a place where you've once been happy.' Even more ruinous would have been the insertion, or retention, of this self-analytical confession from Gatsby: ' "But the truth is I'm empty and I guess people feel it . . . Daisy's all I've got left from a world that was so wonderful that when I think of it I feel sick all over." He looked round with wild regret. "Let me sing you a song – I want to sing you a song . . . the sound of it makes me happy. But I don't sing it often because I'm afraid I'll use it up." ' The song, something he wrote when he was fourteen – fourteen! This man's future really is the past – is quoted in full and amply justifies Nick's comment on his 'appalling sentimentality'. All this disastrous, self-reducing explicitness was, unerringly as ever, cut. Fitzgerald left in only the last paragraph of the passage quoted above. The deletions increase the unknowability of Gatsby, while the retained paragraph suggests that whatever chord of nostalgia, memory and desire the figure of Gatsby might touch, it remains irrecoverable, uncommunicable, inarticulable – lost (like, indeed, the American Dream). And it is no longer clear where the sentimentality, and the regressive impulses, are coming from. We sense only that they are in the air – in the air of the writing. And the writing is Nick's.

Perhaps the following is the most famous paragraph of the book.

I suppose he'd had the name ready for a long time, even then. His parents were shiftless and unsuccessful farm people – his imagination had never really accepted them as his parents at all. The truth was that Jay Gatsby of West Egg, Long Island, sprang from his Platonic conception of himself. He was a son of God – a phrase which, if it means anything, means just that – and he must be about His Father's business, the service of a vast, vulgar, and meretricious beauty. So he invented just the sort of Jay Gatsby that a seventeen-year-old boy would be likely to invent, and to this conception he was faithful to the end.

He supposes – but goes on to declare 'the truth'. This 'truth' that he asserts about Gatsby – and that audaciously, if not blasphemously, invokes the authority of both Plato and God – springs from the fact that Gatsby never accepted his parents as his parents. Like Rudolph Miller, like Fitzgerald himself, and like many another self-parenting figure in the history of America, life and literature. The reasons for this determination or instinct to reject or deny the parents – more specifically it is mainly a repudiation of the authority, prescriptive and proscriptive, of fathers, biological or Founding – range from the practical (slough off your immigrant identity) to the ideological (throw off the coercive, restrictive, predetermining weight of the past). I am not so foolish as to suggest that the instinct to deny parents is peculiarly American – after all, Freud's 'Family Romance' would suggest that it is more or less universal; but there is no doubt that it is felt with special force in America. Moreover, it receives specific cultural endorsement and support. Indeed, it is embedded in American literature as something of an obligation and a prerequisite for the achievement of an 'American' identity. 'Our age is retrospective. It builds the sepulchres of the fathers.' So starts Emerson's first work, the enormously influential 1836 essay 'Nature'. Building sepulchres to the fathers is just exactly what Americans should not be doing, as far as Emerson was concerned: fathers (and fathering countries, like England) are to be forgotten. 'Why should not we also enjoy an original relation to the universe? . . . The sun shines today also . . . There are new lands, new men, new thoughts.' Emerson, and many writers who followed him, stressed self-reliance, self-sculpting, self-architecturing, self-inventing – the metaphors are many. The American 'self-made man' had a prestigious legitimation and encouragement. (*The Self-Made Man* by Greeley appeared in 1862.) Jay Gatsby is a very American young man.

But what about God and Plato? Here I must bring together a few passages to point up a particular characteristic of Nick's vocabulary. Near the end, after summarizing the legal and logistical business that followed the shooting of Gatsby, Nick writes: 'But all this part of it seemed remote and unessential.' Even nearer the end he refers to the 'inessential houses' melting away as the moon rises. Between 'un–' and 'in–', as prefixes expressing negation, there is not much difference: either way, not essential, not of the essence. When Nick imagines Gatsby's state of mind as he awaits a phone call from Daisy, and instead receives a visit from Wilson, he becomes quite metaphysical.

I have an idea that Gatsby himself didn't believe it would come, and perhaps he no longer cared. If that was true he must have felt that he had lost the old warm world, paid a high price for living too long with a single dream. He must have looked up at an unfamiliar sky through frightening leaves and shivered as he found what a grotesque thing a rose is and how raw the sunlight was upon the scarcely created grass. A new world, material without being real, where poor ghosts, breathing dreams like air, drifted fortuitously about . . . like that ashen, fantastic figure gliding toward him through the amorphous trees.

'Material without being real' is a straightforward neo-Platonic distinction (the really Real is to be found, or sought, in the realm of unchanging Ideas or Forms). But Nick is transcribing something more like a moment of existential panic, such as is described by Sartre in *La Nausée* when Roquentin, staring at a tree, experiences a terrible sense of the sheer, absurd, horrible gratuitousness of things – a negative epiphany in which matter without meaning turns monstrous, 'frightening', 'grotesque'. To Gatsby, thinks Nick, this is how the world empty and bereft of his dream of Daisy must have appeared: to Nick, perhaps, this is how the world without Gatsby, and thus without Gatsby's tenacious but doomed dreaming, is beginning to look.

This passage is followed by Nick's description of what he saw when they hurried down to the pool in which Gatsby had been shot. 'There was a faint, barely perceptible movement of the water as the fresh flow from one end urged its way towards the drain at the other. With little ripples that were hardly the shadows of waves, the laden mattress moved irregularly down the pool. A small gust of wind that scarcely corrugated the surface was enough to disturb its *accidental* course with its *accidental* burden.' (My italics.) In a book in which there is much bad driving and so many accidents, including the fatal one that precipitates the catastrophic conclusion, the italicized word is highly appropriate. But the deliberate repetition serves to remind us of the more general, philosophical meaning of the word – exactly, not essential. Nick tells us that when Gatsby met Daisy he found himself in her house by a 'colossal accident': wittingly or not, he has chosen an ominously apt phrase, for their relationship also ends with and by a 'colossal accident' of a more horribly literal kind. Was it all an 'accidental' matter, from beginning to end? Now that Gatsby is dead, it would seem that Nick feels he is confronting a wholly contingent world. Inessential. Unessential. When Tom Buchanan, confident that he has exposed Gatsby as a common criminal, contemptuously dismisses Gatsby and Daisy to drive back together, Nick writes: 'They were gone, without a word, snapped out, made accidental . . .' In a world dominated by Buchanans, pure contingency reigns: frightening, grotesque.

During the reunion of Gatsby and Daisy, recounted at the very centre of the book, according to Nick Gatsby sometimes 'stared around at his possessions in a dazed way, as though in her actual and astounding presence none of it was any longer real'. More filtered neo-Platonism with the higher 'actual' (ideal) displacing and devaluing, indeed effectively de-materializing, the merely materially real. No wonder that Gatsby feels momentarily ontologically all at sea. 'Once he nearly toppled down a flight of stairs.' Where Gatsby is concerned, just what is 'real', and where it is to be found, becomes problematical, surprising. There is a marvellous scene in which the slightly drunk guest with the owl-eyed spectacles, whom Nick and Jordan come across in Gatsby's library, begins to eulogize admiringly.

'What do you think about that?' he demanded impetuously.

'About what?'

He waved his hand toward the book-shelves.

'About that. As a matter of fact you needn't bother to ascertain. I ascertained. They're real.'

'The books?'

He nodded.

'Absolutely real – have pages and everything. I thought they'd be a nice durable cardboard. Matter of fact, they're absolutely real. Pages and – Here! Lemme show you.'

Taking our scepticism for granted, he rushed to the bookcases and returned with Volume One of the *Stoddard Lectures*.

'See!' he cried triumphantly. 'It's a bona-fide piece of printed matter. It fooled me. This fella's a regular Belasco. It's a triumph. What thoroughness! What realism! Knew when to stop, too – didn't cut the pages, But what do you want? What do you expect?'

David Belasco was a Broadway producer famous for the realism of his sets. Gatsby theatricalizes himself and his surroundings, and it is often difficult to know which parts of the show – how much of what he shows – is 'real'. It can happen that just where you expect, or suspect, the most obvious artifice and artificiality – in the books in his library, say, or in his embarrassingly clichéd account of his life, which does not so much challenge credulity as defy it – you find you have stumbled into authenticity: 'They're real . . . Absolutely real', 'Then it was all true.' Perhaps, then, we should look for the 'real' where we might least expect it, ready in the case of Gatsby (perhaps in the case of America) to discern merit in meretriciousness, value in the vulgar.

It is worth pausing briefly on the word 'absolutely'. It is the first word Jordan Baker says in the opening scene, so seemingly *à propos* of nothing it makes Nick jump; she is also, she says, 'absolutely in training'. 'Is this absolutely where you live, my dearest one?' Daisy gaily asks Nick as they approach Gatsby's house; and on another occasion she indeed calls Nick 'an absolute rose' – a less appropriate description of the somewhat prim and shrinking wallflower, Nick, it would be hard to imagine. Clearly, 'absolutely' has here become one of those empty words that make up part of the bantering argot of a particular social set, or indeed period, and is conceptually meaningless. So we should not lean too heavily on the word, nor hear too much in it, when the man in the owl-eyed spectacles remarks in some amazement on the absolute reality of Gatsby's books. But clearly there is in Nick's narrative discourse a hunger for something absolute, something essential, something that is Real in a more than contingent, material, 'accidental' way. There is a theological and metaphysical yearning – confused and vestigial thought it may be – mixed up with Nick's desire to believe in some form or figure of gorgeousness to offset the dismalness with which he is all too, and now increasingly, familiar, which is why he deliberately and daringly invokes God and Plato in his celebratory elegy of the sentimental American criminal in the pink rag of a suit. At the end of Thomas Pynchon's *The Crying of Lot 49* the heroine, Oedipa Maas, has come to a personal crisis that also involves no less than the meaning of America itself.

Another mode of meaning behind the obvious, or none. Either Oedipa in the orbiting ecstasy of a true paranoia, or a real Tristero. For there either was some Tristero beyond the appearance of legacy America, or there was just America and if there was just America then it seemed the only way she could continue, and manage to be at all relevant to it, was as an alien, unfurrowed, assumed full circle into some paranoia.

Nick is no Oedipa, and Gatsby is not the Tristero (an ambiguous secret society operating beyond or beneath the reach of the official established power structures). But there is a similarity in the stance, and the need, and the perceived alternatives, that is recognizable and may be found throughout American literature. From the time of the Puritans, the idea that it might be 'just America' has been felt to be intolerable and unacceptable. There *must* be 'another mode of meaning behind the obvious'. You may discover and assert it the Puritan way (God) or the Transcendentalist way (Plato), but one way or another the urge to do so, or fear of being unable to do so, is recurrent. It drives and worries Nick, as it does Oedipa Maas, and while Nick gives no indication of having recourse to Oedipa's alternative of paranoia, it could be argued that he finds a refuge in writing and fantasy to console himself in a post-Gatsby world. He catches glimpses of some of the uglier and more sordid social, sexual and economic realities of the story he has to tell, but he refuses to let them dominate his narrative as they do life – if they did, there would be 'just America'. Consequently, writes Richard Godden, 'whenever the contradictions within his subject become too disquieting, he turns social aspiration into "dream", sexual politics into "romance", and translates class conflict as "tragedy" ' (*Fictions of Capital*, Cambridge University Press, 1990, p. 92 – the book contains one of the most striking and probing essays on *The Great Gatsby* I have ever read).

When Nick is introducing himself to us, he speaks about his family with such casual, disarming honesty that it is easy to overlook the implications of what he reveals.

My family have been prominent, well-to-do people in this Middle Western city for three generations. The Carraways are something of a clan, and we have a tradition that we're descended from the Dukes of Buccleuch, but the actual founder of my line was my grandfather's brother, who came here in fifty-one, sent a substitute to the Civil War, and started the wholesale hardware business that my father carries on today.

Underneath the cosmetic vocabulary of 'clan', 'tradition',

'Dukes', etc., *this* 'actual' is a pretty inglorious, cowardly, materially opportunistic affair. Towards the end of *The American Scene* Henry James, having visited the old town of St Augustine in Florida, recalls how the magazine illustrators had contrived, or conspired, to give the town an intensely 'romantic character', investing it, quite falsely, with all sorts of vistas and attributes of 'Spanish antiquity'. This sets James musing:

It points so vividly the homely moral that when you haven't what you like you must perforce like, and above all misrepresent what you have . . . The guardians of real values struck me as, up and down, far to seek. The whole matter indeed would seem to come back, interestingly enough, to the general truth of the aesthetic need, in the country, for much greater values, of certain sorts, than the country and its manners, its aspects and arrangements, its past and present, and perhaps even future, really supply; whereby, as the aesthetic need is also intermixed with a patriotic yearning, a supply has somehow to be extemporized, by any pardonable form of pictorial 'hankey-pankey' – has to be, as the expression goes, cleverly 'faked' . . . the novelists improvise, with the aid of the historians, a romantic local past of costume and compliment and sword-play and gallantry and passion; the dramatists build up, of a thousand pieces, the airy fiction that the life of the people among whom the elements of clash and contrast are simplest and most superficial abounds in the subjects and situations and effects of the theatre; while the genealogists touch up the picture with their pleasant hint of the number, over the land, of families of royal blood . . . It is the public these appearances collectively refer us to that becomes thus again the more attaching subject; the public so placidly uncritical that the whitest thread of the deceptive stitch never makes it blink, and sentimental at once with such inveteracy and such simplicity that, finding everything everywhere perfectly splendid, it fairly goes upon its knees to be humbuggingly humbugged.

Nick certainly doesn't find 'everything everywhere perfectly splendid', and I would never for a moment suggest that even in the most metaphorical way he ever goes upon his knees before Gatsby to be 'humbuggingly humbugged'. But there is about him just a touch of the novelist and dramatist James describes, and once or twice he makes a point of *not* blinking at the white threads of some fairly visible deceptive stitches. And if he himself refuses to go along with the sort of genealogical 'hankey-pankey' that apparently prevails in his family – rather, indeed, blowing the whistle on it, albeit in passing – he nevertheless reveals, or conjures up, a society tolerably permeated with 'hankey-pankey', not to say misrepresentation and fakery, of many kinds.

There is certainly a lot of visible architectural hankey-pankey, starting with Gatsby's own mansion, which is 'a factual imitation of some Hôtel de Ville in Normandy'. In the ambiguous atmosphere in which Gatsby moves and operates factual imitations cannot easily be distinguished from imitation facts. (If you fix the World Series, you have created an imitation fact. Gatsby knows the man who did it: that is part of the company he keeps.) The mansion has a tower that is, as Nick's often entirely unhumbugged eye notes, 'spanking new under a thin beard of raw ivy'. This perfectly exemplifies the practice of 'misrepresentation', the hankey-pankey and fakery that earned James's strictures: the crude super-imposition of a false veneer of antiquity (the thin beard of raw ivy) on the 'spanking newness' of – well, of America, James would say. This desire to affix a prestigious patina of pastness to a less obviously distinguished present can spring from many sources. Gatsby didn't build his phoney French mansion. It was commissioned a decade earlier by a brewer who took his passion to reimpose an alien pastness on the new American landscape to extreme lengths: 'there was a story that he'd agreed to pay five years' taxes on all the neighbouring cottages if the owners would have their roofs thatched with straw.' They wouldn't, and he died. Crazy indeed; but Gatsby also, in his own way, seeks to 'repeat the past' – ' "Why, of course you can!" ' Things aren't so different over on more fashionable East Egg. The Buchanans live in a 'red-and-white Georgian Colonial mansion' with an 'Italian garden'. Tom certainly has the worst kind of 'colonizing' mentality – all others exist only to satisfy his needs and appetites – but he is no more grounded in, or significantly related to, ancient American history than Gatsby. This house originally belonged to 'Demaine, the oil man', and one can see how deftly yet unobtrusively Fitzgerald makes his points. A brewer and an oil man: the money that could afford to erect these grandiose architectural masks, drawing on Europe and history for façades at once to cover and dignify the origins of their wealth, is derived from alcohol and oil, two of the basic raw materials that indeed serve to fuel much of American society, moving both the economy and the people in different and dangerous ways: think how much of this novel is taken up with drinking and driving – and drunken driving. Later in the novel Tom boasts that, while you often hear of people making a garage out of a stable, he is the first man to make a stable out of a garage. It is a suggestive conversion: once you have made enough money – let's say in oil – you can 'thatch' it over with your preferred pastoral fakery. Of course, there are many, many American garages that are doomed to remain always and only garages – unprofitable, unconvertible, irredeemable. Ask Wilson in the valley of ashes.

There is more decorative hankey-pankey in the book – the tapestried furniture covered with 'scenes of ladies swinging in the gardens of Versailles' in Myrtle's apartment, for example – but enough has been noted to indicate that Fitzgerald gives us glimpses of a country where the past is pretty thin on the ground and of a society in which people, once they can afford to, reach out eclectically for all kinds of imported façades (exotic, historic) to cover not just the naked facts of how they make or made their money (which is not unique to them – Victorian England did that too) but also their 'spanking newness'. There is a nice moment recorded by Nick, who, shortly after arriving in West Egg is feeling alone and new when a stranger asks him the way to the village. 'I told him. And as I walked on I was lonely no longer. I was a guide, a pathfinder, an original settler.' This is Nick's tone at its most sympathetic, a kind of tasteful exaggeration that contrives to be at once playful and modest. But in the lightest of ways he is touching on a matter of great import. His instant transformation from lonely newcomer to 'original settler' is a comic version of something that has concerned Americans in various ways since the first settlements. As the inhabitants of America (once the Indians had been effectively erased) have all been, in a sense, displaced newcomers, they have always wanted to 'originate' themselves somehow in America; they have conducted a search, let us call it, for modes of more or less instant racination. In their agonistic confrontation, Tom derides Gatsby as 'Mr Nobody from Nowhere'. He is talking defensive 'gibberish' at the time, as Nick notes, but the phrase does pose an implicit question: can *anybody* in this book be said to be Mr, or Ms, Somebody from Somewhere? They are all restless nomads from the Midwest, simply with more or less money: restlessness is the predominant mood of the novel, and the word and its variants occur frequently. 'There is no there there,' said Gertrude Stein of Oakland: one might, not unfairly, extend the remark to cover the America of this book. 'I didn't want you to think I was just some nobody,' says Gatsby to Nick in their first real conversation, explaining why he has ventured to tell him his life story to date. And if any of these nobodies, driving from nowhere to nowhere, does become Somebody, then, by the grace of Nick's text, it is Gatsby – the *great* Gatsby.

But how and why 'great'? And how much of Gatsby is 'hankey-pankey'? Does Nick to any extent allow himself to be 'humbuggingly humbugged'? There is a most revealing exchange between the two men at the start of their first conversation and Gatsby's life story.

'I'll tell you God's truth.' His right hand suddenly ordered divine retribution to stand by. 'I am the son of some wealthy people in the Middle West – all dead now. I was brought up in America but educated at Oxford, because all my ancestors have been educated there for many years. It is a family tradition.'

He looked at me sideways – and I knew why Jordan Baker had believed he was lying. He hurried the phrase 'educated at Oxford', or swallowed it, or choked on it, as though it had bothered him before. And with this doubt, his whole statement fell to pieces, and I wondered if there wasn't something a little sinister about him, after all.

'What part of the Middle West?' I inquired casually.

'San Francisco.'

'I see.'

'My family all died and I came into a good deal of money.'

His voice was solemn, as if the memory of that sudden extinction of a clan still haunted him. For a moment I suspected that he was pulling my leg, but a glance at him convinced me otherwise.

Incurably dishonest herself, we may perhaps expect Jordan Baker to know a liar when she hears one, and indeed most of this part of Gatsby's story is pure hankey-pankey, even if the Armistice did give him five not-in-the-ancestral-family-tradition months at Oxford. The question is, how much does he expect to be believed? The invoking of God and the theatrical gesture with the right hand, followed by the sideways look . . . Of course his statement falls to pieces. But something odder follows. When he puts San Francisco in the Middle West – rather as if, in Britain, someone told you he came from Glasgow in the Midlands – Nick simply says, 'I see.' Now at this point Gatsby is surely showing Nick the white thread of the deceptive stitch, and Nick chooses not to see it, or rather not to acknowledge or draw attention to it. There is a way of saying 'I see' (it is probably Nick's) that tacitly states: 'I know you're lying, and I know *you* know I know you're lying, but for my own reasons, perhaps politeness, perhaps embarrassment at such brazen mendacity, perhaps something more inscrutable, I choose not to challenge your statement.' It is exactly what Nick says again when Gatsby suddenly and inexplicably dismisses his former staff and fills his house with a bunch of deliberately rude and villainous-looking thugs. Gatsby 'explains': 'They're all brothers and sisters. They used to run a small hotel.' This, surely, is another exposure of the deceptive white thread. I think Richard Godden is absolutely right to suggest that with this sudden and crude termination of his lavish, star-studded, hyper-elegant, conspicuously consuming summer parties Gatsby is deliberately showing Nick (and perhaps, indirectly, Daisy) his *real* milieu, his 'actual' criminal grounding – really rubbing his nose in it, as it were. Nick 'sees' but chooses not to see or, rather, chooses to concentrate on seeing something else.

As Nick has revealed, he knows a thing or two about families inventing ancestors and traditions, and he even extends to Gatsby's relatives his preferred and rather pretentious word 'clan', a more inappropriate appellation, surely, for Gatsby's 'shiftless and unsuccessful farm people' even than for the war-dodging Carraways. It is as if a part of him at least is prepared to participate in Gatsby's hankey-pankey – it runs in the family, we might say. Another part of him knows very well that he is having his leg pulled – Gatsby could hardly have tipped him a more visible wink – but he is extraordinarily quick to be 'convinced otherwise'. We may see this as eager credulity or engaging trust. Constant suspicion and a wary determination never to be taken in are not the most attractive of characteristics, and there is something sympathetic in Nick's tremendous keenness to give Gatsby the benefit of the doubt. How much this is generosity prompted by attraction to the man (and revulsion from the others) and how much is collusion, the willing suspension of disbelief, motivated by a desire for the 'gorgeous', would be impossible to determine. What is clear is that, faced with the Buchanans of this world, Nick will go along with Gatsby's hankey-pankey, will, indeed, justify, amplify and celebrate it in his writing. He is certainly loyal to him to the end, taking charge of his exequies at that sad funeral to which an ungrateful and forgetful 'Nobody' comes except for a few servants, his pathetic father who 'et like a hog' and the man in owl-shaped spectacles who wondered at the absolute reality of Gatsby's books and who pronounces one of his epitaphs, 'The poor son-of-a-bitch.' Nick will write a more encomiastic commemoration.

While waiting for proofs in Rome, Fitzgerald wrote to Maxwell Perkins: 'Strange to say, my notion of Gatsby's vagueness was O.K. . . . *I myself didn't know what Gatsby looked like or was engaged in* . . . Anyhow after careful searching of the files (of a man's mind here) . . . I know Gatsby better than I know my own child. My first instinct was to let him go and have

Tom Buchanan dominate the book . . . but Gatsby sticks in my heart. I had him for a while, then lost him, and now I know I have him again' (*circa* 20 December 1924). And in a letter to John Peale Bishop a little later: 'You are right about Gatsby being blurred and patchy. I never at any one time saw him clear myself' (9 August 1925). This is all exactly right. Nick has Gatsby, loses him, then has him again in a different way. More generally, now you see Gatsby, now you don't. On more than one occasion Nick looks for Gatsby, only to find him 'not there', and, of course, he does not even appear until Chapter Three (a quarter of the way into the book) and disappears before the end. In a way Tom *does* dominate the book; he dominates everyone and every thing, and Nick drinks with him before he meets Gatsby and shakes his hand after Gatsby's death. Buchanans, as a type, go on for ever, survive everything. Gatsby, for all his 'gonnections', is frailer and more vulnerable. And, in a more general epistemological sense he is and remains (for us the readers too) vague as to what he is and what he does. As we have seen, Fitzgerald deliberately contributed to his vagueness by cutting out too explicit dialogue, and this was not a matter of, as it were, withholding information in the interests of mystification; that strange hint of ontological insubstantiality about him is absolutely crucial. Of a look that passes over Gatsby's face while Tom is insulting him Nick states that it was 'definitely unfamiliar and vaguely recognizable'. Notice the perfection, for suggestivity, of the apparent oxymorons: the recognizability is vague, but the unfamiliarity is definite. Gatsby looms and fades, sharpens and blurs. Now you see him, you think; and now you don't, you are almost sure. This wonderfully maintained 'vagueness' is better than 'O.K.': it is an essential part of the magic of the book. For, after even the harshest scrutiny of the figure of Gatsby – which might reduce him to a sentimental roughneck, a criminal with a soppy dream, a ruthless social climber determined to buy himself a very classy piece of female goods – Gatsby does, somehow, stick in the heart.

At times, when he does appear, he reminds people of a popular journal or an advertisement. 'My incredulity was submerged in fascination now; it was like skimming hastily through a dozen magazines,' writes Nick of his response to Gatsby's life story. 'You resemble the advertisement of the man . . . You know the advertisement of the man –' Daisy doesn't finish her sentence. Presumably he looks like the man in any number of advertisements. (Jordan Baker is said to look like a 'good illustration': the effects are everywhere.) In today's parlance we might say that he sometimes strikes people as being all 'simulacra'. Advertising was booming in the America of the Twenties. Gatsby is very much a child of his culture and equips and surrounds himself with all the most fashionable and flamboyant commodities, from shirts to cars. The 'formal note' with the signature in a 'majestic hand' with which he first announces himself to Nick is the first sign of his careful self-fashioning (and observe how quick Nick is to pick up hints of regality in this democratic republic). In a way his ostentatious house and expensive parties are an elaborate advertising display designed to impress Daisy. His certainty that he can repeat the past, his confidence that he can 'fix everything just the way it was', owes a lot to this advertising culture. (In the book I have referred to Richard Godden details how Henry Ford, in 1922, recreated his old home exactly as it had been sixty years earlier. 'In the marketplace, time is reversible,' Godden comments.) In reality, of course, his dream founders on his impossible insistence that time can be not only reversed but erased. He has lost Daisy (and dream) from the moment he tries to make her tell Tom that she had never loved him, 'and it's all wiped out forever'. You can wipe away graffiti and stray shaving soap but not time; time is the one thing Gatsby cannot 'fix'. He cannot even handle it very well: in the central chapter of the book (Five), when he meets Daisy again, he very nearly knocks over a clock. This clock happens to be 'defunct', which perhaps makes it a fitting adjunct and material witness to the attempt he is making to stop time, but elsewhere the clocks are ticking like mad. (There is an unusually large number of time words in the novel – over four hundred.) It is no wonder that he looks at Daisy's child with surprise: 'I don't think he had ever really believed in its existence before.' And Tom has only to cite the times and places of his sexual possession of Daisy, and Gatsby is pretty well done for. I should say 'Gatsby' – ' "Jay Gatsby" had broken up like glass against Tom's hard malice, and the long secret extravaganza was played out.' His constructed identity, the simulacrum, which has been buoyed up and motivated by the cherished notion of a recapturable, repurchasable, Daisy *and* an erasable time, is in ruins. Daisy stays bought.

So is 'great' an irony or a wishful hyperbole that recoils on itself? Is the whole work the self-consoling hankey-pankey of a miserable failure of a bachelor, who invents a 'gorgeous' figure to compensate for the 'dismal' Middle West to which he has retreated – Nick's fakery of Gatsby's fakery? This cannot be all there is to it, although I believe there are those who think so. To the extent that it *is* this, we know it from Nick himself. Just as Gatsby occasionally shows him the white thread of the deceptive stitch, so Nick does to the attentive reader. There is more to Gatsby than the shivered glass of his custom-made identity after his shattering encounter with Tom's 'rock' at its most obdurate, something that in the end he inadequately articulates and imperfectly incarnates but is indeed part of the 'essence' of that self-inventing, self-parented nation of which he is at once so remarkable and so representative a product. We may call it, with Nick, 'an extraordinary gift for hope, a romantic readiness', an adherence to, or gesturing towards, a conviction or a feeling that there must be something more to life than the 'corruption' that surrounds and attends Gatsby, the appetitive, self-gratifying, sheer, mere materiality in which the Buchanans are so heedlessly at home. That this hope takes the form of a romantic dream or impossible obsession, which is at once doomed and unrealizable, does not necessarily invalidate the need or desire that nourished it. If 'the colossal vitality of his illusion' does finally go 'beyond everything', and thus must perforce be disappointed and come too naught, it does not mean that the devitalizing lifelessness that may result from determined disillusion necessarily offers the better way. It does mean that there is a special kind of sadness to the book. For there is pathos (as well as, if you like, puerility) about Gatsby – his aura of loneliness and isolation, the emptiness that seems to flow from his house, his piles of 'beautiful shirts', his always unappreciated generosity (no thanks for covering for Daisy, which costs him his life), his mean death and unattended funeral. And to the extent that Gatsby – 'Gatsby' – is excessive, foolish and foredoomed, so, the whole book suggests, is America.

Not long after the novel was published Fitzgerald wrote to Marya Mannes: 'America's greatest promise is that something is going to happen, and after a while you get tired of waiting because nothing happens to people except that they grow old, and nothing happens to American art because America is the story of the moon that never rose' (October 1925). When the moon famously *does* rise at the end of *The*

Great Gatsby, it prompts one of the most famous paragraphs in American literature:

the inessential houses began to melt away until gradually I became aware of the old island here that flowered once for Dutch sailors' eyes – a fresh, green breast of the new world. Its vanished trees, the trees that had made way for Gatsby's house, had once pandered in whispers to the last and greatest of human dreams; for a transitory enchanted moment man must have held his breath in the presence of this continent, compelled into *an aesthetic contemplation he neither understood or desired*, face to face for the last time in history with something commensurate to his capacity for wonder. (My italics.)

This passage was originally at the end of Chapter One until, with another of those unerring corrections, Fitzgerald moved it to the end, the dusk of the narrative where its crepuscular tone is so fitting. The original early positioning indicates that the book was always going to be an elegy, pervaded with a sense of something muffed, something lost – a chance missed, a dream doomed. The 'green breast of the new world', the pap of a possible new life, might have offered an inexhaustible supply of the 'milk of wonder'. But whatever the sailors came for – all the sailors, from Puritans to pirates – they came not to wonder at America but rather, in various ways, to 'rape' it, to use William Carlos Williams's metaphor for the various and multiple spoliations of the American land. The green breast of the new world has given way, as an image, to the shocking spectacle of Myrtle's left breast, 'swinging loose like a flap' after the road accident. Fitzgerald was very insistent about retaining this spectacle: 'I *want* Myrtle Wilson's breast ripped off – it's exactly the thing, I think' (to Maxwell Perkins *circa* 20 December 1924). Fitzgerald knows, of course, exactly what he is doing. He *wants* to show America desecrated, mutilated, violated.

Whatever the might-have-beens of the new world – and the incoherent, hopeful yet hopeless reachings out of a Gatsby perhaps offer a vague, vestigial and distorted hint of a kind of gladly accepted 'capacity for wonder', desired if not fully understood, that might have made something better out of the great last chance that was America – America has contrived to make itself utterly accidental and accident-prone. Of what might have been a Wonderland (a theme endemic to American literature suggests) we have made a wasteland.

Fitzgerald knew T. S. Eliot's poem of that name pretty much by heart, and of course he created his own wasteland in the valley of ashes (indeed, one title he considered for the novel was *Among the Ash Heaps and Millionaires*): 'a fantastic farm where ashes grow like wheat into ridges and hills and grotesque gardens; where ashes take the forms of houses and chimneys and, finally, with a transcendent effort, of ash-grey men, who move dimly and already crumbling through the powdery air. Occasionally a line of grey cars crawls along an invisible track, gives out a ghastly creak, and comes to rest.' 'Transcendent' is a peculiarly loaded word in America, and it is used here with dark irony. This is negative transcendence, a travesty, the very reverse of what Emerson and his friends had hoped for America, with the land actually producing, *growing*, ashes. Fitzgerald was neither the first nor the last American writer to have an entropic vision of America – the great agrarian continent turning itself into some sort of terminal rubbish heap or wasteland, where, with ultimate perversity, the only thing that grows is death.

Fitzgerald was canny enough to associate this process with the exponential spread of the automobile. As already noted, the book is full of cars, bad driving and accidents, and together they conspire to kill not only people but the land itself. Bad driver Jordan Baker's very name is composed of the brand names of two automobiles. Aptly, Fitzgerald places the garage – Wilson's garage, but let us say the generic garage – at the heart of the valley of ashes that it is producing. Henry Adams, who was the first American writer to employ the word 'entropy' to describe the future he foresaw, related this predicted accelerating entropy to the rapid increase of new discoveries of sources of energy and power, coupled with a decrease in the human ability to control it. In his *Education* he wrote:

Power leaped from every atom, and enough of it to supply the stellar universe showed itself running to waste at every pore of matter. Man could no longer hold it off. Forces grasped his wrists and flung him about as though he had hold of a live wire or a runaway automobile; which was very nearly the exact truth for the purposes of an elderly and timid single gentleman in Paris, who never drove down the Champs Elysées without expecting an accident and commonly witnessing one; or found himself in the neighbourhood of an official without calculating the chances of a bomb. So long as the rates of progress held good, these bombs would double in number and force every ten years.

Fitzgerald chose to double up on the automobile accidents. A contemporary writer might prefer to go for bombs.

Overlooking, though not overseeing, the valley of ashes are, of course, the eyes of Doctor T. J. Eckleburg.

The eyes of Doctor T. J. Eckleburg are blue and gigantic – their retinas are one yard high. They look out of no face, but, instead, from a pair of enormous yellow spectacles which pass over a non-existent nose. Evidently some wild wag of an oculist set them there to fatten his practice in the borough of Queens, and then sank down himself into eternal blindness, or forgot them and moved away. But his eyes, dimmed a little by many paintless days, under sun and rain, brood on over the solemn dumping ground.

André le Vot has most sensitively traced the various subtle ways in which Fitzgerald deploys colours, above all blue and yellow. As le Vot points out, blue is water, the sky, twilight, cool, restful, inviting. Yellow is wheat, sunshine and fertility but also whisky, gold (lucre) and dead, combustible straw, and is thus ambiguous, for what seems attractive and warm may turn combustible, violent, too hot. (Tom is 'straw-haired'.) Ideally the two colours, and all they evoke, should be in harmony with each other, as in Nick's odd but suggestive phrase 'the blue honey of the Mediterranean'. But in this book they seem to drift apart and tend to opposition. Misleadingly, perhaps, Gatsby's car is yellow (though it is part of the dubiety that surrounds him that people disagree about the colour: one describes it as cream-coloured, another light green – like its owner, it appears differently in different lights), while Tom's convertible is blue. But, appropriately, they exchange cars, at Tom's insistence, when their struggle over Daisy heads for climax and show-down.

To return to Doctor T. J. Eckleburg, to the extent that his blue eyes are fading and 'dimming a little' while the yellow spectacles persist untarnished, this may intimate, as le Vot suggests, 'a withering of spiritual power and a corresponding increase in materialism'. Spectacles are designed to help you to see better. But see what? See how? For Nick, after Gatsby's death, 'the East was haunted . . . distorted beyond my eyes' power of correction', so he retreats (one might be tempted to say 'regresses') back home which at the start of his narrative seemed like 'the ragged edge of the universe' but is now again, perhaps, 'the warm centre of the world'. The 'wild wag oculist' whom Nick posits and who has also absented himself from the area, may be an allusion to a God who should oversee the world but who has become a *deus absconditus*, or who no longer cares to turn his eyes on man in the wasteland he has made, or who may simply be dead, having left behind what man hath made – an advertisement. After the accident Michaelis is shocked to see that while Wilson is invoking God, he is looking at the eyes of Doctor T. J. Eckleburg. ' "God sees everything," repeated Wilson. "That's an advertisement," Michaelis assured him.'

Whatever may have been the religious intentions and aspirations of the original Puritan settlers, the landscape is now dominated entirely by commercial and material considerations (though religious and commercial concerns may have been linked from the start. In *America's Coming of Age* Van Wyck Brooks suggests that this is so: 'Thus the literature of the seventeenth century in America is composed in equal parts, one might fairly say, of piety and advertisement.'). As we have seen, Gatsby lives in and through an advertising world and is something of a composite advertisement himself. The question, perhaps, is whether his 'gestures', which result from and express, thinks Nick, 'some heightened sensitivity to the promises of life', are indicative of an inchoate form of a 'piety' all his own.

When Nick says that the East is 'haunted for me like that, distorted beyond my eyes' power of correction', 'that' refers to 'a night scene by El Greco'. El Greco is famous for his elongations and what some might call his feverish exaggerations. Since by Nick's own confession his vision of what happened is uncorrected and uncorrectable, we should perhaps take the hint, intended or not, that he has given us an El Greco-ish version – heightened, enlarged, excitably glorified – of Gatsby and what surrounded him. But El Greco, like Vermeer, whom we may regard as much less inclined to distortion than El Greco (indeed, as painting with as miraculously a correct vision as is possible to attain) is an artist, and all art involves distortion – selection, interpretation, amplification. It could be argued that distortion is inseparable from representation. Whatever the motivation for Nick's writing, even if it was simply a 'winter dream' to occupy and console him in the dismal fastnesses of the Middle West, he has still delivered a work of art; and there can never be any unravelling of the motives that lie behind the making of a work of art.

It is Fitzgerald's book, of course, and in showing us Nick working on the problems and pitfalls involved in 'seeing' his material, working out his way of 'writing' Gatsby, both faking and fêting him, Fitzgerald added a whole new dimension to his work. Henry James once wrote: 'There is the story of one's hero, and then, thanks to the intimate connexion of things, the story of one's story itself.' In giving us not only the story of Gatsby but the story of Nick trying to write that story, Fitzgerald confronts no less a problem than what might be involved, what might be at stake, in trying to see, and *write*, America itself. The result is short (those inspired excisions), deceptively simple, with something of the lean yet pregnant economy of a parable (for a book so explicitly rooted in the Twenties, it contains, as Matthew Bruccoli has noted, surprisingly little 'in the way of sociological or anthropological data'). It is word-perfect and inexhaustible. *The Great Gatsby* is, I believe, the most perfectly crafted work of fiction to have come out of America.

When Nick attends his first party at Gatsby's mansion he is 'on guard against its spectroscopic gaiety': he finds some things 'graceless', others 'vacuous'. After two glasses of champagne 'the scene had changed before my eyes into something significant, elemental, and profound'. There is a touch of self-mockery in the knowing exaggeration (if that's all it takes . . .). A critic such as Richard Godden might say that the champagne is pretty flat (his chapter on the novel is entitled 'Glamour on the Turn'), but this, I think, is to miss something of the undoubted magic of the book and its irreducible polyvalency. Call it undecidability. Some days the car is yellow; on others it looks light green. At times Gatsby may stick in your throat as well as your heart. Perhaps he is like the books in his library: 'absolutely real' where you most expect him to be fake, but finally absolutely unreadable because his inner pages are uncut.

But what do you want?

What do you expect?

Tony Tanner
February 1990

THE GREAT GATSBY

ONCE AGAIN
TO
ZELDA

Then wear the gold hat, if that will move her;
  If you can bounce high, bounce for her too,
Till she cry 'Lover, gold-hatted, high-bouncing lover,
  I must have you!'

THOMAS PARKE D'INVILLIERS

Chapter I

In my younger and more vulnerable years my father gave me some advice that I've been turning over in my mind ever since.

'Whenever you feel like criticizing anyone,' he told me, 'just remember that all the people in this world haven't had the advantages that you've had.'

He didn't say any more, but we've always been unusually communicative in a reserved way, and I understood that he meant a great deal more than that. In consequence, I'm inclined to reserve all judgements, a habit that has opened up many curious natures to me and also made me the victim of not a few veteran bores. The abnormal mind is quick to detect and attach itself to this quality when it appears in a normal person, and so it came about that in college I was unjustly accused of being a politician, because I was privy to the secret griefs of wild, unknown men. Most of the confidences were unsought – frequently I have feigned sleep, preoccupation, or a hostile levity when I realized by some unmistakable sign that an intimate revelation was quivering on the horizon; for the intimate revelations of young men, or at least the terms in which they express them, are usually plagiaristic and marred by obvious suppressions. Reserving judgements is a matter of infinite hope. I am still a little afraid of missing something if I forget that, as my father snobbishly suggested, and I snobbishly repeat, a sense of the fundamental decencies is parcelled out unequally at birth.

And, after boasting this way of my tolerance, I come to the admission that it has a limit. Conduct may be founded on the hard rock or the wet marshes, but after a certain point I don't care what it's founded on. When I came back from the East last autumn I felt that I wanted the world to be in uniform and at a sort of moral attention forever; I wanted no more riotous excursions with privileged glimpses into the human heart. Only Gatsby, the man who gives his name to this book, was exempt from my reaction – Gatsby, who represented everything for which I have an unaffected scorn. If personality is an unbroken series of successful gestures, then there was something gorgeous about him, some heightened sensitivity to the promises of life, as if he were related to one of those intricate machines that register earthquakes ten thousand miles away. This responsiveness had nothing to do with that flabby impressionability which is dignified under the name of the 'creative temperament' – it was an extraordinary gift for hope, a romantic readiness such as I have never found in any other person and which it is not likely I shall ever find again. No – Gatsby turned out all right at the end; it is what preyed on Gatsby, what foul dust floated in the wake of his dreams that temporarily closed out my interest in the abortive sorrows and shortwinded elations of men.

My family have been prominent, well-to-do people in this Middle Western city for three generations. The Carraways are something of a clan, and we have a tradition that we're descended from the Dukes of Buccleuch,[1] but the actual founder of my line was my grandfather's brother, who came here in fifty-one, sent a substitute to the Civil War, and started the wholesale hardware business that my father carries on today.

I never saw this great-uncle, but I'm supposed to look like him – with special reference to the rather hard-boiled painting that hangs in father's office. I graduated from New Haven[2] in 1915, just a quarter of a century after my father, and a little later I participated in that delayed Teutonic migration known as the Great War. I enjoyed the counter-raid so thoroughly that I came back restless. Instead of being the warm centre of the world, the Middle West now seemed like the ragged edge of the universe – so I decided to go East and learn the bond business. Everybody I knew was in the bond business, so I supposed it could support one more single man. All my aunts and uncles talked it over as if they were choosing a prep school for me, and finally said, 'Why – ye-es,' with very grave, hesitant faces. Father agreed to finance me for a year, and after various delays I came East, permanently, I thought, in the spring of twenty-two.

The practical thing was to find rooms in the city, but it was a warm season, and I had just left a country of wide lawns and friendly trees, so when a young man at the office suggested that we take a house together in a commuting town, it sounded like a great idea. He found the house, a weather-beaten cardboard bungalow at eighty a month, but at the last minute the firm ordered him to Washington, and I went out to the country alone. I had a dog – at least I had him for a few days until he ran away – and an old Dodge and a Finnish woman, who made my bed and cooked breakfast and muttered Finnish wisdom to herself over the electric stove.

It was lonely for a day or so until one morning some man, more recently arrived than I, stopped me on the road.

'How do you get to West Egg village?' he asked helplessly.

I told him. And as I walked on I was lonely no longer. I was a guide, a pathfinder, an original settler. He had casually conferred on me the freedom of the neighbourhood.

And so with the sunshine and the great bursts of leaves growing on the trees, just as things grow in fast movies, I had that familiar conviction that life was beginning over again with the summer.

There was so much to read, for one thing, and so much fine health to be pulled down out of the young breath-giving air. I bought a dozen volumes on banking and credit and investment securities, and they stood on my shelf in red and gold like new money from the mint, promising to unfold the shining secrets that only Midas and Morgan and Maecenas knew. And I had the high intention of reading many other books besides. I was rather literary in college – one year I wrote a series of very solemn and obvious editorials for the Yale News – and now I was going to bring back all such things into my life and become again that most limited of all specialists, the 'well-rounded man'. This isn't just an epigram – life is much more successfully looked at from a single window, after all.

It was a matter of chance that I should have rented a house in one of the strangest communities in North America. It was on that slender riotous island which extends itself due east of New York – and where there are, among other natural curiosities, two unusual formations of land. Twenty miles from the city a pair of enormous eggs, identical in contour and separated only by a courtesy bay, jut out into the most domesticated body of salt water in the Western hemisphere, the great wet barnyard of Long Island Sound. They are not perfect ovals – like the egg in the Columbus story, they are both crushed flat at the contact end – but their physical resemblance must be a source of perpetual wonder to the gulls that fly overhead. To the wingless a more interesting phenomenon is their dissimilarity in every particular except shape and size.

I lived at West Egg, the – well, the less fashionable of the two, though this is a most superficial tag to express the bizarre and not a little sinister contrast between them. My house was at the very tip of the egg, only fifty yards from the Sound, and squeezed between two huge places that rented for twelve or fifteen thousand a season. The one on my right was a colossal affair by any standard – it was a factual imitation of some Hôtel de Ville in Normandy, with a tower on one side, spanking new under a thin beard of raw ivy, and a marble swimming pool, and more than forty acres of lawn and garden. It was Gatsby's mansion. Or, rather, as I didn't know Mr Gatsby, it was a mansion inhabited by a gentleman of that name. My own house was an eyesore, but it was a small eyesore, and it had been overlooked, so I had a view of the water, a partial view of my neighbour's lawn, and the consoling proximity of millionaires – all for eighty dollars a month.

Across the courtesy bay the white palaces of fashionable East Egg glittered along the water, and the history of the summer really begins on the evening I drove over there to have dinner with the Tom Buchanans. Daisy was my second cousin once removed, and I'd known Tom in college. And just after the war I spent two days with them in Chicago.

Her husband, among various physical accomplishments, had been one of the most powerful ends that ever played football at New Haven – a national figure in a way, one of those men who reach such an acute limited excellence at twenty-one that everything afterward savours of anti-climax. His family were enormously wealthy – even in college his freedom with money was a matter for reproach – but now he'd left Chicago and come East in a fashion that rather took your breath away: for instance, he'd brought down a string of polo ponies from Lake Forest.[3] It was hard to realize that a man in my own generation was wealthy enough to do that.

Why they came East I don't know. They had spent a year in France for no particular reason, and then drifted here and there unrestfully wherever people played polo and were rich together. This was a permanent move, said Daisy over the telephone, but I didn't believe it – I had no sight into Daisy's heart, but I felt that Tom would drift on forever seeking, a little wistfully, for the dramatic turbulence of some irrecoverable football game.

And so it happened that on a warm windy evening I drove over to East Egg to see two old friends whom I scarcely knew at all. Their house was even more elaborate than I expected, a cheerful red-and-white Georgian Colonial mansion, over-looking the bay. The lawn started at the beach and ran to-wards the front door for a quarter of a mile, jumping over sundials and brick walks and burning gardens – finally when it reached the house drifting up the side in bright vines as though from the momentum of its run. The front was broken by a line of french windows, glowing now with reflected gold and wide open to the warm windy afternoon, and Tom Buchanan in riding clothes was standing with his legs apart on the front porch.

He had changed since his New Haven years. Now he was a sturdy straw-haired man of thirty, with a rather hard mouth and a supercilious manner. Two shining arrogant eyes had established dominance over his face and gave him the appear-ance of always leaning aggressively forward. Not even the effeminate swank of his riding clothes could hide the enormous power of that body – he seemed to fill those glistening boots until he strained the top lacing, and you could see a great pack of muscle shifting when his shoulder moved under his thin coat. It was a body capable of enormous leverage – a cruel body.

His speaking voice, a gruff husky tenor, added to the impres-sion of fractiousness he conveyed. There was a touch of paternal contempt in it, even toward people he liked – and there were men at New Haven who had hated his guts.

'Now, don't think my opinion on these matters is final,' he seemed to say, 'just because I'm stronger and more of a man than you are.' We were in the same senior society,[4] and while we were never intimate I always had the impression that he approved of me and wanted me to like him with some harsh, defiant wistfulness of his own.

We talked for a few minutes on the sunny porch.

'I've got a nice place here,' he said, his eyes flashing about restlessly.

Turning me around by one arm, he moved a broad flat hand along the front vista, including in its sweep a sunken Italian garden, a half acre of deep, pungent roses, and a snub-nosed motor-boat that bumped the tide offshore.

'It belonged to Demaine, the oil man.' He turned me around again, politely and abruptly. 'We'll go inside.'

We walked through a high hallway into a bright rosy-coloured space, fragilely bound into the house by french windows at either end. The windows were ajar and gleaming white against the fresh grass outside that seemed to grow a little way into the house. A breeze blew through the room, blew curtains in at one end and out the other like pale flags, twisting them up toward the frosted wedding-cake of the ceiling, and then rippled over the wine-coloured rug, making a shadow on it as wind does on the sea.

The only completely stationary object in the room was an enormous couch on which two young women were buoyed up as though upon an anchored balloon. They were both in white, and their dresses were rippling and fluttering as if they had just been blown back in after a short flight around the house. I must have stood for a few moments listening to the whip and snap of the curtains and the groan of a picture on the wall. Then there was a boom as Tom Buchanan shut the rear windows and the caught wind died out about the room, and the curtains and the rugs and the two young women ballooned slowly to the floor.

The younger of the two was a stranger to me. She was extended full length at her end of the divan, completely motionless, and with her chin raised a little, as if she were balancing something on it which was quite likely to fall. If she saw me out of the corner of her eyes she gave no hint of it – indeed, I was almost surprised into murmuring an apology for having disturbed her by coming in.

The other girl, Daisy, made an attempt to rise – she leaned slightly forward with a conscientious expression – then she laughed, an absurd, charming little laugh, and I laughed too and came forward into the room.

'I'm p-paralysed with happiness.'

She laughed again, as if she said something very witty, and held my hand for a moment, looking up into my face, promising that there was no one in the world she so much wanted to see. That was a way she had. She hinted in a murmur that the surname of the balancing girl was Baker. (I've heard it said that Daisy's murmur was only to make people lean toward her; an irrelevant criticism that made it no less charming.)

At any rate, Miss Baker's lips fluttered, she nodded at me almost imperceptibly, and then quickly tipped her head back again – the object she was balancing had obviously tottered a little and given her something of a fright. Again a sort of apology arose to my lips. Almost any exhibition of complete self-sufficiency draws a stunned tribute from me.

I looked back at my cousin, who began to ask me questions in her low, thrilling voice. It was the kind of voice that the ear follows up and down, as if each speech is an arrangement of notes that will never be played again. Her face was sad and lovely with bright things in it, bright eyes and a bright passionate mouth, but there was an excitement in her voice that men who had cared for her found difficult to forget: a singing compulsion, a whispered 'Listen', a promise that she had done gay, exciting things just a while since and that there were gay, exciting things hovering in the next hour.

I told her how I had stopped off in Chicago for a day on my way East, and how a dozen people had sent their love through me.

'Do they miss me?' she cried ecstatically.

'The whole town is desolate. All the cars have the left rear wheel painted black as a mourning wreath, and there's a persistent wail all night along the north shore.'

'How gorgeous! Let's go back, Tom. Tomorrow!' Then she added irrelevantly: 'You ought to see the baby.'

'I'd like to.'

'She's asleep. She's three years old. Haven't you ever seen her?'

'Never.'

'Well, you ought to see her. She's –'

Tom Buchanan, who had been hovering restlessly about the room, stopped and rested his hand on my shoulder.

'What you doing, Nick?'

'I'm a bond man.'

'Who with?'

I told him.

'Never heard of them,' he remarked decisively.

This annoyed me.

'You will,' I answered shortly. 'You will if you stay in the East.'

'Oh, I'll stay in the East, don't you worry,' he said, glancing at Daisy and then back at me, as if he were alert for something more. 'I'd be a God damned fool to live anywhere else.'

At this point Miss Baker said: 'Absolutely!' with such suddenness that I started – it was the first word she had uttered since I came into the room. Evidently it surprised her as much as it did me, for she yawned and with a series of rapid, deft movements stood up into the room.

'I'm stiff,' she complained, 'I've been lying on that sofa for as long as I can remember.'

'Don't look at me,' Daisy retorted, 'I've been trying to get you to New York all afternoon.'

'No, thanks,' said Miss Baker to the four cocktails just in from the pantry. 'I'm absolutely in training.'

Her host looked at her incredulously.

'You are!' He took down his drink as if it were a drop in the bottom of a glass. 'How you ever get anything done is beyond me.'

I looked at Miss Baker, wondering what it was she 'got done'. I enjoyed looking at her. She was a slender, small-breasted girl, with an erect carriage, which she accentuated by throwing her body backward at the shoulders like a young cadet. Her grey sun-strained eyes looked back at me with polite reciprocal curiosity out of a wan, charming, discontented face. It occurred to me now that I had seen her, or a picture of her, somewhere before.

'You live in West Egg,' she remarked contemptuously. 'I know somebody there.'

'I don't know a single –'

'You must know Gatsby.'

'Gatsby?' demanded Daisy. 'What Gatsby?'

Before I could reply that he was my neighbour dinner was announced; wedging his tense arm imperatively under mine, Tom Buchanan compelled me from the room as though he were moving a checker to another square.

Slenderly, languidly, their hands set lightly on their hips, the two young women preceded us out on to a rosy-coloured porch, open toward the sunset, where four candles flickered on the table in the diminished wind.

'Why *candles*?' objected Daisy, frowning. She snapped them out with her fingers. 'In two weeks it'll be the longest day in the year.' She looked at us all radiantly. 'Do you always watch for the longest day of the year and then miss it? I always watch for the longest day in the year and then miss it.'

'We ought to plan something,' yawned Miss Baker, sitting down at the table as if she were getting into bed.

'All right,' said Daisy. 'What'll we plan?' She turned to me helplessly: 'What do people plan?'

Before I could answer her eyes fastened with an awed expression on her little finger.

'Look!' she complained; 'I hurt it.'

We all looked – the knuckle was black and blue.

'You did it, Tom,' she said accusingly. 'I know you didn't mean to, but you *did* do it. That's what I get for marrying a brute of a man, a great, big, hulking physical specimen of a –'

'I hate that word hulking,' objected Tom crossly, 'even in kidding.'

'Hulking,' insisted Daisy.

Sometimes she and Miss Baker talked at once, unobtrusively and with a bantering inconsequence that was never quite chatter, that was as cool as their white dresses and their impersonal eyes in the absence of all desire. They were here, and they accepted Tom and me, making only a polite pleasant effort to entertain or to be entertained. They knew that presently dinner would be over and a little later the evening too would be over and casually put away. It was sharply different from the West, where an evening was hurried from phase to phase towards its close, in a continually disappointed anticipation or else in sheer nervous dread of the moment itself.

'You make me feel uncivilized, Daisy,' I confessed on my

second glass of corky but rather impressive claret. 'Can't you talk about crops or something?'

I meant nothing in particular by this remark, but it was taken up in an unexpected way.

'Civilization's going to pieces,' broke out Tom violently. 'I've gotten to be a terrible pessimist about things. Have you read *The Rise of the Coloured Empires*[5] by this man Goddard?'

'Why, no,' I answered, rather surprised by his tone.

'Well, it's a fine book, and everybody ought to read it. The idea is if we don't look out the white race will be – will be utterly submerged. It's all scientific stuff; it's been proved.'

'Tom's getting very profound,' said Daisy, with an expression of unthoughtful sadness. 'He reads deep books with long words in them. What was that word we –'

'Well, these books are all scientific,' insisted Tom, glancing at her impatiently. 'This fellow has worked out the whole thing. It's up to us, who are the dominant race, to watch out or these other races will have control of things.'

'We've got to beat them down,' whispered Daisy, winking ferociously toward the fervent sun.

'You ought to live in California –' began Miss Baker, but Tom interrupted her by shifting heavily in his chair.

'This idea is that we're Nordics. I am, and you are, and you are, and –' After an infinitesimal hesitation he included Daisy with a slight nod, and she winked at me again. '– And we've produced all the things that go to make civilization – oh, science and art, and all that. Do you see?'

There was something pathetic in his concentration, as if his complacency, more acute than of old, was not enough to him any more. When, almost immediately, the telephone rang inside and the butler left the porch Daisy seized upon the momentary interruption and leaned towards me.

'I'll tell you a family secret,' she whispered enthusiastically.

'It's about the butler's nose. Do you want to hear about the butler's nose?'

'That's why I came over tonight.'

'Well, he wasn't always a butler; he used to be the silver polisher for some people in New York that had a silver service for two hundred people. He had to polish it from morning till night, until finally it began to affect his nose –'

'Things went from bad to worse,' suggested Miss Baker.

'Yes. Things went from bad to worse, until finally he had to give up his position.'

For a moment the last sunshine fell with romantic affection upon her glowing face; her voice compelled me forward breathlessly as I listened – then the glow faded, each light deserting her with lingering regret, like children leaving a pleasant street at dusk.

The butler came back and murmured something close to Tom's ear, whereupon Tom frowned, pushed back his chair, and without a word went inside. As if his absence quickened something within her, Daisy leaned forward again, her voice glowing and singing.

'I love to see you at my table, Nick. You remind me of a – of a rose, an absolute rose. Doesn't he?' She turned to Miss Baker for confirmation: 'An absolute rose?'

This was untrue. I am not even faintly like a rose. She was only extemporizing, but a stirring warmth flowed from her, as if her heart was trying to come out to you concealed in one of those breathless, thrilling words. Then suddenly she threw her napkin on the table and excused herself and went into the house.

Miss Baker and I exchanged a short glance consciously devoid of meaning. I was about to speak when she sat up alertly and said 'Sh!' in a warning voice. A subdued impassioned murmur was audible in the room beyond, and Miss

Baker leaned forward unashamed, trying to hear. The murmur trembled on the verge of coherence, sank down, mounted excitedly, and then ceased altogether.

'This Mr Gatsby you spoke of is my neighbour –' I began.

'Don't talk. I want to hear what happens.'

'Is something happening?' I inquired innocently.

'You mean to say you don't know?' said Miss Baker, honestly surprised. 'I thought everybody knew.'

'I don't.'

'Why –' she said hesitantly. 'Tom's got some woman in New York.'

'Got some woman?' I repeated blankly.

Miss Baker nodded.

'She might have the decency not to telephone him at dinner time. Don't you think?'

Almost before I had grasped her meaning there was the flutter of a dress and the crunch of leather boots, and Tom and Daisy were back at the table.

'It couldn't be helped!' cried Daisy with tense gaiety.

She sat down, glanced searchingly at Miss Baker and then at me, and continued: 'I looked outdoors for a minute, and it's very romantic outdoors. There's a bird on the lawn that I think must be a nightingale come over on the Cunard or White Star Line. He's singing away –' Her voice sang: 'It's romantic, isn't it, Tom?'

'Very romantic,' he said, and then miserably to me: 'If it's light enough after dinner, I want to take you down to the stables.'

The telephone rang inside, startlingly, and as Daisy shook her head decisively at Tom the subject of the stables, in fact all subjects, vanished into air. Among the broken fragments of the last five minutes at table I remember the candles being lit again, pointlessly, and I was conscious of wanting to look squarely at every one, and yet to avoid all eyes. I couldn't guess what Daisy and Tom were thinking, but I doubt if even Miss Baker, who seemed to have mastered a certain hardy scepticism, was able utterly to put this fifth guest's shrill metallic urgency out of mind. To a certain temperament the situation might have seemed intriguing – my own instinct was to telephone immediately for the police.

The horses, needless to say, were not mentioned again. Tom and Miss Baker, with several feet of twilight between them, strolled back into the library, as if to a vigil beside a perfectly tangible body, while, trying to look pleasantly interested and a little deaf, I followed Daisy around a chain of connecting verandas to the porch in front. In its deep gloom we sat down side by side on a wicker settee.

Daisy took her face in her hands as if feeling its lovely shape, and her eyes moved gradually out into the velvet dusk. I saw that turbulent emotions possessed her, so I asked what I thought would be some sedative questions about her little girl.

'We don't know each other very well, Nick,' she said suddenly. 'Even if we are cousins. You didn't come to my wedding.'

'I wasn't back from the war.'

'That's true.' She hesitated. 'Well, I've had a very bad time, Nick, and I'm pretty cynical about everything.'

Evidently she had reason to be. I waited but she didn't say any more, and after a moment I returned rather feebly to the subject of her daughter.

'I suppose she talks, and – eats, and everything.'

'Oh, yes.' She looked at me absently. 'Listen, Nick; let me tell you what I said when she was born. Would you like to hear?'

'Very much.'

'It'll show you how I've gotten to feel about – things. Well, she was less than an hour old and Tom was God knows where. I woke up out of the ether with an utterly abandoned feeling, and asked the nurse right away if it was a boy or a girl. She told me it was a girl, and so I turned my head away and wept. "All right," I said, "I'm glad it's a girl. And I hope she'll be a fool – that's the best thing a girl can be in this world, a beautiful little fool."

'You see I think everything's terrible anyhow,' she went on in a convinced way. 'Everybody thinks so – the most advanced people. And I *know*. I've been everywhere and seen everything and done everything.' Her eyes flashed around her in a defiant way, rather like Tom's, and she laughed with thrilling scorn. 'Sophisticated – God, I'm sophisticated!'

The instant her voice broke off, ceasing to compel my attention, my belief, I felt the basic insincerity of what she had said. It made me uneasy, as though the whole evening had been a trick of some sort to exact a contributory emotion from me. I waited, and sure enough, in a moment she looked at me with an absolute smirk on her lovely face, as if she had asserted her membership in a rather distinguished secret society to which she and Tom belonged.

Inside, the crimson room bloomed with light. Tom and Miss Baker sat at either end of the long couch and she read aloud to him from the *Saturday Evening Post* – the words, murmurous and uninflected, running together in a soothing tune. The lamp-light, bright on his boots and dull on the autumn-leaf yellow of her hair, glinted along the paper as she turned a page with a flutter of slender muscles in her arms.

When we came in she held us silent for a moment with a lifted hand.

'To be continued,' she said, tossing the magazine on the table, 'in our very next issue.'

Her body asserted itself with a restless movement of her knee, and she stood up.

'Ten o'clock,' she remarked, apparently finding the time on the ceiling. 'Time for this good girl to go to bed.'

'Jordan's going to play in the tournament tomorrow,' explained Daisy, 'over at Westchester.'[6]

'Oh – you're *Jor*dan Baker.'[7]

I knew now why her face was familiar – its pleasing contemptuous expression had looked out at me from many rotogravure pictures of the sporting life at Asheville and Hot Springs and Palm Beach.[8] I had heard some story of her too, a critical, unpleasant story, but what it was I had forgotten long ago.

'Good night,' she said softly. 'Wake me at eight, won't you.'

'If you'll get up.'

'I will. Good night, Mr Carraway. See you anon.'

'Of course you will,' confirmed Daisy. 'In fact I think I'll arrange a marriage. Come over often, Nick, and I'll sort of – oh – fling you together. You know – lock you up accidentally in linen closets and push you out to sea in a boat, and all that sort of thing –'

'Good night,' called Miss Baker from the stairs. 'I haven't heard a word.'

'She's a nice girl,' said Tom after a moment. 'They oughtn't to let her run around the country this way.'

'Who oughtn't to?' inquired Daisy coldly.

'Her family.'

'Her family is one aunt about a thousand years old. Besides, Nick's going to look after her, aren't you, Nick? She's going to spend lots of week-ends out here this summer. I think the home influence will be very good for her.'

Daisy and Tom looked at each other for a moment in silence.

'Is she from New York?' I asked quickly.

'From Louisville. Our white girlhood was passed together there. Our beautiful white –'

'Did you give Nick a little heart to heart talk on the veranda?' demanded Tom suddenly.

'Did I?' She looked at me. 'I can't seem to remember, but I think we talked about the Nordic race. Yes, I'm sure we did. It sort of crept up on us and first thing you know –'

'Don't believe everything you hear, Nick,' he advised me.

I said lightly that I had heard nothing at all, and a few minutes later I got up to go home. They came to the door with me and stood side by side in a cheerful square of light. As I started my motor Daisy peremptorily called: 'Wait!

'I forgot to ask you something, and it's important. We heard you were engaged to a girl out West.'

'That's right,' corroborated Tom kindly. 'We heard that you were engaged.'

'It's a libel. I'm too poor.'

'But we heard it,' insisted Daisy, surprising me by opening up again in a flower-like way. 'We heard it from three people, so it must be true.'

Of course I knew what they were referring to, but I wasn't even vaguely engaged. The fact that gossip had published the banns was one of the reasons I had come East. You can't stop going with an old friend on account of rumours, and on the other hand I had no intention of being rumoured into marriage.

Their interest rather touched me and made them less remotely rich – nevertheless, I was confused and a little disgusted as I drove away. It seemed to me that the thing for Daisy to do was to rush out of the house, child in arms – but apparently there were no such intentions in her head. As for Tom, the fact that he 'had some woman in New York' was really less surprising than that he had been depressed by a book. Something was making him nibble at the edge of stale ideas as if his sturdy physical egotism no longer nourished his peremptory heart.

Already it was deep summer on roadhouse roofs and in front of wayside garages, where new red petrol-pumps sat out in pools of light, and when I reached my estate at West Egg I ran the car under its shed and sat for a while on an abandoned grass roller in the yard. The wind had blown off, leaving a loud, bright night, with wings beating in the trees and a persistent organ sound as the full bellows of the earth blew the frogs full of life. The silhouette of a moving cat wavered across the moonlight, and, turning my head to watch it, I saw that I was not alone – fifty feet away a figure had emerged from the shadow of my neighbour's mansion and was standing with his hands in his pockets regarding the silver pepper of the stars. Something in his leisurely movements and the secure position of his feet upon the lawn suggested that it was Mr Gatsby himself, come out to determine what share was his of our local heavens.

I decided to call to him. Miss Baker had mentioned him at dinner, and that would do for an introduction. But I didn't call to him, for he gave a sudden intimation that he was content to be alone – he stretched out his arms toward the dark water in a curious way, and, far as I was from him, I could have sworn he was trembling. Involuntarily I glanced seaward – and distinguished nothing except a single green light, minute and far away, that might have been the end of a dock. When I looked once more for Gatsby he had vanished, and I was alone again in the unquiet darkness.

colour ?

Chapter II

ABOUT half-way between West Egg and New York the motor
road hastily joins the railroad and runs beside it for a quarter
of a mile, so as to shrink away from a certain desolate area of
land. This is a valley of ashes[9] – a fantastic farm where ashes
grow like wheat into ridges and hills and grotesque gardens;
where ashes take the forms of houses and chimneys and rising
smoke and, finally, with a transcendent effort, of ash-grey men,
who move dimly and already crumbling through the powdery
air. Occasionally a line of grey cars crawls along an invisible
track, gives out a ghastly creak, and comes to rest, and immediately the ash-grey men swarm up with leaden spades and stir
up an impenetrable cloud, which screens their obscure opera-
tions from your sight.

But above the grey land and the spasms of bleak dust which
drift endlessly over it, you perceive, after a moment, the eyes
of Doctor T. J. Eckleburg. The eyes of Doctor T. J. Eckleburg
are blue and gigantic – their retinas are one yard high. They
look out of no face, but, instead, from a pair of enormous
yellow spectacles which pass over a non-existent nose. Evidently some wild wag of an oculist set them there to fatten his
practice in the borough of Queens, and then sank down himself
into eternal blindness, or forgot them and moved away. But
his eyes, dimmed a little by many paintless days, under sun and
rain, brood on over the solemn dumping ground.

The valley of ashes is bounded on one side by a small foul
river, and, when the drawbridge is up to let barges through,
the passengers on waiting trains can stare at the dismal scene

for as long as half an hour. There is always a halt there of at least a minute, and it was because of this that I first met Tom Buchanan's mistress.

The fact that he had one was insisted upon wherever he was known. His acquaintances resented the fact that he turned up in popular cafés with her and, leaving her at a table, sauntered about, chatting with whomsoever he knew. Though I was curious to see her, I had no desire to meet her – but I did. I went up to New York with Tom on the train one afternoon, and when we stopped by the ashheaps he jumped to his feet and, taking hold of my elbow, literally forced me from the car.

'We're getting off,' he insisted. 'I want you to meet my girl.'

I think he'd tanked up a good deal at luncheon, and his determination to have my company bordered on violence. The supercilious assumption was that on Sunday afternoon I had nothing better to do.

I followed him over a low whitewashed railroad fence, and we walked back a hundred yards along the road under Doctor Eckleburg's persistent stare. The only building in sight was a small block of yellow brick sitting on the edge of the waste land, a sort of compact Main Street ministering to it, and contiguous to absolutely nothing. One of the three shops it contained was for rent and another was an all-night restaurant, approached by a trail of ashes; the third was a garage – *Repairs*. GEORGE B. WILSON. *Cars bought and sold*. – and I followed Tom inside.

The interior was unprosperous and bare; the only car visible was the dust-covered wreck of a Ford which crouched in a dim corner. It had occurred to me that this shadow of a garage must be a blind, and that sumptuous and romantic apartments were concealed overhead, when the proprietor himself appeared in the door of an office, wiping his hands on a piece of waste. He was a blond, spiritless man, anaemic, and faintly handsome. When he saw us a damp gleam of hope sprang into his light blue eyes.

'Hello, Wilson, old man,' said Tom, slapping him jovially on the shoulder. 'How's business?'

'I can't complain,' answered Wilson unconvincingly. 'When are you going to sell me that car?'

'Next week; I've got my man working on it now.'

'Works pretty slow, don't he?'

'No, he doesn't,' said Tom coldly. 'And if you feel that way about it, maybe I'd better sell it somewhere else after all.'

'I don't mean that,' explained Wilson quickly. 'I just meant –'

His voice faded off and Tom glanced impatiently around the garage. Then I heard footsteps on a stairs, and in a moment the thickish figure of a woman blocked out the light from the office door. She was in the middle thirties, and faintly stout, but she carried her flesh sensuously as some women can. Her face, above a spotted dress of dark blue crêpe-de-chine, contained no facet or gleam of beauty, but there was an immediately perceptible vitality about her as if the nerves of her body were continually smouldering. She smiled slowly and, walking through her husband as if he were a ghost, shook hands with Tom, looking him flush in the eye. Then she wet her lips, and without turning around spoke to her husband in a soft, coarse voice:

'Get some chairs, why don't you, so somebody can sit down.'

'Oh, sure,' agreed Wilson hurriedly, and went toward the little office, mingling immediately with the cement colour of the walls. A white ashen dust veiled his dark suit and his pale hair as it veiled everything in the vicinity – except his wife, who moved close to Tom.

'I want to see you,' said Tom intently. 'Get on the next train.'

'All right.'

'I'll meet you by the news-stand on the lower level.'

She nodded and moved away from him just as George Wilson emerged with two chairs from his office door.

We waited for her down the road and out of sight. It was a few days before the Fourth of July, and a grey, scrawny Italian child was setting torpedoes in a row along the railroad track.

'Terrible place, isn't it,' said Tom, exchanging a frown with Doctor Eckleburg.

'Awful.'

'It does her good to get away.'

'Doesn't her husband object?'

'Wilson? He thinks she goes to see her sister in New York. He's so dumb he doesn't know he's alive.'

So Tom Buchanan and his girl and I went up together to New York – or not quite together, for Mrs Wilson sat discreetly in another car. Tom deferred that much to the sensibilities of those East Eggers who mig: be on the train.

She had changed her dress to a brown figured muslin, which stretched tight over her rather wide hips as Tom helped her to the platform in New York. At the news-stand she bought a copy of *Town Tattle* and a moving-picture magazine, and in the station drug-store some cold cream and a small flask of perfume. Upstairs, in the solemn echoing drive she let four taxicabs drive away before she selected a new one, lavender-coloured with grey upholstery, and in this we slid out from the mass of the station into the glowing sunshine. But immediately she turned sharply from the window and, leaning forward, tapped on the front glass.

'I want to get one of those dogs,' she said earnestly. 'I want to get one for the apartment. They're nice to have – a dog.'

We backed up to a grey old man who bore an absurd

resemblance to John D. Rockefeller. In a basket swung from his neck cowered a dozen very recent puppies of an indeterminate breed.

'What kind are they?' asked Mrs Wilson eagerly, as he came to the taxi-window.

'All kinds. What kind do you want, lady?'

'I'd like to get one of those police dogs; I don't suppose you got that kind?'

The man peered doubtfully into the basket, plunged in his hand and drew one up, wriggling, by the back of the neck.

'That's no police dog,' said Tom.

'No, it's not exactly a police dog,' said the man with disappointment in his voice. 'It's more of an Airedale.' He passed his hand over the brown washrag of a back. 'Look at that coat. Some coat. That's a dog that'll never bother you with catching cold.'

'I think it's cute,' said Mrs Wilson enthusiastically. 'How much is it?'

'That dog?' He looked at it admiringly. 'That dog will cost you ten dollars.'

The Airedale – undoubtedly there was an Airedale concerned in it somewhere, though its feet were startlingly white – changed hands and settled down into Mrs Wilson's lap, where she fondled the weather-proof coat with rapture.

'Is it a boy or a girl?' she asked delicately.

'That dog? That dog's a boy.'

'It's a bitch,' said Tom decisively. 'Here's your money. Go and buy ten more dogs with it.'

We drove over to Fifth Avenue, warm and soft, almost pastoral, on the summer Sunday afternoon. I wouldn't have been surprised to see a great flock of white sheep turn the corner.

'Hold on,' I said, 'I have to leave you here.'

'No you don't,' interposed Tom quickly. 'Myrtle'll be hurt if you don't come up to the apartment. Won't you, Myrtle?'

'Come on,' she urged. 'I'll telephone my sister Catherine. She's said to be very beautiful by people who ought to know.'

'Well, I'd like to, but –'

We went on, cutting back again over the Park toward the West Hundreds. At 158th Street the cab stopped at one slice in a long white cake of apartment-houses. Throwing a regal homecoming glance around the neighbourhood, Mrs Wilson gathered up her dog and her other purchases, and went haughtily in.

'I'm going to have the McKees come up,' she announced as we rose in the elevator. 'And, of course, I got to call up my sister, too.'

The apartment was on the top floor – a small living-room, a small dining-room, a small bedroom, and a bath. The living-room was crowded to the doors with a set of tapestried furniture entirely too large for it, so that to move about was to stumble continually over scenes of ladies swinging in the gardens of Versailles. The only picture was an over-enlarged photograph, apparently a hen sitting on a blurred rock. Looked at from a distance, however, the hen resolved itself into a bonnet, and the countenance of a stout old lady beamed down into the room. Several old copies of *Town Tattle*[10] lay on the table together with a copy of *Simon Called Peter*,[11] and some of the small scandal magazines of Broadway. Mrs Wilson was first concerned with the dog. A reluctant elevator boy went for a box full of straw and some milk, to which he added on his own initiative a tin of large, hard dog biscuits – one of which decomposed apathetically in the saucer of milk all afternoon. Meanwhile Tom brought out a bottle of whisky from a locked bureau door.

I have been drunk just twice in my life, and the second time was that afternoon; so everything that happened has a dim, hazy cast over it, although until after eight o'clock the apartment was full of cheerful sun. Sitting on Tom's lap Mrs Wilson called up several people on the telephone; then there were no cigarettes, and I went out to buy some at the drugstore on the corner. When I came back they had both disappeared, so I sat down discreetly in the living-room and read a chapter of *Simon Called Peter* – either it was terrible stuff or the whisky distorted things, because it didn't make any sense to me.

Just as Tom and Myrtle (after the first drink Mrs Wilson and I called each other by our first names) reappeared, company commenced to arrive at the apartment door.

The sister, Catherine, was a slender, worldly girl of about thirty, with a solid, sticky bob of red hair, and a complexion powdered milky white. Her eyebrows had been plucked and then drawn on again at a more rakish angle, but the efforts of nature toward the restoration of the old alignment gave a blurred air to her face. When she moved about there was an incessant clicking as innumerable pottery bracelets jingled up and down upon her arms. She came in with such a proprietary haste, and looked around so possessively at the furniture that I wondered if she lived here. But when I asked her she laughed immoderately, repeated my question aloud, and told me she lived with a girl friend at a hotel.

Mr McKee was a pale, feminine man from the flat below. He had just shaved, for there was a white spot of lather on his cheekbone, and he was most respectful in his greeting to every one in the room. He informed me that he was in the 'artistic game', and I gathered later that he was a photographer and had made the dim enlargement of Mrs Wilson's mother which hovered like an ectoplasm on the wall. His wife was shrill, languid, handsome, and horrible. She told me with pride that her husband had photographed her a hundred and twenty-seven times since they had been married.

Mrs Wilson had changed her costume some time before, and was now attired in an elaborate afternoon dress of cream-coloured chiffon, which gave out a continual rustle as she swept about the room. With the influence of the dress her personality had also undergone a change. The intense vitality that had been so remarkable in the garage was converted into impressive *hauteur*. Her laughter, her gestures, her assertions became more violently affected moment by moment, and as she expanded the room grew smaller around her, until she seemed to be revolving on a noisy, creaking pivot through the smoky air.

'My dear,' she told her sister in a high, mincing shout, 'most of these fellas will cheat you every time. All they think of is money. I had a woman up here last week to look at my feet, and when she gave me the bill you'd of thought she had my appendicitus out.'

'What was the name of the woman?' asked Mrs McKee.

'Mrs Eberhardt. She goes around looking at people's feet in their own homes.'

'I like your dress,' remarked Mrs McKee, 'I think it's adorable.'

Mrs Wilson rejected the compliment by raising her eyebrow in disdain.

'It's just a crazy old thing,' she said. 'I just slip it on sometimes when I don't care what I look like.'

'But it looks wonderful on you, if you know what I mean,' pursued Mrs McKee. 'If Chester could only get you in that pose I think he could make something of it.'

We all looked in silence at Mrs Wilson, who removed a strand of hair from over her eyes and looked back at us with a brilliant smile. Mr McKee regarded her intently with his head on one side, and then moved his hand back and forth slowly in front of his face.

'I should change the light,' he said after a moment. 'I'd like to bring out the modelling of the features. And I'd try to get hold of all the back hair.'

'I wouldn't think of changing the light,' cried Mrs McKee. 'I think it's –'

Her husband said '*Sh!*' and we all looked at the subject again, whereupon Tom Buchanan yawned audibly and got to his feet.

'You McKees have something to drink,' he said. 'Get some more ice and mineral water, Myrtle, before everybody goes to sleep.'

'I told that boy about the ice.' Myrtle raised her eyebrows in despair at the shiftlessness of the lower orders. 'These people! You have to keep after them all the time.'

She looked at me and laughed pointlessly. Then she flounced over to the dog, kissed it with ecstasy, and swept into the kitchen, implying that a dozen chefs awaited her orders there.

'I've done some nice things out on Long Island,' asserted Mr McKee.

Tom looked at him blankly.

'Two of them we have framed downstairs.'

'Two what?' demanded Tom.

'Two studies. One of them I call "Montauk Point – The Gulls", and the other I call "Montauk Point – the Sea".'[12]

The sister Catherine sat down beside me on the couch.

'Do you live down on Long Island, too?' she inquired.

'I live at West Egg.'

'Really? I was down there at a party about a month ago. At a man named Gatsby's. Do you know him?'

'I live next door to him.'

'Well, they say he's a nephew or a cousin of Kaiser Wilhelm's. That's where all his money comes from.'

'Really?'

She nodded.

'I'm scared of him. I'd hate to have him get anything on me.'

This absorbing information about my neighbour was interrupted by Mrs McKee's pointing suddenly at Catherine:

'Chester, I think you could do something with *her*,' she broke out, but Mr McKee only nodded in a bored way, and turned his attention to Tom.

'I'd like to do more work on Long Island, if I could get the entry. All I ask is that they should give me a start.'

'Ask Myrtle,' said Tom, breaking into a short shout of laughter as Mrs Wilson entered with a tray. 'She'll give you a letter of introduction, won't you, Myrtle?'

'Do what?' she asked, startled.

'You'll give McKee a letter of introduction to your husband, so he can do some studies of him.' His lips moved silently for a moment as he invented, ' "George B. Wilson at the Gasoline Pump", or something like that.'

Catherine leaned close to me and whispered in my ear:

'Neither of them can stand the person they're married to.'

'Can't they?'

'Can't *stand* them.' She looked at Myrtle and then at Tom. 'What I say is, why go on living with them if they can't stand them? If I was them I'd get a divorce and get married to each other right away.'

'Doesn't she like Wilson either?'

The answer to this was unexpected. It came from Myrtle, who had overheard the question, and it was violent and obscene.

'You see,' cried Catherine triumphantly. She lowered her

voice again. 'It's really his wife that's keeping them apart. She's a Catholic, and they don't believe in divorce.'

Daisy was not a Catholic, and I was a little shocked at the elaborateness of the lie.

'When they do get married,' continued Catherine, 'they're going West to live for a while until it blows over.'

'It'd be more discreet to go to Europe.'

'Oh, do you like Europe?' she exclaimed surprisingly. 'I just got back from Monte Carlo.'

'Really.'

'Just last year. I went over there with another girl.'

'Stay long?'

'No, we just went to Monte Carlo and back. We went by way of Marseilles. We had over twelve hundred dollars when we started, but we got gyped out of it all in two days in the private rooms. We had an awful time getting back, I can tell you. God, how I hated that town!'

The late afternoon sky bloomed in the window for a moment like the blue honey of the Mediterranean – then the shrill voice of Mrs McKee called me back into the room.

'I almost made a mistake, too,' she declared vigorously. 'I almost married a little kyke who'd been after me for years. I knew he was below me. Everybody kept saying to me: "Lucille, that man's 'way below you!" But if I hadn't met Chester, he'd of got me sure.'

'Yes, but listen,' said Myrtle Wilson, nodding her head up and down, 'at least you didn't marry him.'

'I know I didn't.'

'Well, I married him,' said Myrtle, ambiguously. 'And that's the difference between your case and mine.'

'Why did you, Myrtle?' demanded Catherine. 'Nobody forced you to.'

Myrtle considered.

36

'I married him because I thought he was a gentleman,' she said finally. 'I thought he knew something about breeding, but he wasn't fit to lick my shoe.'

'You were crazy about him for a while,' said Catherine.

'Crazy about him!' cried Myrtle incredulously. 'Who said I was crazy about him? I never was any more crazy about him than I was about that man there.'

She pointed suddenly at me, and every one looked at me accusingly. I tried to show by my expression that I expected no affection.

'The only *crazy* I was was when I married him. I knew right away I made a mistake. He borrowed somebody's best suit to get married in, and never even told me about it, and the man came after it one day when he was out: "Oh, is that your suit?" I said. "This is the first I ever heard about it." But I gave it to him and then I lay down and cried to beat the band all afternoon.'

'She really ought to get away from him,' resumed Catherine to me. 'They've been living over that garage for eleven years. And Tom's the first sweetie she ever had.'

The bottle of whisky – a second one – was now in constant demand by all present, excepting Catherine, who 'felt just as good on nothing at all'. Tom rang for the janitor and sent him for some celebrated sandwiches, which were a complete supper in themselves. I wanted to get out and walk eastward toward the park through the soft twilight, but each time I tried to go I became entangled in some wild, strident argument which pulled me back, as if with ropes, into my chair. Yet high over the city our line of yellow windows must have contributed their share of human secrecy to the casual watcher in the darkening streets, and I saw him too, looking up and wondering. I was within and without, simultaneously enchanted and repelled by the inexhaustible variety of life.

Myrtle pulled her chair close to mine, and suddenly her warm breath poured over me the story of her first meeting with Tom.

'It was on the two little seats facing each other that are always the last ones left on the train. I was going up to New York to see my sister and spend the night. He had on a dress suit and patent leather shoes, and I couldn't keep my eyes off him, but every time he looked at me I had to pretend to be looking at the advertisement over his head. When we came into the station he was next to me, and his white shirt-front pressed against my arm, and so I told him I'd have to call a policeman, but he knew I lied. I was so excited that when I got into a taxi with him I didn't hardly know I wasn't getting into a subway train. All I kept thinking about, over and over, was "You can't live forever; you can't live forever."'

She turned to Mrs McKee and the room rang full of her artificial laughter.

'My dear,' she cried, 'I'm going to give you this dress as soon as I'm through with it. I've got to get another one tomorrow. I'm going to make a list of all the things I've got to get. A massage and a wave, and a collar for the dog, and one of those cute little ash-trays where you touch a spring, and a wreath with a black silk bow for mother's grave that'll last all summer. I got to write down a list so I won't forget all the things I got to do.'

It was nine o'clock – almost immediately afterward I looked at my watch and found it was ten. Mr McKee was asleep on a chair with his fists clenched in his lap, like a photograph of a man of action. Taking out my handkerchief I wiped from his cheek the spot of dried lather that had worried me all the afternoon.

The little dog was sitting on the table looking with blind eyes through the smoke, and from time to time groaning faintly. People disappeared, reappeared, made plans to go somewhere, and then lost each other, searched for each other, found each other a few feet away. Some time toward midnight Tom Buchanan and Mrs Wilson stood face to face discussing, in impassioned voices, whether Mrs Wilson had any right to mention Daisy's name.

'Daisy! Daisy! Daisy!' shouted Mrs Wilson. 'I'll say it whenever I want to! Daisy! Dai –' *recording sum of his reality*

Making a short deft movement, Tom Buchanan broke her nose with his open hand.

Then there were bloody towels upon the bathroom floor, and women's voices scolding, and high over the confusion a long broken wail of pain. Mr McKee awoke from his doze and started in a daze toward the door. When he had gone half-way he turned around and stared at the scene – his wife and Catherine scolding and consoling as they stumbled here and there among the crowded furniture with articles of aid, and the despairing figure on the couch, bleeding fluently, and trying to spread a copy of *Town Tattle* over the tapestry scenes of Versailles. Then Mr McKee turned and continued on out the door. Taking my hat from the chandelier, I followed.

'Come to lunch some day,' he suggested, as we groaned down in the elevator.

'Where?'

'Anywhere.'

'Keep your hands off the lever,' snapped the elevator boy.

'I beg your pardon,' said Mr McKee with dignity, 'I didn't know I was touching it.'

'All right,' I agreed, 'I'll be glad to.'

... I was standing beside his bed and he was sitting up between the sheets, clad in his underwear, with a great portfolio in his hands.

'Beauty and the Beast ... Loneliness ... Old Grocery Horse ... Brook'n Bridge ...'

Then I was lying half asleep in the cold lower level of the Pennsylvania Station, staring at the morning *Tribune*, and waiting for the four o'clock train.

Chapter III

THERE was music from my neighbour's house through the summer nights. In his blue gardens men and girls came and went like moths among the whisperings and the champagne and the stars. At high tide in the afternoon I watched his guests diving from the tower of his raft, or taking the sun on the hot sand of his beach while his two motor-boats slit the waters of the Sound, drawing aquaplanes over cataracts of foam. On week-ends his Rolls-Royce became an omnibus, bearing parties to and from the city between nine in the morning and long past midnight, while his station wagon scampered like a brisk yellow bug to meet all trains. And on Mondays eight servants, including an extra gardener, toiled all day with mops and scrubbing-brushes and hammers and garden-shears, repairing the ravages of the night before.

Every Friday five crates of oranges and lemons arrived from a fruiterer in New York – every Monday these same oranges and lemons left his back door in a pyramid of pulpless halves. There was a machine in the kitchen which could extract the juice of two hundred oranges in half an hour if a little button was pressed two hundred times by a butler's thumb.

At least once a fortnight a corps of caterers came down with several hundred feet of canvas and enough coloured lights to make a Christmas tree of Gatsby's enormous garden. On buffet tables, garnished with glistening hors-d'oeuvre, spiced baked hams crowded against salads of harlequin designs and pastry pigs and turkeys bewitched to a dark gold. In the main hall a bar with a real brass rail was set up, and stocked with gins and liquors and with cordials so long forgotten that most of his female guests were too young to know one from another.

By seven o'clock the orchestra has arrived, no thin five-piece affair, but a whole pitful of oboes and trombones and saxophones and viols and cornets and piccolos, and low and high drums. The last swimmers have come in from the beach now and are dressing upstairs; the cars from New York are parked five deep in the drive, and already the halls and salons and verandas are gaudy with primary colours, and hair bobbed in strange new ways, and shawls beyond the dreams of Castile. The bar is in full swing, and floating rounds of cocktails permeate the garden outside, until the air is alive with chatter and laughter, and casual innuendo and introductions forgotten on the spot, and enthusiastic meetings between women who never knew each other's names.

The lights grow brighter as the earth lurches away from the sun, and now the orchestra is playing yellow cocktail music, and the opera of voices pitches a key higher. Laughter is easier minute by minute, spilled with prodigality, tipped out at a cheerful word. The groups change more swiftly, swell with new arrivals, dissolve and form in the same breath; already there are wanderers, confident girls who weave here and there among the stouter and more stable, become for a sharp, joyous moment the centre of a group, and then, excited with triumph, glide on through the sea-change of faces and voices and colour under the constantly changing light.

Suddenly one of these gypsies, in trembling opal, seizes a cocktail out of the air, dumps it down for courage and, moving her hands like Frisco,[13] dances out alone on the canvas platform. A momentary hush; the orchestra leader varies his rhythm obligingly for her, and there is a burst of chatter as the erroneous news goes around that she is Gilda Gray's[14] understudy from the Follies. The party has begun.

I believe that on the first night I went to Gatsby's house I was one of the few guests who had actually been invited. People were not invited – they went there. They got into automobiles which bore them out to Long Island, and somehow they ended up at Gatsby's door. Once there they were introduced by somebody who knew Gatsby, and after that they conducted themselves according to the rules of behaviour associated with an amusement park. Sometimes they came and went without having met Gatsby at all, came for the party with a simplicity of heart that was its own ticket of admission.

I had been actually invited. A chauffeur in a uniform of robin's-egg blue crossed my lawn early that Saturday morning with a surprisingly formal note from his employer: the honour would be entirely Gatsby's, it said, if I would attend his 'little party' that night. He had seen me several times, and had intended to call on me long before, but a peculiar combination of circumstances had prevented it – signed Jay Gatsby, in a majestic hand.

Dressed up in white flannels I went over to his lawn a little after seven, and wandered around rather ill at ease among swirls and eddies of people I didn't know – though here and there was a face I had noticed on the commuting train. I was immediately struck by the number of young Englishmen dotted about; all well dressed, all looking a little hungry, and all talking in low, earnest voices to solid and prosperous Americans. I was sure that they were selling something: bonds or insurance or automobiles. They were at least agonizingly aware of the easy money in the vicinity and convinced that it was theirs for a few words in the right key.

As soon as I arrived I made an attempt to find my host, but the two or three people of whom I asked his whereabouts stared at me in such an amazed way, and denied so vehemently any knowledge of his movements, that I slunk off in the direction of the cocktail table – the only place in the garden where a single man could linger without looking purposeless and alone.

I was on my way to get roaring drunk from sheer embarrassment when Jordan Baker came out of the house and stood at the head of the marble steps, leaning a little backward and looking with contemptuous interest down into the garden.

Welcome or not, I found it necessary to attach myself to some one before I should begin to address cordial remarks to the passers-by.

'Hello!' I roared, advancing toward her. My voice seemed unnaturally loud across the garden.

'I thought you might be here,' she responded absently as I came up. 'I remembered you lived next door to –'

She held my hand impersonally, as a promise that she'd take care of me in a minute, and gave ear to two girls in twin yellow dresses, who stopped at the foot of the steps.

'Hello!' they cried together. 'Sorry you didn't win.'

That was for the golf tournament. She had lost in the finals the week before.

'You don't know who we are,' said one of the girls in yellow, 'but we met you here about a month ago.'

'You've dyed your hair since then,' remarked Jordan, and I started, but the girls had moved casually on and her remark was addressed to the premature moon, produced like the supper, no doubt, out of a caterer's basket. With Jordan's slender golden arm resting in mine, we descended the steps and sauntered about the garden. A tray of cocktails floated at us through the twilight, and we sat down at a table with the two girls in yellow and three men, each one introduced to us as Mr Mumble.

'Do you come to these parties often?' inquired Jordan of the girl beside her.

'The last one was the one I met you at,' answered the girl,

in an alert confident voice. She turned to her companion: 'Wasn't it for you, Lucille?'

It was for Lucille, too.

'I like to come,' Lucille said. 'I never care what I do, so I always have a good time. When I was here last I tore my gown on a chair, and he asked me my name and address – inside of a week I got a package from Croirier's with a new evening gown in it.'

'Did you keep it?' asked Jordan.

'Sure I did. I was going to wear it tonight, but it was too big in the bust and had to be altered. It was gas blue with lavender beads. Two hundred and sixty-five dollars.'

'There's something funny about a fellow that'll do a thing like that,' said the other girl eagerly. 'He doesn't want any trouble with *any*body.'

'Who doesn't?' I inquired.

'Gatsby. Somebody told me –'

The two girls and Jordan leaned together confidentially.

'Somebody told me they thought he killed a man once.'

A thrill passed over all of us. The three Mr Mumbles bent forward and listened eagerly.

'I don't think it's so much *that*,' argued Lucille sceptically; 'It's more that he was a German spy during the war.'

One of the men nodded in confirmation.

'I heard that from a man who knew all about him, grew up with him in Germany,' he assured us positively.

'Oh, no,' said the first girl, 'it couldn't be that, because he was in the American army during the war.' As our credulity switched back to her she leaned forward with enthusiasm. 'You look at him sometimes when he thinks nobody's looking at him. I'll bet he killed a man.'

She narrowed her eyes and shivered. Lucille shivered. We all turned and looked around for Gatsby. It was testimony to

45

the romantic speculation he inspired that there were whispers about him from those who had found little that it was necessary to whisper about in this world.

The first supper – there would be another one after midnight – was now being served, and Jordan invited me to join her own party, who were spread around a table on the other side of the garden. There were three married couples and Jordan's escort, a persistent undergraduate given to violent innuendo, and obviously under the impression that sooner or later Jordan was going to yield him up her person to a greater or lesser degree. Instead of rambling, this party had preserved a dignified homogeneity, and assumed to itself the function of representing the staid nobility of the countryside – East Egg condescending to West Egg and carefully on guard against its spectroscopic gaiety.

'Let's get out,' whispered Jordan, after a somehow wasteful and inappropriate half-hour; 'this is much too polite for me.'

We got up, and she explained that we were going to find the host: I had never met him, she said, and it was making me uneasy. The undergraduate nodded in a cynical, melancholy way.

The bar, where we glanced first, was crowded, but Gatsby was not there. She couldn't find him from the top of the steps, and he wasn't on the veranda. On a chance we tried an important-looking door, and walked into a high Gothic library, panelled with carved English Oak, and probably transported complete from some ruin overseas.

A stout, middle-aged man, with enormous owl-eyed spectacles, was sitting somewhat drunk on the edge of a great table, staring with unsteady concentration at the shelves of books. As we entered he wheeled excitedly around and examined Jordan from head to foot.

'What do you think?' he demanded impetuously.

'About what?'

He waved his hand toward the book-shelves.

'About that. As a matter of fact you needn't bother to ascertain. I ascertained. They're real.'

'The books?'

He nodded.

'Absolutely real – have pages and everything. I thought they'd be a nice durable cardboard. Matter of fact, they're absolutely real. Pages and – Here! Lemme show you.'

Taking our scepticism for granted, he rushed to the bookcases and returned with Volume One of the *Stoddard Lectures*.[15]

'See!' he cried triumphantly. 'It's a bona-fide piece of printed matter. It fooled me. This fella's a regular Belasco.[16] It's a triumph. What thoroughness! What realism! Knew when to stop, too – didn't cut the pages. But what do you want? What do you expect?'

He snatched the book from me and replaced it hastily on its shelf, muttering that if one brick was removed the whole library was liable to collapse.

'Who brought you?' he demanded. 'Or did you just come? I was brought. Most people were brought.'

Jordan looked at him alertly, cheerfully, without answering.

'I was brought by a woman named Roosevelt,' he continued. 'Mrs Claud Roosevelt. Do you know her? I met her somewhere last night. I've been drunk for about a week now, and I thought it might sober me up to sit in a library.'

'Has it?'

'A little bit, I think. I can't tell yet. I've only been here an hour. Did I tell you about the books? They're real. They're –'

'You told us.'

We shook hands with him gravely and went back outdoors.

There was dancing now on the canvas in the garden; old men pushing young girls backward in eternal graceless circles, superior couples holding each other tortuously, fashionably, and keeping in the corners – and a great number of single girls dancing individualistically or re ieving the orchestra for a moment of the burden of the banjo or the traps. By midnight the hilarity had increased. A celebrated tenor had sung in Italian, and a notorious contralto had sung in jazz, and between the numbers people were doing 'stunts' all over the garden, while happy, vacuous bursts of laughter rose toward the summer sky. A pair of stage twins, who turned out to be the girls in yellow, did a baby act in costume, and champagne was served in glasses bigger than finger-bowls. The moon had risen higher, and floating in the Sound was a triangle of silver scales, trembling a little to the stiff, tinny drip of the banjoes on the lawn.

I was still with Jordan Baker. We were sitting at a table with a man of about my age and a rowdy little girl, who gave way upon the slightest provocation to uncontrollable laughter. I was enjoying myself now. I had taken two finger-bowls of champagne, and the scene had changed before my eyes into something significant, elemental, and profound.

At a lull in the entertainment the man looked at me and smiled.

'Your face is familiar,' he said politely. 'Weren't you in the First Division during the war?'

'Why, yes. I was in the Twenty-eighth Infantry.'

'I was in the Sixteenth until June nineteen-eighteen.[17] I knew I'd seen you somewhere before.'

We talked for a moment about some wet, grey little villages in France. Evidently he lived in this vicinity, for he told me that he had just bought a hydroplane,[18] and was going to try it out in the morning.

'Want to go with me, old sport? Just near the shore along the Sound.'

'What time?'

'Any time that suits you best.'

It was on the tip of my tongue to ask his name when Jordan looked around and smiled.

'Having a gay time now?' she inquired.

'Much better.' I turned again to my new acquaintance. 'This is an unusual party for me. I haven't even seen the host. I live over there –' I waved my hand at the invisible hedge in the distance, 'and this man Gatsby sent over his chauffeur with an invitation.'

For a moment he looked at me as if he failed to understand.

'I'm Gatsby,' he said suddenly.

'What!' I exclaimed. 'Oh, I beg your pardon.'

'I thought you knew, old sport. I'm afraid I'm not a very good host.'

He smiled understandingly – much more than understandingly. It was one of those rare smiles with a quality of eternal reassurance in it, that you may come across four or five times in life. It faced – or seemed to face – the whole eternal world for an instant, and then concentrated on *you* with an irresistible prejudice in your favour. It understood you just so far as you wanted to be understood, believed in you as you would like to believe in yourself, and assured you that it had precisely the impression of you that, at your best, you hoped to convey. Precisely at that point it vanished – and I was looking at an elegant young rough-neck, a year or two over thirty, whose elaborate formality of speech just missed being absurd. Some time before he introduced himself I'd got a strong impression that he was picking his words with care.

Almost at the moment when Mr Gatsby identified himself a butler hurried toward him with the information that Chicago was calling him on the wire. He excused himself with a small bow that included each of us in turn.

'If you want anything just ask for it, old sport,' he urged me. 'Excuse me. I will rejoin you later.'

When he was gone I turned immediately to Jordan – constrained to assure her of my surprise. I had expected that Mr Gatsby would be a florid and corpulent person in his middle years.

'Who is he?' I demanded. 'Do you know?'

'He's just a man named Gatsby.'

'Where is he from, I mean? And what does he do?'

'Now *you*'re started on the subject,' she answered with a wan smile. 'Well, he told me once he was an Oxford man.'

A dim background started to take shape behind him, but at her next remark it faded away.

'However, I don't believe it.'

'Why not?'

'I don't know,' she insisted, 'I just don't think he went there.'

Something in her tone reminded me of the other girl's 'I think he killed a man', and had the effect of stimulating my curiosity. I would have accepted without question the information that Gatsby sprang from the swamps of Louisiana or from the lower East Side of New York. That was comprehensible. But young men didn't – at least in my provincial inexperience I believed they didn't – drift coolly out of nowhere and buy a palace on Long Island Sound.

'Anyhow, he gives large parties,' said Jordan, changing the subject with an urban distaste for the concrete. 'And I like large parties. They're so intimate. At small parties there isn't any privacy.'

There was the boom of a bass drum, and the voice of the orchestra leader rang out suddenly above the echolalia of the garden.

'Ladies and gentlemen,' he cried. 'At the request of Mr

Gatsby we are going to play for you Mr Vladmir Tostoff's latest work, which attracted so much attention at Carnegie Hall last May. If you read the papers you know there was a big sensation.' He smiled with jovial condescension, and added: 'Some sensation!' Whereupon everybody laughed.

'The piece is known,' he concluded lustily, 'as "Vladmir Tostoff's Jazz History of the World!".'

The nature of Mr Tostoff's composition eluded me, because just as it began my eyes fell on Gatsby, standing alone on the marble steps and looking from one group to another with approving eyes. His tanned skin was drawn attractively tight on his face and his short hair looked as though it were trimmed every day. I could see nothing sinister about him. I wondered if the fact that he was not drinking helped to set him off from his guests, for it seemed to me that he grew more correct as the fraternal hilarity increased. When the 'Jazz History of the World' was over, girls were putting their heads on men's shoulders in a puppyish, convivial way, girls were swooning backward playfully into men's arms, even into groups, knowing that some one would arrest their falls – but no one swooned backward on Gatsby, and no French bob touched Gatsby's shoulder, and no singing quartets were formed with Gatsby's head for one link.

'I beg your pardon.'

Gatsby's butler was suddenly standing beside us.

'Miss Baker?' he inquired. 'I beg your pardon, but Mr Gatsby would like to speak to you alone.'

'With me?' she exclaimed in surprise.

'Yes, madame.'

She got up slowly, raising her eyebrows at me in astonishment, and followed the butler toward the house. I noticed that she wore her evening-dress, all her dresses, like sports clothes – there was a jauntiness about her movements as if she had first learned to walk upon golf courses on clean, crisp mornings.

I was alone and it was almost two. For some time confused and intriguing sounds had issued from a long, many-windowed room which overhung the terrace. Eluding Jordan's undergraduate, who was now engaged in an obstetrical conversation with two chorus girls, and who implored me to join him, I went inside.

The large room was full of people. One of the girls in yellow was playing the piano, and beside her stood a tall, red-haired young lady from a famous chorus, engaged in song. She had drunk a quantity of champagne, and during the course of her song she had decided, ineptly, that everything was very, very sad – she was not only singing, she was weeping too. Whenever there was a pause in the song she filled it with gasping, broken sobs, and then took up the lyric again in a quavering soprano. The tears coursed down her cheeks – not freely, however, for when they came into contact with her heavily beaded eyelashes they assumed an inky colour, and pursued the rest of their way in slow black rivulets. A humorous suggestion was made that she sing the notes on her face, whereupon she threw up her hands, sank into a chair, and went off into a deep vinous sleep.

'She had a fight with a man who says he's her husband,' explained a girl at my elbow.

I looked around. Most of the remaining women were now having fights with men said to be their husbands. Even Jordan's party, the quartet from East Egg, were rent asunder by dissension. One of the men was talking with curious intensity to a young actress, and his wife, after attempting to laugh at the situation in a dignified and indifferent way, broke down entirely and resorted to flank attacks – at intervals she appeared suddenly at his side like an angry diamond, and hissed: 'You promised!' into his ear.

The reluctance to go home was not confined to wayward men. The hall was at present occupied by two deplorably sober men and their highly indignant wives. The wives were sympathizing with each other in slightly raised voices.

'Whenever he sees I'm having a good time he wants to go home.'

'Never heard anything so selfish in my life.'

'We're always the first ones to leave.'

'So are we.'

'Well, we're almost the last tonight,' said one of the men sheepishly. 'The orchestra left half an hour ago.'

In spite of the wives' agreement that such malevolence was beyond credibility, the dispute ended in a short struggle, and both wives were lifted, kicking, into the night.

As I waited for my hat in the hall the door of the library opened and Jordan Baker and Gatsby came out together. He was saying some last word to her, but the eagerness in his manner tightened abruptly into formality as several people approached him to say good-bye.

Jordan's party were calling impatiently to her from the porch, but she lingered for a moment to shake hands.

'I've just heard the most amazing thing,' she whispered. 'How long were we in there?'

'Why, about an hour.'

'It was . . . simply amazing,' she repeated abstractedly. 'But I swore I wouldn't tell it and here I am tantalizing you.' She yawned gracefully in my face. 'Please come and see me . . . Phone book . . . Under the name of Mrs Sigourney Howard . . . My aunt . . .' She was hurrying off as she talked – her brown hand waved a jaunty salute as she melted into her party at the door.

Rather ashamed that on my first appearance I had stayed so late, I joined the last of Gatsby's guests, who were clustered around him. I wanted to explain that I'd hunted for him early in the evening and to apologize for not having known him in the garden.

'Don't mention it,' he enjoined me eagerly. 'Don't give it another thought, old sport.' The familiar expression held no more familiarity than the hand which reassuringly brushed my shoulder. 'And don't forget we're going up in the hydroplane tomorrow morning, at nine o'clock.'

Then the butler, behind his shoulder:

'Philadelphia wants you on the phone, sir.'

'All right, in a minute. Tell them I'll be right there ... Good night.'

'Good night.'

'Good night.' He smiled – and suddenly there seemed to be a pleasant significance in having been among the last to go, as if he had desired it all the time. 'Good night, old sport ... Good night.'

But as I walked down the steps I saw that the evening was not quite over. Fifty feet from the door a dozen headlights illuminated a bizarre and tumultuous scene. In the ditch beside the road, right side up, but violently shorn of one wheel, rested a new coupe which had left Gatsby's drive not two minutes before. The sharp jut of a wall accounted for the detachment of the wheel, which was now getting considerable attention from half a dozen curious chauffeurs. However, as they had left their cars blocking the road, a harsh, discordant din from those in the rear had been audible for some time, and added to the already violent confusion of the scene.

A man in a long duster had dismounted from the wreck and now stood in the middle of the road, looking from the car to the tyre and from the tyre to the observers in a pleasant, puzzled way.

'See!' he explained. 'It went in the ditch.'

54

The fact was infinitely astonishing to him, and I recognized first the unusual quality of wonder, and then the man – it was the late patron of Gatsby's library.

'How'd it happen?'

He shrugged his shoulders.

'I know nothing whatever about mechanics,' he said decisively.

'But how did it happen? Did you run into the wall?'

'Don't ask me,' said Owl Eyes, washing his hands of the whole matter. 'I know very little about driving – next to nothing. It happened, and that's all I know.'

'Well, if you're a poor driver you oughtn't to try driving at night.'

'But I wasn't even trying,' he explained indignantly, 'I wasn't even trying.'

An awed hush fell upon the bystanders.

'Do you want to commit suicide?'

'You're lucky it was just a wheel! A bad driver and not even *try*ing!'

'You don't understand,' explained the criminal. 'I wasn't driving. There's another man in the car.'

The shock that followed this declaration found voice in a sustained 'Ah-h-h!' as the door of the coupé swung slowly open. The crowd – it was now a crowd – stepped back involuntarily, and when the door had opened wide there was a ghostly pause. Then, very gradually, part by part, a pale, dangling individual stepped out of the wreck, pawing tentatively at the ground with a large uncertain dancing shoe.

Blinded by the glare of the headlights and confused by the incessant groaning of the horns, the apparition stood swaying for a moment before he perceived the man in the duster.

'Wha's matter?' he inquired calmly. 'Did we run outa gas?'

'Look!'

55

Half a dozen fingers pointed at the amputated wheel – he stared at it for a moment, and then looked upward as though he suspected that it had dropped from the sky.

'It came off,' someone explained.

He nodded.

'At first I din' notice we'd stopped.'

A pause. Then, taking a long breath and straightening his shoulders, he remarked in a determined voice:

'Wonder'ff tell me where there's a gas'line station?'

At least a dozen men, some of them a little better off than he was, explained to him that wheel and car were no longer joined by any physical bond.

'Back out,' he suggested after a moment. 'Put her in reverse.'

'But the *wheel*'s off!'

He hesitated.

'No harm in trying,' he said.

The caterwauling horns had reached a crescendo and I turned away and cut across the lawn toward home. I glanced back once. A wafer of a moon was shining over Gatsby's house, making the night fine as before, and surviving the laughter and the sound of his still glowing garden. A sudden emptiness seemed to flow now from the windows and the great doors, endowing with complete isolation the figure of the host, who stood on the porch, his hand up in a formal gesture of farewell.

Reading over what I have written so far, I see I have given the impression that the events of three nights several weeks apart were all that absorbed me. On the contrary, they were merely casual events in a crowded summer, and, until much later, they absorbed me infinitely less than my personal affairs.

Most of the time I worked. In the early morning the sun threw my shadow westward as I hurried down the white chasms of lower New York to the Probity Trust. I knew the other clerks and young bond-salesmen by their first names, and lunched with them in dark, crowded restaurants on little pig sausages and mashed potatoes and coffee. I even had a short affair with a girl who lived in Jersey City and worked in the accounting department, but her brother began throwing mean looks in my direction, so when she went on her vacation in July I let it blow quietly away.

I took dinner usually at the Yale Club – for some reason it was the gloomiest event of my day – and then I went upstairs to the library and studied investments and securities for a conscientious hour. There were generally a few rioters around, but they never came into the library, so it was a good place to work. After that, if the night was mellow, I strolled down Madison Avenue past the old Murray Hill Hotel, and over 33rd Street to the Pennsylvania Station.

I began to like New York, the racy, adventurous feel of it at night, and the satisfaction that the constant flicker of men and women and machines gives to the restless eye. I liked to walk up Fifth Avenue and pick out romantic women from the crowd and imagine that in a few minutes I was going to enter into their lives, and no one would ever know or disapprove. Sometimes, in my mind, I followed them to their apartments on the corners of hidden streets, and they turned and smiled back at me before they faded through a door into warm darkness. At the enchanted metropolitan twilight I felt a haunting loneliness sometimes, and felt it in others – poor young clerks who loitered in front of windows waiting until it was time for a solitary restaurant dinner – young clerks in the dusk, wasting the most poignant moments of night and life.

Again at eight o'clock, when the dark lanes of the Forties were lined five deep with throbbing taxicabs, bound for the theatre district, I felt a sinking in my heart. Forms leaned together in the taxis as they waited, and voices sang, and there was laughter from unheard jokes, and lighted cigarettes made unintelligible circles inside. Imagining that I, too, was hurrying towards gaiety and sharing their intimate excitement, I wished them well.

For a while I lost sight of Jordan Baker, and then in midsummer I found her again. At first I was flattered to go places with her, because she was a golf champion, and everyone knew her name. Then it was something more. I wasn't actually in love, but I felt a sort of tender curiosity. The bored haughty face that she turned to the world concealed something – most affectations conceal something eventually, even though they don't in the beginning – and one day I found what it was. When we were on a house-party together up in Warwick, [19] she left a borrowed car out in the rain with the top down, and then lied about it – and suddenly I remembered the story about her that had eluded me that night at Daisy's. At her first big gold tournament there was a row that nearly reached the newspapers – a suggestion that she had moved her ball from a bad lie in the semi-final round. The thing approached the proportions of a scandal – then died away. A caddy retracted his statement, and the only other witness admitted that he might have been mistaken. The incident and the name had remained together in my mind.

Jordan Baker instinctively avoided clever, shrewd men, and now I saw that this was because she felt safer on a plane where any divergence from a code would be thought impossible. She was incurably dishonest. She wasn't able to endure being at a disadvantage and, given this unwillingness, I suppose she had begun dealing in subterfuges when she was very young in order to keep that cool, insolent smile turned to the world and yet satisfy the demands of her hard, jaunty body.

It made no difference to me. Dishonesty in a woman is a

thing you never blame deeply – I was casually sorry, and then I forgot. It was on that same house-party that we had a curious conversation about driving a car. It started because she passed so close to some workmen that our fender flicked a button on one man's coat.

'You're a rotten driver,' I protested. 'Either you ought to be more careful, or you oughtn't to drive at all.'

'I am careful.'

'No, you're not.'

'Well, other people are,' she said lightly.

'What's that got to do with it?'

'They'll keep out of my way,' she insisted. 'It takes two to make an accident.'

'Suppose you met somebody just as careless as yourself.'

'I hope I never will,' she answered. 'I hate careless people. That's why I like you.'

Her grey, sun-strained eyes stared straight ahead, but she had deliberately shifted our relations, and for a moment I thought I loved her. But I am slow-thinking and full of interior rules that act as brakes on my desires, and I knew that first I had to get myself definitely out of that tangle back home. I'd been writing letters once a week and signing them: 'Love, Nick,' and all I could think of was how, when that certain girl played tennis, a faint moustache of perspiration appeared on her upper lip. Nevertheless there was a vague understanding that had to be tactfully broken off before I was free.

Every one suspects himself of at least one of the cardinal virtues, and this is mine: I am one of the few honest people that I have ever known.

Chapter IV

ON Sunday morning while church bells rang in the villages alongshore, the world and its mistress returned to Gatsby's house and twinkled hilariously on his lawn.

'He's a bootlegger,' said the young ladies,[20] moving somewhere between his cocktails and his flowers. 'One time he killed a man who had found out that he was nephew to Von Hindenburg[21] and second cousin to the devil. Reach me a rose, honey, and pour me a last drop into that there crystal glass.'

Once I wrote down on the empty spaces of a time-table the names of those who came to Gatsby's house that summer. It is an old time-table now, disintegrating at its folds, and headed 'This schedule in effect July 5th, 1922'. But I can still read the grey names, and they will give you a better impression than my generalities of those who accepted Gatsby's hospitality and paid him the subtle tribute of knowing nothing whatever about him.

From East Egg, then, came the Chester Beckers and the Leeches, and a man named Bunsen, whom I knew at Yale, and Doctor Webster Civet, who was drowned last summer up in Maine. And the Hornbeams and the Willie Voltaires, and a whole clan named Blackbuck, who always gathered in a corner and flipped up their noses like goats at whosoever came near. And the Ismays and the Chrysties (or rather Hubert Auerbach and Mr Chrystie's wife), and Edgar Beaver, whose hair, they say, turned cotton-white one winter afternoon for no good reason at all.

Clarence Endive was from East Egg, as I remember. He

came only once, in white knickerbockers, and had a fight with a bum named Etty in the garden. From farther out on the Island came the Cheadles and the O. R. P. Schraeders, and the Stonewall Jackson Abrams of Georgia, and the Fishguards and the Ripley Snells. Snell was there three days before he went to the penitentiary, so drunk out on the gravel drive that Mrs Ulysses Swett's automobile ran over his right hand. The Dancies came, too, and S. B. Whitebait, who was well over sixty, and Maurice A. Flink, and the Hammerheads, and Beluga the tobacco importer, and Beluga's girls.

From West Egg came the Poles and the Mulreadys and Cecil Roebuck and Cecil Schoen and Gulick the State senator and Newton Orchid, who controlled Films Par Excellence, and Eckhaust and Clyde Cohen and Don S. Schwartz (the son) and Arthur McCarty, all connected with the movies in one way or another. And the Catlips and the Bembergs and G. Earl Muldoon, brother to that Muldoon who afterward strangled his wife. Da Fontano the promoter came there, and Ed Legros and James B. ('Rot-Gut') Ferret and the De Jongs and Ernest Lilly – they came to gamble, and when Ferret wandered into the garden it meant he was cleaned out and Associated Traction would have to fluctuate profitably next day.

A man named Klipspringer was there so often that he became known as 'the boarder' – I doubt if he had any other home. Of theatrical people there were Gus Waize and Horace O'Donavan and Lester Myer and George Duckweed and Francis Bull. Also from New York were the Chromes and the Backhyssons and the Dennickers and Russel Betty and the Corrigans and the Kellehers and the Dewars and the Scullys and S. W. Belcher and the Smirkes and the young Quinns, divorced now, and Henry L. Palmetto, who killed himself by jumping in front of a subway train in Times Square.

Benny McClenahan arrived always with four girls. They were never quite the same ones in physical person, but they were so identical one with another that it inevitably seemed they had been there before. I have forgotten their names – Jaqueline, I think, or else Consuela, or Gloria or Judy or June, and their last names were either the melodious names of flowers and months or the sterner ones of the great American capitalists whose cousins, if pressed, they would confess themselves to be.

In addition to all these I can remember that Faustina O'Brien came there at least once and the Baedeker girls and young Brewer, who had his nose shot off in the war, and Mr Albrucksburger and Miss Haag, his fiancée, and Ardita Fitz-Peters and Mr P. Jewett, once head of the American Legion, and Miss Claudia Hip, with a man reputed to be her chauffeur, and a prince of something, whom we called Duke, and whose name, if I ever knew it, I have forgotten.

All these people came to Gatsby's house in the summer.

At nine o'clock, one morning late in July, Gatsby's gorgeous car lurched up the rocky drive to my door and gave out a burst of melody from its three-noted horn. It was the first time he had called on me, though I had gone to two of his parties, mounted in his hydroplane, and, at his urgent invitation, made frequent use of his beach.

'Good morning, old sport. You're having lunch with me to-day and I thought we'd ride up together.'

He was balancing himself on the dashboard of his car with that resourcefulness of movement that is so peculiarly American – that comes, I suppose, with the absence of lifting work in youth and, even more, with the formless grace of our nervous, sporadic games. This quality was continually breaking through his punctilious manner in the shape of restlessness. He was never quite still; there was always a tapping foot somewhere or the impatient opening and closing of a hand.

He saw me looking with admiration at his car.

'It's pretty, isn't it, old sport?' He jumped off to give me a better view. 'Haven't you ever seen it before?'

I'd seen it. Everybody had seen it. It was a rich cream colour, bright with nickel, swollen here and there in its monstrous length with triumphant hat-boxes and supper-boxes and tool-boxes, and terraced with a labyrinth of wind-shields that mirrored a dozen suns. Sitting down behind many layers of glass in a sort of green leather conservatory, we started to town.

I had talked with him perhaps half a dozen times in the past month and found, to my disappointment, that he had little to say. So my first impression, that he was a person of some undefined consequence, had gradually faded and he had become simply the proprietor of an elaborate road-house next door.

And then came that disconcerting ride. We hadn't reached West Egg village before Gatsby began leaving his elegant sentences unfinished and slapping himself indecisively on the knee of his caramel-coloured suit.

'Look here, old sport,' he broke out surprisingly, 'what's your opinion of me, anyhow?'

A little overwhelmed, I began the generalized evasions which that question deserves.

'Well, I'm going to tell you something about my life,' he interrupted. 'I don't want you to get a wrong idea of me from all these stories you hear.'

So he was aware of the bizarre accusations that flavoured conversation in his halls.

'I'll tell you God's truth.' His right hand suddenly ordered divine retribution to stand by. 'I am the son of some wealthy people in the Middle West – all dead now. I was brought up in America but educated at Oxford, because all my ancestors have been educated there for many years. It is a family tradition.'

He looked at me sideways – and I knew why Jordan Baker had believed he was lying. He hurried the phrase 'educated at Oxford', or swallowed it, or choked on it, as though it had bothered him before. And with this doubt, his whole statement fell to pieces, and I wondered if there wasn't something a little sinister about him, after all.

'What part of the Middle West?' I inquired casually.

'San Francisco.'

'I see.'

'My family all died and I came into a good deal of money.'

His voice was solemn, as if the memory of that sudden extinction of a clan still haunted him. For a moment I suspected that he was pulling my leg, but a glance at him convinced me otherwise.

'After that I lived like a young rajah in all the capitals of Europe – Paris, Venice, Rome – collecting jewels, chiefly rubies, hunting big game, painting a little, things for myself only, and trying to forget something very sad that had happened to me long ago.'

With an effort I managed to restrain my incredulous laughter. The very phrases were worn so threadbare that they evoked no image except that of a turbaned 'character' leaking sawdust at every pore as he pursued a tiger through the Bois de Boulogne.

'Then came the war, old sport. It was a great relief, and I tried very hard to die, but I seemed to bear an enchanted life. I accepted a commission as first lieutenant when it began. In the Argonne Forest I took the remains of my machine-gun battalion so far forward that there was a half mile gap on either side of us where the infantry couldn't advance. We stayed there two days and two nights, a hundred and thirty men with sixteen Lewis guns, and when the infantry came up at last they found the insignia of three German divisions among the piles of dead. I was promoted to be a major, and every Allied government gave me a decoration – even Montenegro, little Montenegro down on the Adriatic Sea!'

Little Montenegro! He lifted up the words and nodded at them – with his smile. The smile comprehended Montenegro's troubled history and sympathized with the brave struggles of the Montenegrin people. It appreciated fully the chain of national circumstances which had elicited this tribute from Montenegro's warm little heart. My incredulity was submerged in fascination now; it was like skimming hastily through a dozen magazines.

He reached in his pocket, and a piece of metal, slung on a ribbon, fell into my palm.

'That's the one from Montenegro.'

To my astonishment, the thing had an authentic look. 'Orderi di Danilo', ran the circular legend, 'Montenegro, Nicolas Rex'.[22]

'Turn it.'

'Major Jay Gatsby,' I read, 'For Valour Extraordinary.'

'Here's another thing I always carry. A souvenir of Oxford days. It was taken in Trinity Quad[23] – the man on my left is now the Earl of Doncaster.'

It was a photograph of half a dozen young men in blazers loafing in an archway through which were visible a host of spires. There was Gatsby, looking a little, not much, younger – with a cricket bat in his hand.

Then it was all true. I saw the skins of tigers flaming in his palace on the Grand Canal; I saw him opening a chest of rubies to ease, with their crimson-lighted depths, the gnawings of his broken heart.

'I'm going to make a big request of you today,' he said, pocketing his souvenirs with satisfaction, 'so I thought you ought to know something about me. I didn't want you to think I was just some nobody. You see, I usually find myself among strangers because I drift here and there trying to forget the sad things that happened to me.' He hesitated. 'You'll hear about it this afternoon.'

'At lunch?'

'No, this afternoon. I happened to find out that you're taking Miss Baker to tea.'

'Do you mean you're in love with Miss Baker?'

'No, old sport, I'm not. But Miss Baker has kindly consented to speak to you about this matter.'

I hadn't the faintest idea what 'this matter' was, but I was more annoyed than interested. I hadn't asked Jordan to tea in order to discuss Mr Jay Gatsby. I was sure the request would be something utterly fantastic, and for a moment I was sorry I'd ever set foot upon his over-populated lawn.

He wouldn't say another word. His correctness grew on him as we neared the city. We passed Port Roosevelt,[24] where there was a glimpse of red-belted ocean-going ships, and sped along a cobbled slum lined with the dark, undeserted saloons of the faded-gilt nineteen-hundreds. Then the valley of ashes opened out on both sides of us, and I had a glimpse of Mrs Wilson straining at the garage pump with panting vitality as we went by.

With fenders spread like wings we scattered light through half Astoria – only half, for as we twisted among the pillars of the elevated I heard the familiar 'jug-jug-*spat*!' of a motor-cycle, and a frantic policeman rode alongside.

'All right, old sport,' called Gatsby. We slowed down.

Taking a white card from his wallet, he waved it before the man's eyes.

'Right you are,' agreed the policeman, tipping his cap. 'Know you next time, Mr Gatsby. Excuse *me*!'

'What was that?' I inquired. 'The picture of Oxford?'

'I was able to do the commissioner a favour once, and he sends me a Christmas card every year.'

Over the great bridge, with the sunlight through the girders making a constant flicker upon the moving cars, with the city rising up across the river in white heaps and sugar lumps all built with a wish out of nonolfactory money. The city seen from the Queensboro Bridge is always the city seen for the first time, in its first wild promise of all the mystery and the beauty in the world.

A dead man passed us in a hearse heaped with blooms, followed by two carriages with drawn blinds, and by more cheerful carriages for friends. The friends looked out at us with the tragic eyes and short upper lips of south-eastern Europe, and I was glad that the sight of Gatsby's splendid car was included in their sombre holiday. As we crossed Blackwell's Island a limousine passed us, driven by a white chauffeur, in which sat three modish negroes, two bucks and a girl. I laughed aloud as the yolks of their eyeballs rolled toward us in haughty rivalry.

'Anything can happen now that we've slid over this bridge,' I thought; 'anything at all ...'

Even Gatsby could happen, without any particular wonder.

Roaring noon. In a well-fanned Forty-second Street cellar I met Gatsby for lunch. Blinking away the brightness of the street outside, my eyes picked him out obscurely in the ante-room, talking to another man.

'Mr Carraway, this is my friend Mr Wolfshiem.'[25]

A small, flat-nosed Jew raised his large head and regarded me with two fine growths of hair which luxuriated in either nostril. After a moment I discovered his tiny eyes in the half-darkness.

' – So I took one look at him,' said Mr Wolfshiem, shaking my hand earnestly, 'and what do you think I did?'

'What?' I inquired politely.

But evidently he was not addressing me, for he dropped my hand and covered Gatsby with his expressive nose.

'I handed the money to Katspaugh and I said: "All right, Katspaugh, don't pay him a penny till he shuts his mouth." He shut it then and there.'

Gatsby took an arm of each of us and moved forward into the restaurant, whereupon Mr Wolfshiem swallowed a new sentence he was starting and lapsed into a somnambulatory abstraction.

'Highballs?' asked the head waiter.

'This is a nice restaurant here,' said Mr Wolfshiem, looking at the presbyterian nymphs on the ceiling. 'But I like across the street better!'

'Yes, highballs,' agreed Gatsby, and then to Mr Wolfshiem: 'It's too hot over there.'

'Hot and small – yes,' said Mr Wolfshiem, 'but full of memories.'

'What place is that?' I asked.

'The old Metropole.'

'The old Metropole,' brooded Mr Wolfshiem gloomily. 'Filled with faces dead and gone. Filled with friends gone now forever. I can't forget so long as I live the night they shot Rosy Rosenthal there. It was six of us at the table, and Rosy had eat and drunk a lot all evening. When it was almost morning the waiter came up to him with a funny look and says somebody wants to speak to him outside. "All right," says Rosy, and begins to get up, and I pulled him down in his chair.

' "Let the bastards come in here if they want you, Rosy, but don't you, so help me, move outside this room."

'It was four o'clock in the morning then, and if we'd of raised the blinds we'd of seen daylight.'

'Did he go?' I asked innocently.

'Sure he went.' Mr Wolfshiem's nose flashed at me indignantly. 'He turned around in the door and says: "Don't let that waiter take away my coffee!" Then he went out on the sidewalk, and they shot him three times in his full belly and drove away.'

'Four of them were electrocuted,' I said, remembering.

'Five, with Becker.' His nostrils turned to me in an interested way. 'I understand you're looking for a business gonnegtion.'

The juxtaposition of these two remarks was startling. Gatsby answered for me:

'Oh, no,' he exclaimed, 'this isn't the man.'

'No?' Mr Wolfshiem seemed disappointed.

'This is just a friend. I told you we'd talk about that some other time.'

'I beg your pardon,' said Mr Wolfshiem, 'I had a wrong man.'

A succulent hash arrived, and Mr Wolfshiem, forgetting the more sentimental atmosphere of the old Metropole, began to eat with ferocious delicacy. His eyes, meanwhile, roved very slowly all around the room – he completed the arc by turning to inspect the people directly behind. I think that, except for my presence, he would have taken one short glance beneath our own table.

'Look here, old sport,' said Gatsby, leaning toward me, 'I'm afraid I made you a little angry this morning in the car.'

There was the smile again, but this time I held out against it.

'I don't like mysteries,' I answered, 'and I don't understand why you won't come out frankly and tell me what you want. Why has it all got to come through Miss Baker?'

'Oh, it's nothing underhand,' he assured me. 'Miss Baker's a great sportswoman, you know, and she'd never do anything that wasn't all right.'

Suddenly he looked at his watch, jumped up, and hurried from the room, leaving me with Mr Wolfshiem at the table.

'He has to telephone,' said Mr Wolfshiem, following him with his eyes. 'Fine fellow, isn't he? Handsome to look at and a perfect gentleman.'

'Yes.'

'He's an Oggsford man.'

'Oh!'

'He went to Oggsford College in England. You know Oggsford College?'

'I've heard of it.'

'It's one of the most famous colleges in the world.'

'Have you known Gatsby for a long time?' I inquired.

'Several years,' he answered in a gratified way. 'I made the pleasure of his acquaintance just after the war. But I knew I had discovered a man of fine breeding after I talked with him an hour. I said to myself: "There's the kind of man you'd like to take home and introduce to your mother and sister." ' He paused. 'I see you're looking at my cuff buttons.'

I hadn't been looking at them, but I did now. They were composed of oddly familiar pieces of ivory.

'Finest specimens of human molars,' he informed me.

'Well!' I inspected them. 'That's a very interesting idea.'

'Yeah.' He flipped his sleeves up under his coat. 'Yeah, Gatsby's very careful about women. He would never so much as look at a friend's wife.'

When the subject of this instinctive trust returned to the

table and sat down Mr Wolfshiem drank his coffee with a jerk and got to his feet.

'I have enjoyed my lunch,' he said, 'and I'm going to run off from you two young men before I outstay my welcome.'

'Don't hurry, Meyer,' said Gatsby, without enthusiasm. Mr Wolfshiem raised his hand in a sort of benediction.

'You're very polite, but I belong to another generation,' he announced solemnly. 'You sit here and discuss your sports and your young ladies and your –' He supplied an imaginary noun with another wave of his hand. 'As for me, I am fifty years old, and I won't impose myself on you any longer.'

As he shook hands and turned away his tragic nose was trembling. I wondered if I had said anything to offend him.

'He becomes very sentimental sometimes,' explained Gatsby. 'This is one of his sentimental days. He's quite a character around New York – a denizen of Broadway.'

'Who is he, anyhow, an actor?'

'No.'

'A dentist?'

'Meyer Wolfshiem? No, he's a gambler.' Gatsby hesitated, then added, coolly: 'He's the man who fixed the World's Series back in 1919.'[26]

'Fixed the World's Series?' I repeated.

The idea staggered me. I remembered, of course, that the World's Series had been fixed in 1919, but if I had thought of it at all I would have thought of it as a thing that merely *happened*, the end of some inevitable chain. It never occurred to me that one man could start to play with the faith of fifty million people – with the single-mindedness of a burglar blowing a safe.

'How did he happen to do that?' I asked after a minute.

'He just saw the opportunity.'

'Why isn't he in jail?'

'They can't get him, old sport. He's a smart man.'

I insisted on paying the check. As the waiter brought my change I caught sight of Tom Buchanan across the crowded room.

'Come along with me for a minute,' I said; 'I've got to say hello to someone.'

When he saw us Tom jumped up and took half a dozen steps in our direction.

'Where've you been?' he demanded eagerly. 'Daisy's furious because you haven't called up.'

'This is Mr Gatsby, Mr Buchanan.'

They shook hands briefly, and a strained, unfamiliar look of embarrassment came over Gatsby's face.

'How've you been, anyhow?' demanded Tom of me. 'How'd you happen to come up this far to eat?'

'I've been having lunch with Mr Gatsby.'

I turned toward Mr Gatsby, but he was no longer there.

One October day in nineteen-seventeen –

(said Jordan Baker that afternoon, sitting up very straight on a straight chair in the tea-garden at the Plaza Hotel)

– I was walking along from one place to another, half on the sidewalks and half on the lawns. I was happier on the lawns because I had on shoes from England with rubber knobs on the soles that bit into the soft ground. I had on a new plaid skirt also that blew a little in the wind, and whenever this happened the red, white, and blue banners in front of all the houses stretched out stiff and said *tut-tut-tut-tut*, in a disapproving way.

The largest of the banners and the largest of the lawns belonged to Daisy Fay's house. She was just eighteen, two years older than me, and by far the most popular of all the young girls in Louisville. She dressed in white, and had a little white roadster, and all day long the telephone rang in her house and excited young officers from Camp Taylor[27] demanded the privilege of monopolizing her that night. 'Anyways, for an hour!'

When I came opposite her house that morning her white roadster was beside the kerb, and she was sitting in it with a lieutenant I had never seen before. They were so engrossed in each other that she didn't see me until I was five feet away.

'Hello, Jordan,' she called unexpectedly. 'Please come here.'

I was flattered that she wanted to speak to me, because of all the older girls I admired her most. She asked me if I was going to the Red Cross to make bandages. I was. Well, then, would I tell them that she couldn't come that day? The officer looked at Daisy while she was speaking, in a way that every young girl wants to be looked at sometime, and because it seemed romantic to me I have remembered the incident ever since. His name was Jay Gatsby, and I didn't lay eyes on him again for over four years – even after I'd met him on Long Island I didn't realize it was the same man.

That was nineteen-seventeen. By the next year I had a few beaux myself, and I began to play in tournaments, so I didn't see Daisy very often. She went with a slightly older crowd – when she went with anyone at all. Wild rumours were circulating about her – how her mother had found her packing her bag one winter night to go to New York and say good-bye to a soldier who was going overseas. She was effectually prevented, but she wasn't on speaking terms with her family for several weeks. After that she didn't play around with the soldiers any more, but only with a few flat-footed, short-sighted young men in town, who couldn't get into the army at all.

By the next autumn she was gay again, gay as ever. She had

a début after the armistice, and in February she was presumably engaged to a man from New Orleans. In June she married Tom Buchanan of Chicago, with more pomp and circumstance than Louisville ever knew before. He came down with a hundred people in four private cars, and hired a whole floor of the Muhlbach Hotel, and the day before the wedding he gave her a string of pearls valued at three hundred and fifty thousand dollars.

I was a bridesmaid. I came into her room half an hour before the bridal dinner, and found her lying on her bed as lovely as the June night in her flowered dress – and as drunk as a monkey. She had a bottle of Sauterne in one hand and a letter in the other.

''Gratulate me,' she muttered. 'Never had a drink before, but oh how I do enjoy it.'

'What's the matter, Daisy?'

I was scared, I can tell you; I'd never seen a girl like that before.

'Here, deares'.' She groped around in a waste-basket she had with her on the bed and pulled out the string of pearls. 'Take 'em downstairs and give 'em back to whoever they belong to. Tell 'em all Daisy's change' her mine. Say: "Daisy's change' her mine!"'

She began to cry – she cried and cried. I rushed out and found her mother's maid, and we locked the door and got her into a cold bath. She wouldn't let go of the letter. She took it into the tub with her and squeezed it up in a wet ball, and only let me leave it in the soap-dish when she saw that it was coming to pieces like snow.

But she didn't say another word. We gave her spirits of ammonia and put ice on her forehead and hooked her back into her dress, and half an hour later, when we walked out of the room, the pearls were around her neck and the incident was over. Next day at five o'clock she married Tom Buchanan without so much as a shiver, and started off on a three months' trip to the South Seas.

I saw them in Santa Barbara when they came back, and I thought I'd never seen a girl so mad about her husband. If he left the room for a minute she'd look around uneasily, and say: 'Where's Tom gone?' and wear the most abstracted expression until she saw him coming in the door. She used to sit on the sand with his head in her lap by the hour, rubbing her fingers over his eyes and looking at him with unfathomable delight. It was touching to see them together – it made you laugh in a hushed, fascinated way. That was in August. A week after I left Santa Barbara Tom ran into a wagon on the Ventura road one night, and ripped a front wheel off his car. The girl who was with him got into the papers, too, because her arm was broken – she was one of the chambermaids in the Santa Barbara Hotel.

The next April Daisy had her little girl, and they went to France for a year. I saw them one spring in Cannes, and later in Deauville, and then they came back to Chicago to settle down. Daisy was popular in Chicago, as you know. They moved with a fast crowd, all of them young and rich and wild, but she came out with an absolutely perfect reputation. Perhaps because she doesn't drink. It's a great advantage not to drink among hard-drinking people. You can hold your tongue and, moreover, you can time any little irregularity of your own so that everybody else is so blind that they don't see or care. Perhaps Daisy never went in for amour at all – and yet there's something in that voice of hers . . .

Well, about six weeks ago, she heard the name Gatsby for the first time in years. It was when I asked you – do you remember? – if you knew Gatsby in West Egg. After you had gone home she came into my room and woke me up, and said:

'What Gatsby?' and when I described him – I was half asleep – she said in the strangest voice that it must be the man she used to know. It wasn't until then that I connected this Gatsby with the officer in her white car.

When Jordan Baker had finished telling all this we had left the Plaza for half an hour and were driving in a victoria through Central Park. The sun had gone down behind the tall apartments of the movie stars in the West Fifties, and the clear voices of children, already gathered like crickets on the grass, rose through the hot twilight:

> 'I'm the Sheik of Araby.
> Your love belongs to me.
> At night when you're asleep
> Into your tent I'll creep –'

'It was a strange coincidence,' I said.

'But it wasn't a coincidence at all.'

'Why not?'

'Gatsby bought that house so that Daisy would be just across the bay.'

Then it had not been merely the stars to which he had aspired on that June night. He came alive to me, delivered suddenly from the womb of his purposeless splendour.

'He wants to know,' continued Jordan, 'if you'll invite Daisy to your house some afternoon and then let him come over.'

The modesty of the demand shook me. He had waited five years and bought a mansion where he dispensed starlight to casual moths – so that he could 'come over' some afternoon to a stranger's garden.

'Did I have to know all this before he could ask such a little thing?'

'He's afraid, he's waited so long. He thought you might be offended. You see, he's regular tough underneath it all.'

Something worried me.

'Why didn't he ask you to arrange a meeting?'

'He wants her to see his house,' she explained. 'And your house is right next door.'

'Oh!'

'I think he half expected her to wander into one of his parties, some night,' went on Jordan, 'but she never did. Then he began asking people casually if they knew her, and I was the first one he found. It was that night he sent for me at his dance, and you should have heard the elaborate way he worked up to it. Of course, I immediately suggested a luncheon in New York – and I thought he'd go mad:

' "I don't want to do anything out of the way!" he kept saying. "I want to see her right next door."

'When I said you were a particular friend of Tom's, he started to abandon the whole idea. He doesn't know very much about Tom, though he says he's read a Chicago paper for years just on the chance of catching a glimpse of Daisy's name.'

It was dark now, and as we dipped under a little bridge I put my arm around Jordan's golden shoulder and drew her toward me and asked her to dinner. Suddenly I wasn't thinking of Daisy and Gatsby any more, but of this clean, hard, limited person, who dealt in universal scepticism, and who leaned back jauntily just within the circle of my arm. A phrase began to beat in my ears with a sort of heady excitement: 'There are only the pursued, the pursuing, the busy, and the tired.'

'And Daisy ought to have something in her life,' murmured Jordan to me.

'Does she want to see Gatsby?'

'She's not to know about it. Gatsby doesn't want her to know. You're just supposed to invite her to tea.'

We passed a barrier of dark trees, and then the façade of Fifty-ninth Street, a block of delicate pale light, beamed down into the park. Unlike Gatsby and Tom Buchanan, I had no girl whose disembodied face floated along the dark cornices and blinding signs, and so I drew up the girl beside me, tightening my arms. Her wan, scornful mouth smiled, and so I drew her up again closer, this time to my face.

Chapter V

WHEN I came home to West Egg that night I was afraid for a moment that my house was on fire. Two o'clock and the whole corner of the peninsula was blazing with light, which fell unreal on the shrubbery and made thin elongating glints upon the roadside wires. Turning a corner, I saw that it was Gatsby's house, lit from tower to cellar.

At first I thought it was another party, a wild rout that had resolved itself into 'hide-and-go-seek' or 'sardines-in-the-box' with all the house thrown open to the game. But there wasn't a sound. Only wind in the trees, which blew the wires and made the lights go off and on again as if the house had winked into the darkness. As my taxi groaned away I saw Gatsby walking toward me across his lawn.

'Your place looks like the World's Fair,' I said.

'Does it?' He turned his eyes toward it absently. 'I have been glancing into some of the rooms. Let's go to Coney Island, old sport.[28] In my car.'

'It's too late.'

'Well, suppose we take a plunge in the swimming-pool? I haven't made use of it all summer.'

'I've got to go to bed.'

'All right.'

He waited, looking at me with suppressed eagerness.

'I talked with Miss Baker,' I said after a moment. 'I'm going to call up Daisy tomorrow and invite her over here to tea.'

'Oh, that's all right,' he said carelessly. 'I don't want to put you to any trouble.'

'What day would suit you?'

'What day would suit *you*?' he corrected me quickly. 'I don't want to put you to any trouble, you see.'

'How about the day after tomorrow?'

He considered for a moment. Then, with reluctance: 'I want to get the grass cut,' he said.

We both looked down at the grass – there was a sharp line where my ragged lawn ended and the darker, well-kept expanse of his began. I suspected that he meant my grass.

'There's another little thing,' he said uncertainly, and hesitated.

'Would you rather put it off for a few days?' I asked.

'Oh, it isn't about that. At least –' He fumbled with a series of beginnings. 'Why, I thought – why, look here, old sport, you don't make much money, do you?'

'Not very much.'

This seemed to reassure him and he continued more confidently.

'I thought you didn't, if you'll pardon my – you see, I carry on a little business on the side, a sort of side line, you understand. And I thought that if you don't make very much – You're selling bonds, aren't you, old sport?'

'Trying to.'

'Well, this would interest you. It wouldn't take up much of your time and you might pick up a nice bit of money. It happens to be a rather confidential sort of thing.'

I realize now that under different circumstances that conversation might have been one of the crises of my life. But, because the offer was obviously and tactlessly for a service to be rendered, I had no choice except to cut him off there.

'I've got my hands full,' I said. 'I'm much obliged but I couldn't take on any more work.'

'You wouldn't have to do any business with Wolfshiem.'

Evidently he thought that I was shying away from the 'gon-negtion' mentioned at lunch, but I assured him he was wrong. He waited a moment longer, hoping I'd begin a conversation, but I was too absorbed to be responsive, so he went unwillingly home.

The evening had made me light-headed and happy; I think I walked into a deep sleep as I entered my front door. So I don't know whether or not Gatsby went to Coney Island, or for how many hours he 'glanced into rooms' while his house blazed gaudily on. I called up Daisy from the office next morning, and invited her to come to tea.

'Don't bring Tom,' I warned her.

'What?'

'Don't bring Tom.'

'Who is "Tom"?' she asked innocently.

The day agreed upon was pouring rain. At eleven o'clock a man in a raincoat, dragging a lawn-mower, tapped at my front door and said that Mr Gatsby had sent him over to cut my grass. This reminded me that I had forgotten to tell my Finn to come back, so I drove into West Egg Village to search for her among soggy whitewashed alleys and to buy some cups and lemons and flowers.

The flowers were unnecessary, for at two o'clock a green-house arrived from Gatsby's, with innumerable receptacles to contain it. An hour later the front door opened nervously, and Gatsby, in a white flannel suit, silver shirt, and gold-coloured tie, hurried in. He was pale, and there were dark signs of sleeplessness beneath his eyes.

'Is everything all right?' he asked immediately.

'The grass looks fine, if that's what you mean.'

'What grass?' he inquired blankly. 'Oh, the grass in the yard.' He looked out the window at it, but, judging from his expression, I don't believe he saw a thing.

'Looks very good,' he remarked vaguely. 'One of the papers said they thought the rain would stop about four. I think it was *The Journal*.[29] Have you got everything you need in the shape of – of tea?'

I took him into the pantry, where he looked a little reproachfully at the Finn. Together we scrutinized the twelve lemon cakes from the delicatessen shop.

'Will they do?' I asked.

'Of course, of course! They're fine!' and he added hollowly, '. . . old sport.'

The rain cooled about half-past three to a damp mist, through which occasional thin drops swam like dew. Gatsby looked with vacant eyes through a copy of Clay's *Economics*,[30] starting at the Finnish tread that shook the kitchen floor, and peering towards the bleared windows from time to time as if a series of invisible but alarming happenings were taking place outside. Finally he got up and informed me, in an uncertain voice, that he was going home.

'Why's that?'

'Nobody's coming to tea. It's too late!' He looked at his watch as if there was some pressing demand on his time elsewhere. 'I can't wait all day.'

'Don't be silly; it's just two minutes to four.'

He sat down miserably, as if I had pushed him, and simultaneously there was the sound of a motor turning into my lane. We both jumped up, and, a little harrowed myself, I went out into the yard.

Under the dripping bare lilac-trees a large open car was coming up the drive. It stopped. Daisy's face, tipped sideways beneath a three-cornered lavender hat, looked out at me with a bright ecstatic smile.

'Is this absolutely where you live, my dearest one?'

The exhilarating ripple of her voice was a wild tonic in the rain. I had to follow the sound of it for a moment, up and down, with my ear alone, before any words came through. A damp streak of hair lay like a dash of blue paint across her cheek, and her hand was wet with glistening drops as I took it to help her from the car.

'Are you in love with me,' she said low in my ear, 'or why did I have to come alone?'

'That's the secret of Castle Rackrent.[31] Tell your chauffeur to go far away and spend an hour.'

'Come back in an hour, Ferdie.' Then in a grave murmur: 'His name is Ferdie.'

'Does the gasoline affect his nose?'

'I don't think so,' she said innocently. 'Why?'

We went in. To my overwhelming surprise the living-room was deserted.

'Well, that's funny,' I exclaimed.

'What's funny?'

She turned her head as there was a light dignified knocking at the front door. I went out and opened it. Gatsby, pale as death, with his hands plunged like weights in his coat pockets, was standing in a puddle of water glaring tragically into my eyes.

With his hands still in his coat pockets he stalked by me into the hall, turned sharply as if he were on a wire, and disappeared into the living-room. It wasn't a bit funny. Aware of the loud beating of my own heart I pulled the door to against the increasing rain.

For half a minute there wasn't a sound. Then from the living-room I heard a sort of choking murmur and part of a laugh, followed by Daisy's voice on a clear artificial note:

'I certainly am awfully glad to see you again.'

A pause; it endured horribly. I had nothing to do in the hall, so I went into the room.

Gatsby, his hands still in his pockets, was reclining against the mantelpiece in a strained counterfeit of perfect ease, even of boredom. His head leaned back so far that it rested against the face of a defunct mantelpiece clock, and from this position his distraught eyes stared down at Daisy, who was sitting, frightened but graceful, on the edge of a stiff chair.

'We've met before,' muttered Gatsby. His eyes glanced momentarily at me, and his lips parted with an abortive attempt at a laugh. Luckily the clock took this moment to tilt dangerously at the pressure of his head, whereupon he turned and caught it with trembling fingers, and set it back in place. Then he sat down, rigidly, his elbow on the arm of the sofa and his chin in his hand.

'I'm sorry about the clock,' he said.

My own face had now assumed a deep tropical burn. I couldn't muster up a single commonplace out of the thousand in my head.

'It's an old clock,' I told them idiotically.

I think we all believed for a moment that it had smashed in pieces on the floor.

'We haven't met for many years,' said Daisy, her voice as matter-of-fact as it could ever be.

'Five years next November.'

The automatic quality of Gatsby's answer set us all back at least another minute. I had them both on their feet with the desperate suggestion that they help me make tea in the kitchen when the demoniac Finn brought it in on a tray.

Amid the welcome confusion of cups and cakes a certain physical decency established itself. Gatsby got himself into a shadow and, while Daisy and I talked, looked conscientiously from one to the other of us with tense, unhappy eyes. However, as calmness wasn't an end in itself, I made an excuse at the first possible moment, and got to my feet.

'Where are you going?' demanded Gatsby in immediate alarm.

'I'll be back.'

'I've got to speak to you about something before you go.'

He followed me wildly into the kitchen, closed the door, and whispered: 'Oh, God!' in a miserable way.

'What's the matter?'

'This is a terrible mistake,' he said, shaking his head from side to side, 'a terrible, terrible mistake.'

'You're just embarrassed, that's all,' and luckily I added: 'Daisy's embarrassed too.'

'She's embarrassed?' he repeated incredulously.

'Just as much as you are.'

'Don't talk so loud.'

'You're acting like a little boy,' I broke out impatiently. 'Not only that, but you're rude. Daisy's sitting in there all alone.'

He raised his hand to stop my words, looked at me with unforgettable reproach, and, opening the door cautiously, went back into the other room.

I walked out the back way – just as Gatsby had when he had made his nervous circuit of the house half an hour before – and ran for a huge black knotted tree, whose massed leaves made a fabric against the rain. Once more it was pouring, and my irregular lawn, well-shaved by Gatsby's gardener, abounded in small muddy swamps and prehistoric marshes. There was nothing to look at from under the tree except Gatsby's enormous house, so I stared at it, like Kant at his church steeple,[32] for half an hour. A brewer had built it early in the 'period' craze, a decade before, and there was a story that he'd agreed to pay five years' taxes on all the neighbouring cottages if the owners would have their roofs thatched with straw. Perhaps their refusal took the heart out of his plan to Found a Family

– he went into an immediate decline. His children sold his house with the black wreath still on the door. Americans, while willing, even eager, to be serfs, have always been obstinate about being peasantry.

After half an hour, the sun shone again, and the grocer's automobile rounded Gatsby's drive with the raw material for his servants' dinner – I felt sure he wouldn't eat a spoonful. A maid began opening the upper windows of his house, appeared momentarily in each, and, leaning from the large central bay, spat meditatively into the garden. It was time I went back. While the rain continued it had seemed like the murmur of their voices, rising and swelling a little now and then with gusts of emotion. But in the new silence I felt that silence had fallen within the house too.

I went in – after making every possible noise in the kitchen, short of pushing over the stove – but I don't believe they heard a sound. They were sitting at either end of the couch, looking at each other as if some question had been asked, or was in the air, and every vestige of embarrassment was gone. Daisy's face was smeared with tears, and when I came in she jumped up and began wiping at it with her handkerchief before a mirror. But there was a change in Gatsby that was simply confounding. He literally glowed; without a word or a gesture of exultation a new well-being radiated from him and filled the little room.

'Oh, hello, old sport,' he said, as if he hadn't seen me for years. I thought for a moment he was going to shake hands.

'It's stopped raining.'

'Has it?' When he realized what I was talking about, that there were twinkle-bells of sunshine in the room, he smiled like a weather man, like an ecstatic patron of recurrent light, and repeated the news to Daisy. 'What do you think of that? It's stopped raining.'

'I'm glad, Jay.' Her throat, full of aching, grieving beauty, told only of her unexpected joy.

'I want you and Daisy to come over to my house,' he said, 'I'd like to show her around.'

'You're sure you want me to come?'

'Absolutely, old sport.'

Daisy went upstairs to wash her face – too late I thought with humiliation of my towels – while Gatsby and I waited on the lawn.

'My house looks well, doesn't it?' he demanded. 'See how the whole front of it catches the light.'

I agreed that it was splendid.

'Yes.' His eyes went over it, every arched door and square tower. 'It took me just three years to earn the money that bought it.'

'I thought you inherited your money.'

'I did, old sport,' he said automatically, 'but I lost most of it in the big panic – the panic of the war.'

I think he hardly knew what he was saying, for when I asked him what business he was in he answered: 'That's my affair', before he realized that it wasn't an appropriate reply.

'Oh, I've been in several things,' he corrected himself. 'I was in the drug business and then I was in the oil business. But I'm not in either one now.' He looked at me with more attention. 'Do you mean you've been thinking over what I proposed the other night?'

Before I could answer, Daisy came out of the house and two rows of brass buttons on her dress gleamed in the sunlight.

'That huge place *there?*' she cried pointing.

'Do you like it?'

'I love it, but I don't see how you live there all alone.'

'I keep it always full of interesting people, night and day. People who do interesting things. Celebrated people.'

Instead of taking the short cut along the Sound we went down to the road and entered by the big postern. With enchanting murmurs Daisy admired this aspect or that of the feudal silhouette against the sky, admired the gardens, the sparkling odour of jonquils and the frothy odour of hawthorn and plum blossoms and the pale gold odour of kiss-me-at-the-gate. It was strange to reach the marble steps and find no stir of bright dresses in and out the door, and hear no sound but bird voices in the trees.

And inside, as we wandered through Marie Antoinette music-rooms and Restoration Salons, I felt that there were guests concealed behind every couch and table, under orders to be breathlessly silent until we had passed through. As Gatsby closed the door of 'the Merton College Library' I could have sworn I heard the owl-eyed man break into ghostly laughter.

We went upstairs, through period bedrooms swathed in rose and lavender silk and vivid with new flowers, through dressing-rooms and poolrooms, and bath-rooms with sunken baths – intruding into one chamber where a dishevelled man in pyjamas was doing liver exercises on the floor. It was Mr Klipspringer, the 'boarder'. I had seen him wandering hungrily about the beach that morning. Finally we came to Gatsby's own apartment, a bedroom and a bath, and an Adam's study,[33] where we sat down and drank a glass of some Chartreuse he took from a cupboard in the wall.

He hadn't once ceased looking at Daisy, and I think he revalued everything in his house according to the measure of response it drew from her well-loved eyes. Sometimes too, he stared around at his possessions in a dazed way, as though in her actual and astounding presence none of it was any longer real. Once he nearly toppled down a flight of stairs.

His bedroom was the simplest room of all – except where the

dresser was garnished with a toilet set of pure dull gold. Daisy took the brush with delight, and smoothed her hair, where-upon Gatsby sat down and shaded his eyes and began to laugh.

'It's the funniest thing, old sport,' he said hilariously. 'I can't – When I try to –'

He had passed visibly through two states and was entering upon a third. After his embarrassment and his unreasoning joy he was consumed with wonder at her presence. He had been full of the idea so long, dreamed it right through to the end, waited with his teeth set, so to speak, at an inconceivable pitch of intensity. Now, in the reaction, he was running down like an over-wound clock.

Recovering himself in a minute he opened for us two hulking patent cabinets which held his massed suits and dressing-gowns and ties, and his shirts, piled like bricks in stacks a dozen high.

'I've got a man in England who buys me clothes. He sends over a selection of things at the beginning of each season, spring and fall.'

He took out a pile of shirts and began throwing them, one by one, before us, shirts of sheer linen and thick silk and fine flannel, which lost their folds as they fell and covered the table in many coloured disarray. While we admired he brought more and the soft rich heap mounted higher – shirts with stripes and scrolls and plaids in coral and apple-green and lavender and faint orange, with monograms of indian blue. Suddenly, with a strained sound, Daisy bent her head into the shirts and began to cry stormily.

'They're such beautiful shirts,' she sobbed, her voice muffled in the thick folds. 'It makes me sad because I've never seen such – such beautiful shirts before.'

*

After the house, we were to see the grounds and the swimming-pool, and the hydroplane, and the midsummer flowers – but outside Gatsby's window it began to rain again, so we stood in a row looking at the corrugated surface of the Sound.

'If it wasn't for the mist we could see your home across the bay,' said Gatsby. 'You always have a green light that burns all night at the end of your dock.'

Daisy put her arm through his abruptly, but he seemed absorbed in what he had just said. Possibly it had occurred to him that the colossal significance of that light had now vanished forever. Compared to the great distance that had separated him from Daisy it had seemed very near to her, almost touching her. It had seemed as close as a star to the moon. Now it was again a green light on a dock. His count of enchanted objects had diminished by one.

I began to walk about the room, examining various indefinite objects in the half darkness. A large photograph of an elderly man in yachting costume attracted me, hung on the wall over his desk.

'Who's this?'

'That? That's Mr Dan Cody, old sport.'

The name sounded faintly familiar.

'He's dead now. He used to be my best friend years ago.'

There was a small picture of Gatsby, also in yachting costume, on the bureau – Gatsby with his head thrown back defiantly – taken apparently when he was about eighteen.

'I adore it,' exclaimed Daisy. 'The pompadour! You never told me you had a pompadour – or a yacht.'

'Look at this,' said Gatsby quickly. 'Here's a lot of clippings – about you.'

They stood side by side examining it. I was going to ask to see the rubies when the phone rang, and Gatsby took up the receiver.

'Yes ... Well, I can't talk now ... I can't talk now, old sport ... I said a *small* town ... He must know what a small town is ... Well, he's no use to us if Detroit is his idea of a small town ...'

He rang off.

'Come here *quick*!' cried Daisy at the window.

The rain was still falling, but the darkness had parted in the west, and there was a pink and golden billow of foamy clouds above the sea.

'Look at that,' she whispered, and then after a moment: 'I'd like to just get one of those pink clouds and put you in it and push you around.'

I tried to go then, but they wouldn't hear of it; perhaps my presence made them feel more satisfactorily alone.

'I know what we'll do,' said Gatsby, 'we'll have Klipspringer play the piano.'

He went out of the room calling 'Ewing!' and returned in a few minutes accompanied by an embarrassed, slightly worn young man, with shell-rimmed glasses and scanty blond hair. He was now decently clothed in a 'sport shirt', open at the neck, sneakers, and duck trousers of a nebulous hue.

'Did we interrupt your exercise?' inquired Daisy politely.

'I was asleep,' cried Mr Klipspringer, in a spasm of embarrassment. 'That is, I'd *been* asleep. Then I got up ...'

'Klipspringer plays the piano,' said Gatsby, cutting him off. 'Don't you, Ewing, old sport?'

'I don't play well. I don't – hardly play at all. I'm all out of prac –'

'We'll go downstairs,' interrupted Gatsby. He flipped a switch. The grey windows disappeared as the house glowed full of light.

In the music-room Gatsby turned on a solitary lamp beside the piano. He lit Daisy's cigarette from a trembling match, and sat down with her on a couch far across the room, where there was no light save what the gleaming floor bounced in from the hall.

When Klipspringer had played 'The Love Nest' he turned around on the bench and searched unhappily for Gatsby in the gloom.

'I'm all out of practice, you see. I told you I couldn't play. I'm all out of prac –'

'Don't talk so much, old sport,' commanded Gatsby. 'Play!'

> 'In the morning,
>   In the evening,
>   Ain't we got fun –'

Outside the wind was loud and there was a faint flow of thunder along the Sound. All the lights were going on in West Egg now; the electric trains, men-carrying, were plunging home through the rain from New York. It was the hour of a profound human change, and excitement was generating on the air.

> 'One thing's sure and nothing's surer
> The rich get richer and the poor get – children.
>   In the meantime,
>   In between time –'

As I went over to say good-bye I saw that the expression of bewilderment had come back into Gatsby's face, as though a faint doubt had occurred to him as to the quality of his present happiness. Almost five years! There must have been moments even that afternoon when Daisy tumbled short of his dreams – not through her own fault, but because of the colossal vitality of his illusion. It had gone beyond her, beyond everything. He had thrown himself into it with a creative passion, adding to it all the time, decking it out with every bright feather that drifted his way. No amount of fire or freshness can challenge what a man can store up in his ghostly heart.

As I watched him he adjusted himself a little, visibly. His hand took hold of hers, and as she said something low in his ear he turned toward her with a rush of emotion. I think that voice held him most, with its fluctuating, feverish warmth, because it couldn't be over-dreamed – that voice was a deathless song.

They had forgotten me, but Daisy glanced up and held out her hand; Gatsby didn't know me now at all. I looked once more at them and they looked back at me, remotely, possessed by intense life. Then I went out of the room and down the marble steps into the rain, leaving them there together.

Chapter VI

ABOUT this time an ambitious young reporter from New York arrived one morning at Gatsby's door and asked him if he had anything to say.

'Anything to say about what?' inquired Gatsby politely.

'Why – any statement to give out.'

It transpired after a confused five minutes that the man had heard Gatsby's name around his office in a connection which he either wouldn't reveal or didn't fully understand. This was his day off and with laudable initiative he had hurried out 'to see'.

It was a random shot, and yet the reporter's instinct was right. Gatsby's notoriety, spread about by the hundreds who had accepted his hospitality and so become authorities upon his past, had increased all summer until he fell just short of being news. Contemporary legends such as the 'underground pipe-line to Canada' attached themselves to him,[34] and there was one persistent story that he didn't live in a house at all, but in a boat that looked like a house and was moved secretly up and down the Long Island shore. Just why these inventions were a source of satisfaction to James Gatz of North Dakota, isn't easy to say.

James Gatz – that was really, or at least legally, his name. He had changed it at the age of seventeen and at the specific moment that witnessed the beginning of his career – when he saw Dan Cody's yacht drop anchor over the most insidious flat on Lake Superior. It was James Gatz who had been loafing along the beach that afternoon in a torn green jersey and a pair of canvas pants, but it was already Jay Gatsby who borrowed a rowboat, pulled out to the *Tuolomee,* and informed Cody that a wind might catch him and break him up in half an hour.

I suppose he'd had the name ready for a long time, even then. His parents were shiftless and unsuccessful farm people – his imagination had never really accepted them as his parents at all. The truth was that Jay Gatsby of West Egg, Long Island, sprang from his Platonic conception of himself. He was a son of God – a phrase which, if it means anything, means just that – and he must be about His Father's business, the service of a vast, vulgar, and meretricious beauty. So he invented just the sort of Jay Gatsby that a seventeen-year-old boy would be likely to invent, and to this conception he was faithful to the end.

For over a year he had been beating his way along the south shore of Lake Superior as a clam-digger and a salmon-fisher or in any other capacity that brought him food and bed. His brown, hardening body lived naturally through the half-fierce, half-lazy work of the bracing days. He knew women early, and since they spoiled him he became contemptuous of them, of young virgins because they were ignorant, of the others because they were hysterical about things which in his overwhelming self-absorption he took for granted.

But his heart was in a constant, turbulent riot. The most grotesque and fantastic conceits haunted him in his bed at night. A universe of ineffable gaudiness spun itself out in his brain while the clock ticked on the washstand and the moon soaked with wet light his tangled clothes upon the floor. Each night he added to the pattern of his fancies until drowsiness closed down upon some vivid scene with an oblivious embrace. For a while these reveries provided an outlet for his imagination; they were a satisfactory hint of the unreality of reality, a promise that the rock of the world was founded securely on a fairy's wing.

An instinct toward his future glory had led him, some months before, to the small Lutheran College of St Olaf's in southern Minnesota. He stayed there two weeks, dismayed at its ferocious indifference to the drums of his destiny, to destiny itself, and despising the janitor's work with which he was to pay his way through. Then he drifted back to Lake Superior, and he was still searching for something to do on the day that Dan Cody's yacht dropped anchor in the shallows alongshore.

Cody was fifty years old then, a product of the Nevada silver fields, of the Yukon, of every rush for metal since seventy-five. The transactions in Montana copper that made him many times a millionaire found him physically robust but on the verge of soft-mindedness, and, suspecting this, an infinite number of women tried to separate him from his money. The none too savoury ramifications by which Ella Kaye, the newspaper woman, played Madame de Maintenon[35] to his weakness and sent him to sea in a yacht, were common property of the turgid journalism in 1902. He had been coasting along all too hospitable shores for five years when he turned up as James Gatz's destiny in Little Girl Bay.

To young Gatz, resting on his oars and looking up at the railed deck, that yacht represented all the beauty and glamour in the world. I suppose he smiled at Cody – he had probably discovered that people liked him when he smiled. At any rate Cody asked him a few questions (one of them elicited the brand new name) and found that he was quick and extravagantly ambitious. A few days later he took him to Duluth and bought him a blue coat, six pairs of white duck trousers, and a yachting cap. And when the *Tuolomee* left for the West Indies and the Barbary Coast, Gatsby left too.

He was employed in a vague personal capacity – while he

remained with Cody he was in turn steward, mate, skipper, secretary, and even jailor, for Dan Cody sober knew what lavish doings Dan Cody drunk might soon be about, and he provided for such contingencies by reposing more and more trust in Gatsby. The arrangement lasted five years, during which the boat went three times around the Continent. It might have lasted indefinitely except for the fact that Ella Kaye came on board one night in Boston and a week later Dan Cody inhospitably died.

I remember the portrait of him up in Gatsby's bedroom, a grey, florid man with a hard, empty face – the pioneer debauchee, who during one phase of American life brought back to the Eastern seaboard the savage violence of the frontier brothel and saloon. It was indirectly due to Cody that Gatsby drank so little. Sometimes in the course of gay parties women used to rub champagne into his hair; for himself he formed the habit of letting liquor alone.

And it was from Cody that he inherited money – a legacy of twenty-five thousand dollars. He didn't get it. He never understood the legal device that was used against him, but what remained of the millions went intact to Ella Kaye. He was left with his singularly appropriate education; the vague contour of Jay Gatsby had filled out to the substantiality of a man.

He told me all this very much later, but I've put it down here with the idea of exploding those first wild rumours about his antecedents, which weren't even faintly true. Moreover he told it to me at a time of confusion, when I had reached the point of believing everything and nothing about him. So I take advantage of this short halt, while Gatsby, so to speak, caught his breath, to clear this set of misconceptions away.

It was a halt, too, in my association with his affairs. For several weeks I didn't see him or hear his voice on the phone – mostly I was in New York, trotting around with Jordan and trying to ingratiate myself with her senile aunt – but finally I went over to his house one Sunday afternoon. I hadn't been there two minutes when somebody brought Tom Buchanan in for a drink. I was startled, naturally, but the really surprising thing was that it hadn't happened before.

They were a party of three on horseback – Tom and a man named Sloane and a pretty woman in a brown riding-habit, who had been there previously.

'I'm delighted to see you,' said Gatsby, standing on his porch. 'I'm delighted that you dropped in.'

As though they cared!

'Sit right down. Have a cigarette or a cigar.' He walked around the room quickly, ringing bells. 'I'll have something to drink for you in just a minute.'

He was profoundly affected by the fact that Tom was there. But he would be uneasy anyhow until he had given them something, realizing in a vague way that that was all they came for. Mr Sloane wanted nothing. A lemonade? No, thanks. A little champagne? Nothing at all, thanks ... I'm sorry –

'Did you have a nice ride?'

'Very good roads around here.'

'I suppose the automobiles –'

'Yeah.'

Moved by an irresistible impulse, Gatsby turned to Tom, who had accepted the introduction as a stranger.

'I believe we've met somewhere before, Mr Buchanan.'

'Oh, yes,' said Tom, gruffly polite, but obviously not re-membering. 'So we did. I remember very well.'

'About two weeks ago.'

'That's right. You were with Nick here.'

'I know your wife,' continued Gatsby, almost aggressively.

'That so?'

Tom turned to me.

'You live near here, Nick?'

'Next door.'

'That so?'

Mr Sloane didn't enter into the conversation, but lounged back haughtily in his chair; the woman said nothing either – until unexpectedly, after two highballs, she became cordial.

'We'll all come over to your next party, Mr Gatsby,' she suggested. 'What do you say?'

'Certainly; I'd be delighted to have you.'

'Be ver' nice,' said Mr Sloane, without gratitude. 'Well – think ought to be starting home.'

'Please don't hurry,' Gatsby urged them. He had control of himself now, and he wanted to see more of Tom. 'Why don't you – why don't you stay for supper? I wouldn't be surprised if some other people dropped in from New York.'

'You come to supper with *me*,' said the lady enthusiastically. 'Both of you.'

This included me. Mr Sloane got to his feet.

'Come along,' he said – but to her only.

'I mean it,' she insisted. 'I'd love to have you. Lots of room.'

Gatsby looked at me questioningly. He wanted to go and he didn't see that Mr Sloane had determined he shouldn't.

'I'm afraid I won't be able to,' I said.

'Well, you come,' she urged, concentrating on Gatsby.

Mr Sloane murmured something close to her ear.

'We won't be late if we start now,' she insisted aloud.

'I haven't got a horse,' said Gatsby. 'I used to ride in the army, but I've never bought a horse. I'll have to follow you in my car. Excuse me for just a minute.'

The rest of us walked out on the porch, where Sloane and the lady began an impassioned conversation aside.

'My God, I believe the man's coming,' said Tom. 'Doesn't he know she doesn't want him?'

'She says she does want him.'

'She has a big dinner party and he won't know a soul there.' He frowned. 'I wonder where in the devil he met Daisy. By God, I may be old-fashioned in my ideas, but women run around too much these days to suit me. They meet all kinds of crazy fish.'

Suddenly Mr Sloane and the lady walked down the steps and mounted their horses.

'Come on,' said Mr Sloane to Tom, 'we're late. We've got to go.' And then to me: 'Tell him we couldn't wait, will you?'

Tom and I shook hands, the rest of us exchanged a cool nod, and they trotted quickly down the drive, disappearing under the August foliage just as Gatsby, with hat and light overcoat in hand, came out the front door.

Tom was evidently perturbed at Daisy's running around alone, for on the following Saturday night he came with her to Gatsby's party. Perhaps his presence gave the evening its peculiar quality of oppressiveness – it stands out in my memory from Gatsby's other parties that summer. There were the same people, or at least the same sort of people, the same profusion of champagne, the same many-coloured, many-keyed commotion, but I felt an unpleasantness in the air, a pervading harshness that hadn't been there before. Or perhaps I had merely grown used to it, grown to accept West Egg as a world complete in itself, with its own standards and its own great figures, second to nothing because it had no consciousness of being so, and now I was looking at it again, through Daisy's eyes. It is invariably saddening to look through new eyes at things upon which you have expended your own powers of adjustment.

They arrived at twilight, and, as we strolled out among the sparkling hundreds, Daisy's voice was playing murmurous tricks in her throat.

'These things excite me *so*,' she whispered. 'If you want to kiss me any time during the evening, Nick, just let me know and I'll be glad to arrange it for you. Just mention my name. Or present a green card. I'm giving out green –'

'Look around,' suggested Gatsby.

'I'm looking around. I'm having a marvellous –'

'You must see the faces of many people you've heard about.'

Tom's arrogant eyes roamed the crowd.

'We don't go around very much,' he said; 'in fact, I was just thinking I don't know a soul here.'

'Perhaps you know that lady.' Gatsby indicated a gorgeous, scarcely human orchid of a woman who sat in state under a white-plum tree. Tom and Daisy stared, with that peculiarly unreal feeling that accompanies the recognition of a hitherto ghostly celebrity of the movies.

'She's lovely,' said Daisy.

'The man bending over her is her director.'

He took them ceremoniously from group to group:

'Mrs Buchanan . . . . and Mr Buchanan –' After an instant's hesitation he added: 'the polo player.'

'Oh no,' objected Tom quickly, 'not me.'

But evidently the sound of it pleased Gatsby for Tom remained 'the polo player' for the rest of the evening.

'I've never met so many celebrities,' Daisy exclaimed. 'I liked that man – what was his name? – with the sort of blue nose.'

Gatsby identified him, adding that he was a small producer.

'Well, I liked him anyhow.'

'I'd a little rather not be the polo player,' said Tom pleasantly, 'I'd rather look at all these famous people in – in oblivion.'

Daisy and Gatsby danced. I remember being surprised by his graceful, conservative fox-trot – I had never seen him dance before. Then they sauntered over to my house and sat on the steps for half an hour, while at her request I remained watchfully in the garden. 'In case there's a fire or a flood,' she explained, 'or any act of God.'

Tom appeared from his oblivion as we were sitting down to supper together. 'Do you mind if I eat with some people over here?' he said. 'A fellow's getting off some funny stuff.'

'Go ahead,' answered Daisy genially, 'and if you want to take down any addresses here's my little gold pencil.' . . . She looked around after a moment and told me the girl was 'common but pretty', and I knew that except for the half-hour she'd been alone with Gatsby she wasn't having a good time.

We were at a particularly tipsy table. That was my fault – Gatsby had been called to the phone, and I'd enjoyed these same people only two weeks before. But what had amused me then turned septic on the air now.

'How do you feel, Miss Baedeker?'

The girl addressed was trying, unsuccessfully, to slump against my shoulder. At this inquiry she sat up and opened her eyes.

'Wha'?'

A massive and lethargic woman, who had been urging Daisy to play golf with her at the local club tomorrow, spoke in Miss Baedeker's defence:

'Oh, she's all right now. When she's had five or six cocktails she always starts screaming like that. I tell her she ought to leave it alone.'

'I do leave it alone,' affirmed the accused hollowly.

'We heard you yelling, so I said to Doc Civet here: "There's somebody that needs your help, Doc." '

'She's much obliged, I'm sure,' said another friend, without gratitude, 'but you got her dress all wet when you stuck her head in the pool.'

'Anything I hate is to get my head stuck in a pool,' mumbled Miss Baedeker. 'They almost drowned me once over in New Jersey.'

'Then you ought to leave it alone,' countered Doctor Civet.

'Speak for yourself!' cried Miss Baedeker violently. 'Your hand shakes. I wouldn't let you operate on me!'

It was like that. Almost the last thing I remember was standing with Daisy and watching the moving-picture director and his Star. They were still under the white-plum tree and their faces were touching except for a pale, thin ray of moonlight between. It occurred to me that he had been very slowly bending toward her all evening to attain this proximity, and even while I watched I saw him stoop one ultimate degree and kiss at her cheek.

'I like her,' said Daisy, 'I think she's lovely.'

But the rest offended her – and inarguably, because it wasn't a gesture but an emotion. She was appalled by West Egg, this unprecedented 'place' that Broadway had begotten upon a Long Island fishing village – appalled by its raw vigour that chafed under the old euphemisms and by the too obtrusive fate that herded its inhabitants along a short-cut from nothing to nothing. She saw something awful in the very simplicity she failed to understand.

I sat on the front steps with them while they waited for their car. It was dark here in front; only the bright door sent ten square feet of light volleying out into the soft black morning. Sometimes a shadow moved against a dressing-room blind above, gave way to another shadow, an indefinite procession of shadows, who rouged and powdered in an invisible glass.

'Who is this Gatsby anyhow?' demanded Tom suddenly. 'Some big bootlegger?'

'Where'd you hear that?' I inquired.

'I didn't hear it. I imagined it. A lot of these newly rich people are just big bootleggers, you know.'

'Not Gatsby,' I said shortly.

He was silent for a moment. The pebbles of the drive crunched under his feet.

'Well, he certainly must have strained himself to get this menagerie together.'

A breeze stirred the grey haze of Daisy's fur collar.

'At least they are more interesting than the people we know,' she said with an effort.

'You didn't look so interested.'

'Well, I was.'

Tom laughed and turned to me.

'Did you notice Daisy's face when that girl asked her to put her under a cold shower?'

Daisy began to sing with the music in a husky, rhythmic whisper, bringing out a meaning in each word that it had never had before and would never have again. When the melody rose her voice broke up sweetly, following it, in a way contralto voices have, and each change tipped out a little of her warm human magic upon the air.

'Lots of people come who haven't been invited,' she said suddenly. 'That girl hadn't been invited. They simply force their way in and he's too polite to object.'

'I'd like to know who he is and what he does,' insisted Tom. 'And I think I'll make a point of finding out.'

'I can tell you right now,' she answered. 'He owned some drug-stores, a lot of drug-stores. He built them up himself.'

The dilatory limousine came rolling up the drive.

'Good night, Nick,' said Daisy.

Her glance left me and sought the lighted top of the steps, where 'Three o'clock in the Morning', a neat, sad little waltz of that year, was drifting out the open door. After all, in the very casualness of Gatsby's party there were romantic possibilities totally absent from her world. What was it up there in the song that seemed to be calling her back inside? What would happen now in the dim, incalculable hours? Perhaps some unbelievable guest would arrive, a person infinitely rare and to be marvelled at, some authentically radiant young girl who with one fresh glance at Gatsby, one moment of magical encounter, would blot out those five years of unwavering devotion.

I stayed late that night. Gatsby asked me to wait until he was free, and I lingered in the garden until the inevitable swimming party had run up, chilled and exalted, from the black beach, until the lights were extinguished in the guest-rooms overhead. When he came down the steps at last the tanned skin was drawn unusually tight on his face, and his eyes were bright and tired.

'She didn't like it,' he said immediately.

'Of course she did.'

'She didn't like it,' he insisted. 'She didn't have a good time.'

He was silent, and I guessed at his unutterable depression.

'I feel far away from her,' he said. 'It's hard to make her understand.'

'You mean about the dance?'

'The dance?' He dismissed all the dances he had given with a snap of his fingers. 'Old sport, the dance is unimportant.'

He wanted nothing less of Daisy than that she should go to Tom and say: 'I never loved you.' After she had obliterated four years with that sentence they could decide upon the more practical measures to be taken. One of them was that, after she was free, they were to go back to Louisville and be married from her house – just as if it were five years ago.

'And she doesn't understand,' he said. 'She used to be able to understand. We'd sit for hours –'

He broke off and began to walk up and down a desolate path of fruit rinds and discarded favours and crushed flowers.

'I wouldn't ask too much of her,' I ventured. 'You can't repeat the past.'

'Can't repeat the past?' he cried incredulously. 'Why of course you can!'

He looked around him wildly, as if the past were lurking here in the shadow of his house, just out of reach of his hand.

'I'm going to fix everything just the way it was before,' he said, nodding determinedly. 'She'll see.'

He talked a lot about the past, and I gathered that he wanted to recover something, some idea of himself perhaps, that had gone into loving Daisy. His life had been confused and disordered since then, but if he could once return to a certain starting place and go over it all slowly, he could find out what that thing was . . .

. . . One autumn night, five years before, they had been walking down the street when the leaves were falling, and they came to a place where there were no trees and the sidewalk was white with moonlight. They stopped here and turned toward each other. Now it was a cool night with that mysterious excitement in it which comes at the two changes of the year. The quiet lights in the houses were humming out into the darkness and there was a stir and bustle among the stars. Out of the corner of his eye Gatsby saw that the blocks of the sidewalks really formed a ladder and mounted to a secret place above the trees – he could climb to it, if he climbed alone, and once there he could suck on the pap of life, gulp down the incomparable milk of wonder.

His heart beat faster as Daisy's white face came up to his own. He knew that when he kissed this girl, and forever wed his unutterable visions to her perishable breath, his mind would never romp again like the mind of God. So he waited, listening for a moment longer to the tuning-fork that had been struck upon a star. Then he kissed her. At his lips' touch she blossomed for him like a flower and the incarnation was complete.

Through all he said, even through his appalling sentimentality, I was reminded of something – an elusive rhythm, a fragment of lost words, that I had heard somewhere a long time ago. For a moment a phrase tried to take shape in my mouth and my lips parted like a dumb man's, as though there was more struggling upon them than a wisp of startled air. But they made no sound, and what I had almost remembered was uncommunicable forever.

Chapter VII

I T was when curiosity about Gatsby was at its highest that the lights in his house failed to go on one Saturday night – and, as obscurely as it had begun, his career as Trimalchio was over. Only gradually did I become aware that the automobiles which turned expectantly into his drive stayed for just a minute and then drove sulkily away. Wondering if he were sick I went over to find out – an unfamiliar butler with a villainous face squinted at me suspiciously from the door.

'Is Mr Gatsby sick?'

'Nope.' After a pause he added 'sir' in a dilatory, grudging way.

'I hadn't seen him around, and I was rather worried. Tell him Mr Carraway came over.'

'Who?' he demanded rudely.

'Carraway.'

'Carraway. All right, I'll tell him.'

Abruptly he slammed the door.

My Finn informed me that Gatsby had dismissed every servant in his house a week ago and replaced them with half a dozen others, who never went into West Egg village to be bribed by the tradesmen, but ordered moderate supplies over the telephone. The grocery boy reported that the kitchen looked like a pigsty, and the general opinion in the village was that the new people weren't servants at all.

Next day Gatsby called me on the phone.

'Going away?' I inquired.

'No, old sport.'

'I hear you fired all your servants.'

'I wanted somebody who wouldn't gossip. Daisy comes over quite often – in the afternoons.'

So the whole caravansary had fallen in like a card house at the disapproval in her eyes.

'They're some people Wolfshiem wanted to do something for. They're all brothers and sisters. They used to run a small hotel.'

'I see.'

He was calling up at Daisy's request – would I come to lunch at her house tomorrow? Miss Baker would be there. Half an hour later Daisy herself telephoned and seemed relieved to find that I was coming. Something was up. And yet I couldn't believe that they would choose this occasion for a scene – especially for the rather harrowing scene that Gatsby had outlined in the garden.

The next day was broiling, almost the last, certainly the warmest, of the summer. As my train emerged from the tunnel into sunlight, only the hot whistles of the National Biscuit Company broke the simmering hush at noon. The straw seats of the car hovered on the edge of combustion; the woman next to me perspired delicately for a while into her white shirtwaist, and then, as her newspaper dampened under her fingers, lapsed despairingly into deep heat with a desolate cry. Her pocket-book slapped to the floor.

'Oh, my!' she gasped.

I picked it up with a weary bend and handed it back to her, holding it at arm's length and by the extreme tip of the corners to indicate that I had no designs upon it – but every one near by, including the woman, suspected me just the same.

'Hot!' said the conductor to familiar faces. 'Some weather! ... Hot! ... Hot! ... Hot! ... Is it hot enough for you? Is it hot? Is it ...?'

My commutation ticket came back to me with a dark stain from his hand. That any one should care in this heat whose flushed lips he kissed, whose head made damp the pyjama pocket over his heart!

. . . Through the hall of the Buchanans' house blew a faint wind, carrying the sound of the telephone bell out to Gatsby and me as we waited at the door.

'The master's body?' roared the butler into the mouthpiece. 'I'm sorry, madame, but we can't furnish it – it's far too hot to touch this noon!'

What he really said was: 'Yes . . . Yes . . . I'll see.'

He set down the receiver and came toward us, glistening slightly, to take our stiff straw hats.

'Madame expects you in the salon!' he cried, needlessly indicating the direction. In this heat every extra gesture was an affront to the common store of life.

The room, shadowed well with awnings, was dark and cool. Daisy and Jordan lay upon an enormous couch, like silver idols weighing down their own white dresses against the singing breeze of the fans.

'We can't move,' they said together.

Jordan's fingers, powdered white over their tan, rested for a moment in mine.

'And Mr Thomas Buchanan, the athlete?' I inquired.

Simultaneously I heard his voice, gruff, muffled, husky, at the hall telephone.

Gatsby stood in the centre of the crimson carpet and gazed around with fascinated eyes. Daisy watched him and laughed, her sweet, exciting laugh; a tiny gust of powder rose from her bosom into the air.

'The rumour is,' whispered Jordan, 'that that's Tom's girl on the telephone.'

We were silent. The voice in the hall rose high with

annoyance: 'Very well, then, I won't sell you the car at all ... I'm under no obligations to you at all ... and as for your bothering me about it at lunch time, I won't stand that at all!'

'Holding down the receiver,' said Daisy cynically.

'No, he's not,' I assured her. 'It's a bona-fide deal. I happen to know about it.'

Tom flung open the door, blocked out its space for a moment with his thick body, and hurried into the room.

'Mr Gatsby!' He put out his broad, flat hand with well-concealed dislike. 'I'm glad to see you, sir. ... Nick ...'

'Make us a cold drink,' cried Daisy.

As he left the room again she got up and went over to Gatsby and pulled his face down, kissing him on the mouth.

'You know I love you,' she murmured.

'You forget there's a lady present,' said Jordan.

Daisy looked around doubtfully.

'You kiss Nick too.'

'What a low, vulgar girl!'

'I don't care!' cried Daisy, and began to clog on the brick fireplace. Then she remembered the heat and sat down guiltily on the couch just as a freshly laundered nurse leading a little girl came into the room.

'Bles-sed pre-cious,' she crooned, holding out her arms. 'Come to your own mother that loves you.'

The child, relinquished by the nurse, rushed across the room and rooted shyly into her mother's dress.

'The bles-sed pre-cious! Did mother get powder on your old yellowy hair? Stand up now, and say – How-de-do.'

Gatsby and I in turn leaned down and took the small reluctant hand. Afterward he kept looking at the child with surprise. I don't think he had ever really believed in its existence before.

'I got dressed before luncheon,' said the child, turning eagerly to Daisy.

'That's because your mother wanted to show you off.' Her face bent into the single wrinkle of the small white neck. 'You dream, you. You absolute little dream.'

'Yes,' admitted the child calmly. 'Aunt Jordan's got on a white dress too.'

'How do you like mother's friends?' Daisy turned her around so that she faced Gatsby. 'Do you think they're pretty?'

'Where's Daddy?'

'She doesn't look like her father,' explained Daisy. 'She looks like me. She's got my hair and shape of the face.'

Daisy sat back upon the couch. The nurse took a step forward and held out her hand.

'Come, Pammy.'

'Good-bye, sweetheart!'

With a reluctant backward glance the well-disciplined child held to her nurse's hand and was pulled out the door, just as Tom came back, preceding four gin rickeys that clicked full of ice.

Gatsby took up his drink.

'They certainly look cool,' he said, with visible tension.

We drank in long, greedy swallows.

'I read somewhere that the sun's getting hotter every year,' said Tom genially. 'It seems that pretty soon the earth's going to fall into the sun – or wait a minute – it's just the opposite – the sun's getting colder every year.

'Come outside,' he suggested to Gatsby, 'I'd like you to have a look at the place.'

I went with them out to the veranda. On the green Sound, stagnant in the heat, one small sail crawled slowly toward the fresher sea. Gatsby's eyes followed it momentarily; he raised his hand and pointed across the bay.

'I'm right across from you.'

'So you are.'

Our eyes lifted over the rose-beds and the hot lawn and the weedy refuse of the dog-days alongshore. Slowly the white wings of the boat moved against the blue cool limit of the sky. Ahead lay the scalloped ocean and the abounding blessed isles.

'There's sport for you,' said Tom, nodding. 'I'd like to be out there with him for about an hour.'

We had luncheon in the dining-room, darkened too against the heat, and drank down nervous gaiety with the cold ale.

'What'll we do with ourselves this afternoon?' cried Daisy, 'and the day after that, and the next thirty years?'

'Don't be morbid,' Jordan said. 'Life starts all over again when it gets crisp in the fall.'

'But it's so hot,' insisted Daisy, on the verge of tears, 'and everything's so confused. Let's all go to town!'

Her voice struggled on through the heat, beating against it, moulding its senselessness into forms.

'I've heard of making a garage out of a stable,' Tom was saying to Gatsby, 'but I'm the first man who ever made a stable out of a garage.'

'Who wants to go to town?' demanded Daisy insistently. Gatsby's eyes floated toward her. 'Ah,' she cried, 'you look so cool.'

Their eyes met, and they stared together at each other, alone in space. With an effort she glanced down at the table.

'You always look so cool,' she repeated.

She had told him that she loved him, and Tom Buchanan saw. He was astounded. His mouth opened a little, and he looked at Gatsby, and then back at Daisy as if he had just recognized her as someone he knew a long time ago.

'You resemble the advertisement of the man,' she went on innocently. 'You know the advertisement of the man –'

'All right,' broke in Tom quickly, 'I'm perfectly willing to go to town. Come on – we're all going to town.'

He got up, his eyes still flashing between Gatsby and his wife. No one moved.

'Come on!' His temper cracked a little. 'What's the matter, anyhow? If we're going to town, let's start.'

His hand, trembling with his effort at self-control, bore to his lips the last of his glass of ale. Daisy's voice got us to our feet and out on to the blazing gravel drive.

'Are we just going to go?' she objected. 'Like this? Aren't we going to let anyone smoke a cigarette first?'

'Everybody smoked all through lunch.'

'Oh, let's have fun,' she begged him. 'It's too hot to fuss.'

He didn't answer.

'Have it your own way,' she said. 'Come on, Jordan.'

They went upstairs to get ready while we three men stood there shuffling the hot pebbles with our feet. A silver curve of the moon hovered already in the western sky. Gatsby started to speak, changed his mind, but not before Tom wheeled and faced him expectantly.

'Have you got your stables here?' asked Gatsby with an effort.

'About a quarter of a mile down the road.'

'Oh.'

A pause.

'I don't see the idea of going to town,' broke out Tom savagely. 'Women get these notions in their heads –'

'Shall we take anything to drink?' called Daisy from an upper window.

'I'll get some whisky,' answered Tom. He went inside.

Gatsby turned to me rigidly:

'I can't say anything in his house, old sport.'

'She's got an indiscreet voice,' I remarked. 'It's full of –' I hesitated.

'Her voice is full of money,' he said suddenly.

That was it. I'd never understood before. It was full of money – that was the inexhaustible charm that rose and fell in it, the jingle of it, the cymbals' song of it . . . High in a white palace the king's daughter, the golden girl . . .

Tom came out of the house wrapping a quart bottle in a towel, followed by Daisy and Jordan wearing small tight hats of metallic cloth and carrying light capes over their arms.

'Shall we all go in my car?' suggested Gatsby. He felt the hot, green leather of the seat. 'I ought to have left it in the shade.'

'Is it standard shift?' demanded Tom.

'Yes.'

'Well, you take my coupé and let me drive your car to town.'

The suggestion was distasteful to Gatsby.

'I don't think there's much gas,' he objected.

'Plenty of gas,' said Tom boisterously. He looked at the gauge. 'And if it runs out I can stop at a drug-store. You can buy anything at a drug-store nowadays.'

A pause followed this apparently pointless remark. Daisy looked at Tom frowning, and an indefinable expression, at once definitely unfamiliar and vaguely recognizable, as if I had only heard it described in words, passed over Gatsby's face.

'Come on, Daisy,' said Tom, pressing her with his hand toward Gatsby's car. 'I'll take you in this circus wagon.'

He opened the door, but she moved out from the circle of his arm.

'You take Nick and Jordan. We'll follow you in the coupé.'

She walked close to Gatsby, touching his coat with her hand.

Jordan and Tom and I got into the front seat of Gatsby's car, Tom pushed the unfamiliar gears tentatively, and we shot off into the oppressive heat, leaving them out of sight behind.

'Did you see that?' demanded Tom.

'See what?'

He looked at me keenly, realizing that Jordan and I must have known all along.

'You think I'm pretty dumb, don't you?' he suggested. 'Perhaps I am, but I have a – almost a second sight, sometimes, that tells me what to do. Maybe you don't believe that, but science –'

He paused. The immediate contingency overtook him, pulled him back from the edge of theoretical abyss.

'I've made a small investigation of this fellow,' he continued. 'I could have gone deeper if I'd known –'

'Do you mean you've been to a medium?' inquired Jordan humorously.

'What?' Confused, he stared at us as we laughed. 'A medium?'

'About Gatsby.'

'About Gatsby! No, I haven't. I said I'd been making a small investigation of his past.'

'And you found he was an Oxford man,' said Jordan helpfully.

'An Oxford man!' He was incredulous. 'Like hell he is! He wears a pink suit.'

'Nevertheless he's an Oxford man.'

'Oxford, New Mexico,' snorted Tom contemptuously, 'or something like that.'

'Listen, Tom. If you're such a snob, why did you invite him to lunch?' demanded Jordan crossly.

'Daisy invited him; she knew him before we were married – God knows where!'

We were all irritable now with the fading ale, and aware of it we drove for a while in silence. Then as Doctor T. J. Eckleburg's faded eyes came into sight down the road, I remembered Gatsby's caution about gasoline.

'We've got enough to get us to town,' said Tom.

'But there's a garage right here,' objected Jordan. 'I don't want to get stalled in this baking heat.'

Tom threw on both brakes impatiently, and we slid to an abrupt dusty stop under Wilson's sign. After a moment the proprietor emerged from the interior of his establishment and gazed hollow-eyed at the car.

'Let's have some gas!' cried Tom roughly. 'What do you think we stopped for – to admire the view?'

'I'm sick,' said Wilson without moving. 'Been sick all day.'

'What's the matter?'

'I'm all run down.'

'Well, shall I help myself?' Tom demanded. 'You sounded well enough on the phone.'

With an effort Wilson left the shade and support of the doorway and, breathing hard, unscrewed the cap of the tank. In the sunlight his face was green.

'I didn't mean to interrupt your lunch,' he said. 'But I need money pretty bad, and I was wondering what you were going to do with your old car.'

'How do you like this one?' inquired Tom. 'I bought it last week.'

'It's a nice yellow one,' said Wilson, as he strained at the handle.

'Like to buy it?'

'Big chance,' Wilson smiled faintly. 'No, but I could make some money on the other.'

'What do you want money for, all of a sudden?'

'I've been here too long. I want to get away. My wife and I want to go West.'

'Your wife does,' exclaimed Tom, startled.

'She's been talking about it for ten years.' He rested for a moment against the pump, shading his eyes. 'And now she's going whether she wants to or not. I'm going to get her away.'

The coupé flashed by us with a flurry of dust and the flash of a waving hand.

'What do I owe you?' demanded Tom harshly.

'I just got wised up to something funny the last two days,' remarked Wilson. 'That's why I want to get away. That's why I been bothering you about the car.'

'What do I owe you?'

'Dollar twenty.'

The relentless beating heat was beginning to confuse me and I had a bad moment there before I realized that so far his suspicions hadn't alighted on Tom. He had discovered that Myrtle had some sort of life apart from him in another world, and the shock had made him physically sick. I stared at him and then at Tom, who had made a parallel discovery less than an hour before – and it occurred to me that there was no difference between men, in intelligence or race, so profound as the difference between the sick and the well. Wilson was so sick that he looked guilty, unforgivably guilty – as if he had just got some poor girl with child.

'I'll let you have that car,' said Tom. 'I'll send it over to-morrow afternoon.'

That locality was always vaguely disquieting, even in the broad glare of afternoon, and now I turned my head as though I had been warned of something behind. Over the ashheaps the giant eyes of Doctor T. J. Eckleburg kept their vigil, but I perceived, after a moment, that other eyes were regarding us with peculiar intensity from less than twenty feet away.

In one of the windows over the garage the curtains had been moved aside a little, and Myrtle Wilson was peering down at the car. So engrossed was she that she had no consciousness of being observed, and one emotion after another crept into her face like objects into a slowly developing picture. Her expression was curiously familiar – it was an expression I had often seen on women's faces, but on Myrtle Wilson's face it seemed purposeless and inexplicable until I realized that her eyes, wide with jealous terror, were fixed not on Tom, but on Jordan Baker, whom she took to be his wife.

There is no confusion like the confusion of a simple mind, and as we drove away Tom was feeling the hot whips of panic. His wife and his mistress, until an hour ago secure and inviolate, were slipping precipitately from his control. Instinct made him step on the accelerator with the double purpose of overtaking Daisy and leaving Wilson behind, and we sped along toward Astoria at fifty miles an hour, until, among the spidery girders of the elevated, we came in sight of the easy-going blue coupé.

'Those big movies around Fiftieth Street are cool,' suggested Jordan. 'I love New York on summer afternoons when everyone's away. There's something very sensuous about it – over-ripe, as if all sorts of funny fruits were going to fall into your hands.'

The word 'sensuous' had the effect of further disquieting Tom, but before he could invent a protest the coupé came to a stop, and Daisy signalled us to draw up alongside.

'Where are we going?' she cried.

'How about the movies?'

'It's so hot,' she complained. 'You go. We'll ride around and meet you after.' With an effort her wit rose faintly. 'We'll meet you on some corner. I'll be the man smoking two cigarettes.'

'We can't argue about it here,' Tom said impatiently, as a truck gave out a cursing whistle behind us. 'You follow me to the south side of Central Park, in front of the Plaza.'

Several times he turned his head and looked back for their car, and if the traffic delayed them he slowed up until they came into sight. I think he was afraid they would dart down a side street and out of his life forever.

But they didn't. And we all took the less explicable step of engaging the parlour of a suite in the Plaza Hotel.

The prolonged and tumultuous argument that ended by herding us into that room eludes me, though I have a sharp physical memory that, in the course of it, my underwear kept climbing like a damp snake around my legs and intermittent beads of sweat raced cool across my back. The notion originated with Daisy's suggestion that we hire five bathrooms and take cold baths, and then assumed more tangible form as 'a place to have a mint julep'. Each of us said over and over that it was a 'crazy idea' – we all talked at once to a baffled clerk and thought, or pretended to think, that we were being very funny ...

The room was large and stifling, and, though it was already four o'clock, opening the windows admitted only a gust of hot shrubbery from the Park. Daisy went to the mirror and stood with her back to us, fixing her hair.

'It's a swell suite,' whispered Jordan respectfully, and everyone laughed.

'Open another window,' commanded Daisy, without turning around.

'There aren't any more.'

'Well, we'd better telephone for an axe –'

'The thing to do is to forget about the heat,' said Tom impatiently. 'You make it ten times worse by crabbing about it.'

He unrolled the bottle of whisky from the towel and put it on the table.

'Why not let her alone, old sport?' remarked Gatsby. 'You're the one that wanted to come to town.'

There was a moment of silence. The telephone book slipped from its nail and splashed to the floor, whereupon Jordan whispered, 'Excuse me' – but this time no one laughed.

'I'll pick it up,' I offered.

'I've got it.' Gatsby examined the parted string, muttered 'Hum!' in an interested way, and tossed the book on a chair.

'That's a great expression of yours, isn't it?' said Tom sharply.

'What is?'

'All this "old sport" business. Where'd you pick that up?'

'Now see here, Tom,' said Daisy, turning around from the mirror, 'if you're going to make personal remarks I won't stay here a minute. Call up and order some ice for the mint julep.'

As Tom took up the receiver the compressed heat exploded into sound and we were listening to the portentous chords of Mendelssohn's Wedding March from the ballroom below.

'Imagine marrying anybody in this heat!' cried Jordan dismally.

'Still – I was married in the middle of June,' Daisy remembered. 'Louisville in June! Somebody fainted. Who was it fainted, Tom?'

'Biloxi,' he answered shortly.

'A man named Biloxi. "Blocks" Biloxi, and he made boxes -- that's a fact – and he was from Biloxi, Tennessee.'

'They carried him into my house,' appended Jordan, 'because we lived just two doors from the church. And he stayed three weeks, until Daddy told him he had to get out. The day after he left Daddy died.' After a moment she added. 'There wasn't any connection.'

'I used to know a Bill Biloxi from Memphis,' I remarked.

'That was his cousin. I knew his whole family history before he left. He gave me an aluminium putter that I use today.'

The music had died down as the ceremony began and now a long cheer floated in at the window, followed by intermittent cries of 'Yea – ea – ea!' and finally by a burst of jazz as the dancing began.

'We're getting old,' said Daisy. 'If we were young we'd rise and dance.'

'Remember Biloxi,' Jordan warned her. 'Where'd you know him, Tom?'

'Biloxi?' He concentrated with an effort. 'I didn't know him. He was a friend of Daisy's.'

'He was not,' she denied. 'I'd never seen him before. He came down in the private car.'

'Well, he said he knew you. He said he was raised in Louisville. Asa Bird brought him around at the last minute and asked if we had room for him.'

Jordan smiled.

'He was probably bumming his way home. He told me he was president of your class at Yale.'

Tom and I looked at each other blankly.

'Biloxi?'

'First place, we didn't have any president – '

Gatsby's foot beat a short, restless tattoo and Tom eyed him suddenly.

'By the way, Mr Gatsby, I understand you're an Oxford man.'

'Not exactly.'

'Oh, yes, I understand you went to Oxford.'

'Yes – I went there.'

A pause. Then Tom's voice, incredulous and insulting:

'You must have gone there about the time Biloxi went to New Haven.'

Another pause. A waiter knocked and came in with crushed mint and ice but the silence was unbroken by his 'thank you' and the soft closing of the door. This tremendous detail was to be cleared up at last.

'I told you I went there,' said Gatsby.

'I heard you, but I'd like to know when.'

'It was in nineteen-nineteen, I only stayed five months. That's why I can't really call myself an Oxford man.'

Tom glanced around to see if we mirrored his unbelief. But we were all looking at Gatsby.

'It was an opportunity they gave to some of the officers after the armistice,' he continued. 'We could go to any of the universities in England or France.'

I wanted to get up and slap him on the back. I had one of those renewals of complete faith in him that I'd experienced before.

Daisy rose, smiling faintly, and went to the table.

'Open the whisky, Tom,' she ordered, 'and I'll make you a mint julep. Then you won't seem so stupid to yourself . . . Look at the mint!'

'Wait a minute,' snapped Tom, 'I want to ask Mr Gatsby one more question.'

'Go on,' Gatsby said politely.

'What kind of a row are you trying to cause in my house anyhow?'

They were out in the open at last and Gatsby was content.

'He isn't causing a row,' Daisy looked desperately from one to the other. 'You're causing a row. Please have a little self-control.'

'Self-control!' repeated Tom incredulously. 'I suppose the latest thing is to sit back and let Mr Nobody from Nowhere make love to your wife. Well, if that's the idea you can count me out ... Nowadays people begin by sneering at family life and family institutions, and next they'll throw everything overboard and have intermarriage between black and white.'

Flushed with his impassioned gibberish, he saw himself standing alone on the last barrier of civilization.

'We're all white here,' murmured Jordan.

'I know I'm not very popular. I don't give big parties. I suppose you've got to make your house into a pigsty in order to have any friends – in the modern world.'

Angry as I was, as we all were, I was tempted to laugh whenever he opened his mouth. The transition from libertine to prig was so complete.

'I've got something to tell *you*, old sport – ' began Gatsby. But Daisy guessed at his intention.

'Please don't!' she interrupted helplessly. 'Please let's all go home. Why don't we all go home?'

'That's a good idea,' I got up. 'Come on, Tom. Nobody wants a drink.'

'I want to know what Mr Gatsby has to tell me.'

'Your wife doesn't love you,' said Gatsby. 'She's never loved you. She loves me.'

'You must be crazy!' exclaimed Tom automatically.

Gatsby sprang to his feet, vivid with excitement.

'She never loved you, do you hear?' he cried. 'She only married you because I was poor and she was tired of waiting for me. It was a terrible mistake, but in her heart she never loved any one except me!'

At this point Jordan and I tried to go, but Tom and Gatsby insisted with competitive firmness that we remain – as though neither of them had anything to conceal and it would be a privilege to partake vicariously of their emotions.

'Sit down, Daisy,' Tom's voice groped unsuccessfully for the

paternal note. 'What's been going on? I want to hear all about it.'

'I told you what's been going on,' said Gatsby. 'Going on for five years – and you didn't know.'

Tom turned to Daisy sharply.

'You've been seeing this fellow for five years?'

'Not seeing,' said Gatsby. 'No, we couldn't meet. But both of us loved each other all that time, old sport, and you didn't know. I used to laugh sometimes' – but there was no laughter in his eyes – 'to think that you didn't know.'

'Oh – that's all.' Tom tapped his thick fingers together like a clergyman and leaned back in his chair.

'You're crazy!' he exploded. 'I can't speak about what happened five years ago, because I didn't know Daisy then – and I'll be damned if I see how you got within a mile of her unless you brought the groceries to the back door. But all the rest of that's a God damned lie. Daisy loved me when she married me and she loves me now.'

'No,' said Gatsby, shaking his head.

'She does, though. The trouble is that sometimes she gets foolish ideas in her head and doesn't know what she's doing.' He nodded sagely. 'And what's more, I love Daisy too. Once in a while I go off on a spree and make a fool of myself, but I always come back, and in my heart I love her all the time.'

'You're revolting,' said Daisy. She turned to me, and her voice, dropping an octave lower, filled the room with thrilling scorn: 'Do you know why we left Chicago? I'm surprised that they didn't treat you to the story of that little spree.'

Gatsby walked over and stood beside her.

'Daisy, that's all over now,' he said earnestly. 'It doesn't matter any more. Just tell him the truth – that you never loved him – and it's all wiped out forever.'

She looked at him blindly. 'Why – how could I love him – possibly?'

'You never loved him.'

She hesitated. Her eyes fell on Jordan and me with a sort of appeal, as though she realized at last what she was doing – and as though she had never, all along, intended doing anything at all. But it was done now. It was too late.

'I never loved him,' she said, with perceptible reluctance.

'Not at Kapiolani?' demanded Tom suddenly.[36]

'No.'

From the ballroom beneath, muffled and suffocating chords were drifting up on hot waves of air.

'Not that day I carried you down from the Punch Bowl to keep your shoes dry?'[37] There was a husky tenderness in his tone . . . 'Daisy?'

'Please don't.' Her voice was cold, but the rancour was gone from it. She looked at Gatsby. 'There, Jay,' she said – but her hand as she tried to light a cigarette was trembling. Suddenly she threw the cigarette and the burning match on the carpet.

'Oh, you want too much!' she cried to Gatsby. 'I love you now – isn't that enough? I can't help what's past.' She began to sob helplessly. 'I did love him once – but I loved you too.'

Gatsby's eyes opened and closed.

'You loved me *too*?' he repeated.

'Even that's a lie,' said Tom savagely. 'She didn't know you were alive. Why – there's things between Daisy and me that you'll never know, things that neither of us can ever forget.'

The words seemed to bite physically into Gatsby.

'I want to speak to Daisy alone,' he insisted. 'She's all excited now – '

'Even alone I can't say I never loved Tom,' she admitted in a pitiful voice. 'It wouldn't be true.'

'Of course it wouldn't,' agreed Tom.

She turned to her husband.

'As if it mattered to you,' she said.

'Of course it matters. I'm going to take better care of you from now on.'

'You don't understand,' said Gatsby, with a touch of panic. 'You're not going to take care of her any more.'

'I'm not?' Tom opened his eyes wide and laughed. He could afford to control himself now. 'Why's that?'

'Daisy's leaving you.'

'Nonsense.'

'I am, though,' she said with a visible effort.

'She's not leaving me!' Tom's words suddenly leaned down over Gatsby. 'Certainly not for a common swindler who'd have to steal the ring he put on her finger.'

'I won't stand this!' cried Daisy. 'Oh, please let's get out.'

'Who are you, anyhow?' broke out Tom. 'You're one of that bunch that hangs around with Meyer Wolfshiem – that much I happen to know. I've made a little investigation into your affairs – and I'll carry it further tomorrow.'

'You can suit yourself about that, old sport,' said Gatsby steadily.

'I found out what your "drug-stores" were.'[38] He turned to us and spoke rapidly. 'He and this Wolfshiem bought up a lot of side-street drug-stores here and in Chicago and sold grain alcohol over the counter. That's one of his little stunts. I picked him for a bootlegger the first time I saw him, and I wasn't far wrong.'

'What about it?' said Gatsby politely. 'I guess your friend Walter Chase wasn't too proud to come in on it.'

'And you left him in the lurch, didn't you? You let him go to jail for a month over in New Jersey. God! You ought to hear Walter on the subject of *you*.'

'He came to us dead broke. He was very glad to pick up some money, old sport.'

'Don't you call me "old sport"!' cried Tom. Gatsby said nothing. 'Walter could have you up on the betting laws too, but Wolfshiem scared him into shutting his mouth.'

That unfamiliar yet recognizable look was back again in Gatsby's face.

'That drug-store business was just small change,' continued Tom slowly, 'but you've got something on now that Walter's afraid to tell me about.'

I glanced at Daisy, who was staring terrified between Gatsby and her husband, and at Jordan, who had begun to balance an invisible but absorbing object on the tip of her chin. Then I turned back to Gatsby – and was startled at his expression. He looked – and this is said in all contempt for the babbled slander of his garden – as if he had 'killed a man'. For a moment the set of his face could be described in just that fantastic way.

It passed, and he began to talk excitedly to Daisy, denying everything, defending his name against accusations that had not been made. But with every word she was drawing further and further into herself, so he gave that up, and only the dead dream fought on as the afternoon slipped away, trying to touch what was no longer tangible, struggling unhappily, undespairingly, toward that lost voice across the room.

The voice begged again to go.

'*Please*, Tom! I can't stand this any more.'

Her frightened eyes told that whatever intentions, whatever courage she had had, were definitely gone.

'You two start on home, Daisy,' said Tom. 'In Mr Gatsby's car.'

She looked at Tom, alarmed now, but he insisted with magnanimous scorn.

'Go on. He won't annoy you. I think he realizes that his presumptuous little flirtation is over.'

They were gone, without a word, snapped out, made accidental, isolated, like ghosts, even from our pity.

After a moment Tom got up and began wrapping the unopened bottle of whisky in the towel.

'Want any of this stuff? Jordan? . . . Nick?'

I didn't answer.

'Nick?' He asked again.

'What?'

'Want any?'

'No . . . I just remembered that today's my birthday.'

I was thirty. Before me stretched the portentous, menacing road of a new decade.

It was seven o'clock when we got into the coupé with him and started for Long Island. Tom talked incessantly, exulting and laughing, but his voice was as remote from Jordan and me as the foreign clamour on the sidewalk or the tumult of the elevated overhead. Human sympathy has its limits, and we were content to let all their tragic arguments fade with the city lights behind. Thirty – the promise of a decade of loneliness, a thinning list of single men to know, a thinning brief-case of enthusiasm, thinning hair. But there was Jordan beside me, who, unlike Daisy, was too wise ever to carry well-forgotten dreams from age to age. As we passed over the dark bridge her wan face fell lazily against my coat's shoulder and the formidable stroke of thirty died away with the reassuring pressure of her hand.

So we drove on toward death through the cooling twilight.

The young Greek, Michaelis, who ran the coffee joint beside the ashheaps was the principal witness at the inquest. He had slept through the heat until after five, when he strolled over to the garage, and found George Wilson sick in his office – really sick, pale as his own pale hair and shaking all over. Michaelis advised him to go to bed, but Wilson refused, saying that he'd miss a lot of business if he did. While his neighbour was trying to persuade him a violent racket broke out over-head.

'I've got my wife locked in up there,' explained Wilson calmly. 'She's going to stay there till the day after tomorrow, and then we're going to move away.'

Michaelis was astonished; they had been neighbours for four years, and Wilson had never seemed faintly capable of such a statement. Generally he was one of these worn-out men: when he wasn't working, he sat on a chair in the doorway and stared at the people and the cars that passed along the road. When anyone spoke to him he invariably laughed in an agreeable, colourless way. He was his wife's man and not his own.

So naturally Michaelis tried to find out what had happened, but Wilson wouldn't say a word – instead he began to throw curious, suspicious glances at his visitor and ask him what he'd been doing at certain times on certain days. Just as the latter was getting uneasy, some workmen came past the door bound for his restaurant, and Michaelis took the opportunity to get away, intending to come back later. But he didn't. He supposed he forgot to, that's all. When he came outside again, a little after seven, he was reminded of the conversation because he heard Mrs Wilson's voice, loud and scolding, downstairs in the garage.

'Beat me!' he heard her cry. 'Throw me down and beat me, you dirty little coward!'

A moment later she rushed out into the dusk, waving her hands and shouting – before he could move from his door the business was over.

The 'death car' as the newspapers called it, didn't stop; it came out of the gathering darkness, wavered tragically for a moment, and then disappeared around the next bend. Mavro-michaelis wasn't even sure of its colour – he told the first policeman that it was light green. The other car, the one going toward New York, came to rest a hundred yards beyond, and its driver hurried back to where Myrtle Wilson, her life violently extinguished, knelt in the road and mingled her thick dark blood with the dust.

Michaelis and this man reached her first, but when they had torn open her shirtwaist, still damp with perspiration, they saw that her left breast was swinging loose like a flap, and there was no need to listen for the heart beneath. The mouth was wide open and ripped a little at the corners, as though she had choked a little in giving up the tremendous vitality she had stored so long.

We saw the three or four automobiles and the crowd when we were still some distance away.

'Wreck!' said Tom. 'That's good. Wilson'll have a little business at last.'

He slowed down, but still without any intention of stopping, until, as we came nearer, the hushed, intent faces of the people at the garage door made him automatically put on the brakes.

'We'll take a look,' he said doubtfully, 'just a look.'

I became aware now of a hollow, wailing sound which issued incessantly from the garage, a sound which as we got out of the coupé and walked toward the door resolved itself into the words 'Oh, my God!' uttered over and over in a gasping moan.

'There's some bad trouble here,' said Tom excitedly.

He reached up on tiptoes and peered over a circle of heads

into the garage, which was lit only by a yellow light in a swinging metal basket overhead. Then he made a harsh sound in his throat, and with a violent thrusting movement of his powerful arms pushed his way through.

The circle closed up again with a running murmur of expostulation; it was a minute before I could see anything at all. Then new arrivals deranged the line, and Jordan and I were pushed suddenly inside.

Myrtle Wilson's body, wrapped in a blanket, and then in another blanket, as though she suffered from a chill in the hot night, lay on a work-table by the wall, and Tom, with his back to us, was bending over it, motionless. Next to him stood a motor-cycle policeman taking down names with much sweat and correction in a little book. At first I couldn't find the source of the high, groaning words that echoed clamorously through the bare garage – then I saw Wilson standing on the raised threshold of his office, swaying back and forth and holding to the doorposts with both hands. Some man was talking to him in a low voice and attempting, from time to time, to lay a hand on his shoulder, but Wilson neither heard nor saw. His eyes would drop slowly from the swinging light to the laden table by the wall, and then jerk back to the light again, and he gave out incessantly his high, horrible call:

'Oh, my Ga-od! Oh, my Ga-od! Oh, Ga-od! Oh, my Ga-od!'

Presently Tom lifted his head with a jerk and, after staring around the garage with glazed eyes, addressed a mumbled incoherent remark to the policeman.

'M-a-v –' the policeman was saying, '– o –'

'No, r –' corrected the man, 'M-a-v-r-o –'

'Listen to me!' muttered Tom fiercely.

'r –' said the policeman, 'o –'

'g –'

'g –' He looked up as Tom's broad hand fell sharply on nis shoulder. 'What you want, fella?'

'What happened? – that's what I want to know.'

'Auto hit her. Ins'antly killed.'

'Instantly killed,' repeated Tom, staring.

'She ran out ina road. Son-of-a-bitch didn't even stopus car.'

'There was two cars,' said Michaelis, 'one comin', one goin', see?'

'Going where?' asked the policeman keenly.

'One goin' each way. Well, she' – his hand rose toward the blankets but stopped half-way and fell to his side – 'she ran out there an' the one comin' from N'York knock right into her, goin' thirty or forty miles an hour.'

'What's the name of this place here?' demanded the officer.

'Hasn't got any name.'

A pale well-dressed negro stepped near.

'It was a yellow car,' he said, 'big yellow car. New.'

'See the accident?' asked the policeman.

'No, but the car passed me down the road, going faster'n forty. Going fifty, sixty.'

'Come here and let's have your name. Look out now. I want to get his name.'

Some words of this conversation must have reached Wilson, swaying in the office door, for suddenly a new theme found voice among his grasping cries:

'You don't have to tell me what kind of car it was! I know what kind of car it was!'

Watching Tom, I saw the wad of muscle back of his shoulder tighten under his coat. He walked quickly over to Wilson and, standing in front of him, seized him firmly by the upper arms.

'You've got to pull yourself together,' he said with soothing gruffness.

Wilson's eyes fell upon Tom; he started up on his tiptoes and then would have collapsed to his knees had not Tom held him upright.

'Listen,' said Tom, shaking him a little. 'I just got here a minute ago, from New York. I was bringing you that coupé we've been talking about. That yellow car I was driving this afternoon wasn't mine – do you hear? I haven't seen it all afternoon.'

Only the negro and I were near enough to hear what he said, but the policeman caught something in the tone and looked over with truculent eyes.

'What's all that?' he demanded.

'I'm a friend of his.' Tom turned his head but kept his hands firm on Wilson's body. 'He says he knows the car that did it ... It was a yellow car.'

Some dim impulse moved the policeman to look suspiciously at Tom.

'And what colour's your car?'

'It's a blue car, a coupé.'

'We've come straight from New York,' I said.

Someone who had been driving a little behind us confirmed this, and the policeman turned away.

'Now, if you'll let me have that name again correct –'

Picking up Wilson like a doll, Tom carried him into the office, set him down in a chair, and came back.

'If somebody'll come here and sit with him,' he snapped authoritatively. He watched while the two men standing closest glanced at each other and went unwillingly into the room. Then Tom shut the door on them and came down the single step, his eyes avoiding the table. As he passed close to me he whispered: 'Let's get out.'

Self-consciously, with his authoritative arms breaking the way, we pushed through the still gathering crowd, passing a hurried doctor, case in hand, who had been sent for in wild hope half an hour ago.

Tom drove slowly until we were beyond the bend – then his foot came down hard, and the coupé raced along through the night. In a little while I heard a low husky sob, and saw that the tears were overflowing down his face.

'The God damned coward!' he whimpered. 'He didn't even stop his car.'

The Buchanans' house floated suddenly toward us through the dark rustling trees. Tom stopped beside the porch and looked up at the second floor, where two windows bloomed with light among the vines.

'Daisy's home,' he said. As we got out of the car he glanced at me and frowned slightly.

'I ought to have dropped you in West Egg, Nick. There's nothing we can do tonight.'

A change had come over him, and he spoke gravely, and with decision. As we walked across the moonlight gravel to the porch he disposed of the situation in a few brisk phrases.

'I'll telephone for a taxi to take you home, and while you're waiting you and Jordan better go in the kitchen and have them get you some supper – if you want any.' He opened the door. 'Come in.'

'No, thanks. But I'd be glad if you'd order me the taxi. I'll wait outside.'

Jordan put her hand on my arm.

'Won't you come in, Nick?'

'No, thanks.'

I was feeling a little sick and I wanted to be alone. But Jordan lingered for a moment more.

'It's only half-past nine,' she said.

I'd be damned if I'd go in; I'd had enough of all of them for one day, and suddenly that included Jordan too. She must have seen something of this in my expression, for she turned abruptly away and ran up the porch steps into the house. I sat down for a few minutes with my head in my hands, until I heard the phone taken up inside and the butler's voice calling a taxi. Then I walked slowly down the drive away from the house, intending to wait by the gate.

I hadn't gone twenty yards when I heard my name and Gatsby stepped from between two bushes into the path. I must have felt pretty weird by that time, because I could think of nothing except the luminosity of his pink suit under the moon.

'What are you doing?' I inquired.

'Just standing here, old sport.'

Somehow, that seemed a despicable occupation. For all I knew he was going to rob the house in a moment; I wouldn't have been surprised to see sinister faces, the faces of 'Wolf-shiem's people', behind him in the dark shrubbery.

'Did you see any trouble on the road?' he asked after a minute.

'Yes.'

He hesitated.

'Was she killed?'

'Yes.'

'I thought so; I told Daisy I thought so. It's better that the shock should all come at once. She stood it pretty well.'

He spoke as if Daisy's reaction was the only thing that mattered.

'I got to West Egg by a side road,' he went on, 'and left the car in my garage. I don't think anybody saw us, but of course I can't be sure.'

I disliked him so much by this time that I didn't find it necessary to tell him he was wrong.

'Who was the woman?' he inquired.

'Her name was Wilson. Her husband owns the garage. How the devil did it happen?'

'Well, I tried to swing the wheel –' He broke off, and suddenly I guessed at the truth.

'Was Daisy driving?'

'Yes,' he said after a moment, 'but of course I'll say I was. You see, when we left New York she was very nervous and she thought it would steady her to drive – and this woman rushed out at us just as we were passing a car coming the other way. It all happened in a minute, but it seemed to me that she wanted to speak to us, thought we were somebody she knew. Well, first Daisy turned away from the woman toward the other car, and then she lost her nerve and turned back. The second my hand reached the wheel I felt the shock – it must have killed her instantly.'

'It ripped her open –'

'Don't tell me, old sport.' He winced. 'Anyhow – Daisy stepped on it. I tried to make her stop, but she couldn't, so I pulled on the emergency brake. Then she fell over into my lap and I drove on.

'She'll be all right tomorrow,' he said presently. 'I'm just going to wait here and see if he tries to bother her about that unpleasantness this afternoon. She's locked herself into her room, and if he tries any brutality she's going to turn the light out and on again.'

'He won't touch her,' I said. 'He's not thinking about her.'

'I don't trust him, old sport.'

'How long are you going to wait?'

'All night, if necessary. Anyhow, till they all go to bed.'

A new point of view occurred to me. Suppose Tom found out that Daisy had been driving. He might think he saw a connection in it – he might think anything. I looked at the house; there were two or three bright windows downstairs and the pink glow from Daisy's room on the ground floor.

'You wait here,' I said. 'I'll see if there's any sign of a commotion.'

I walked back along the border of the lawn, traversed the gravel softly, and tiptoed up the veranda steps. The drawing-room curtains were open, and I saw that the room was empty. Crossing the porch where we had dined that June night three months before, I came to a small rectangle of light which I guessed was the pantry window. The blind was drawn, but I found a rift at the sill.

Daisy and Tom were sitting opposite each other at the kitchen table, with a plate of cold fried chicken between them, and two bottles of ale. He was talking intently across the table at her, and in his earnestness his hand had fallen upon and covered her own. Once in a while she looked up at him and nodded in agreement.

They weren't happy, and neither of them had touched the chicken or the ale – and yet they weren't unhappy either. There was an unmistakable air of natural intimacy about the picture, and anybody would have said that they were conspiring together.

As I tiptoed from the porch I heard my taxi feeling its way along the dark road toward the house. Gatsby was waiting where I had left him in the drive.

'Is it all quiet up there?' he asked anxiously.

'Yes, it's all quiet.' I hesitated. 'You'd better come home and get some sleep.'

He shook his head.

'I want to wait here till Daisy goes to bed. Good night, old sport.'

He put his hands in his coat pockets and turned back eagerly to his scrutiny of the house, as though my presence marred the sacredness of the vigil. So I walked away and left him standing there in the moonlight – watching over nothing.

Chapter VIII

I COULDN'T sleep all night; a fog-horn was groaning incessantly on the Sound, and I tossed half-sick between grotesque reality and savage, frightening dreams. Toward dawn I heard a taxi go up Gatsby's drive, and immediately I jumped out of bed and began to dress – I felt that I had something to tell him, something to warn him about, and morning would be too late.

Crossing his lawn, I saw that his front door was still open and he was leaning against a table in the hall, heavy with dejection or sleep.

'Nothing happened,' he said wanly. 'I waited, and about four o'clock she came to the window and stood there for a minute and then turned out the light.'

His house had never seemed so enormous to me as it did that night when we hunted through the great rooms for cigarettes. We pushed aside curtains that were like pavilions, and felt over innumerable feet of dark wall for electric light switches – once I tumbled with a sort of splash upon the keys of a ghostly piano. There was an inexplicable amount of dust everywhere, and the rooms were musty, as though they hadn't been aired for many days. I found the humidor on an unfamiliar table, with two stale, dry cigarettes inside. Throwing open the french windows of the drawing-room, we sat smoking out into the darkness.

'You ought to go away,' I said. 'It's pretty certain they'll trace your car.'

'Go away *now*, old sport?'

'Go to Atlantic City for a week, or up to Montreal.'

He wouldn't consider it. He couldn't possibly leave Daisy until he knew what she was going to do. He was clutching at some last hope and I couldn't bear to shake him free.

It was this night that he told me the strange story of his youth with Dan Cody – told it to me because 'Jay Gatsby' had broken up like glass against Tom's hard malice, and the long secret extravaganza was played out. I think that he would have acknowledged anything now, without reserve, but he wanted to talk about Daisy.

She was the first 'nice' girl he had ever known. In various unrevealed capacities he had come in contact with such people, but always with indiscernible barbed wire between. He found her excitingly desirable. He went to her house, at first with other officers from Camp Taylor, then alone. It amazed him – he had never been in such a beautiful house before. But what gave it an air of breathless intensity, was that Daisy lived there – it was as casual a thing to her as his tent out at camp was to him. There was a ripe mystery about it, a hint of bedrooms upstairs more beautiful and cool than other bedrooms, of gay and radiant activities taking place through its corridors, and of romances that were not musty and laid away already in lavender but fresh and breathing and redolent of this year's shining motor-cars and of dances whose flowers were scarcely withered. It excited him, too, that many men had already loved Daisy – it increased her value in his eyes. He felt their presence all about the house, pervading the air with the shades and echoes of still vibrant emotions.

But he knew that he was in Daisy's house by a colossal accident. However glorious might be his future as Jay Gatsby, he was at present a penniless young man without a past, and at any moment the invisible cloak of his uniform might slip from his shoulders. So he made the most of his time. He took what he could get, ravenously and unscrupulously –

eventually he took Daisy one still October night, took her because he had no real right to touch her hand.

He might have despised himself, for he had certainly taken her under false pretences. I don't mean that he had traded on his phantom millions, but he had deliberately given Daisy a sense of security; he let her believe that he was a person from much the same strata as herself – that he was fully able to take care of her. As a matter of fact, he had no such facilities – he had no comfortable family standing behind him, and he was liable at the whim of an impersonal government to be blown anywhere about the world.

But he didn't despise himself and it didn't turn out as he had imagined. He had intended, probably, to take what he could and go – but now he found that he had committed himself to the following of a grail. He knew that Daisy was extraordinary, but he didn't realize just how extraordinary a 'nice' girl could be. She vanished into her rich house, into her rich, full life, leaving Gatsby – nothing. He felt married to her, that was all.

When they met again, two days later, it was Gatsby who was breathless, who was, somehow, betrayed. Her porch was bright with the bought luxury of star-shine; the wicker of the settee squeaked fashionably as she turned toward him and he kissed her curious and lovely mouth. She had caught a cold, and it made her voice huskier and more charming than ever, and Gatsby was overwhelmingly aware of the youth and mystery that wealth imprisons and preserves, of the freshness of many clothes, and of Daisy, gleaming like silver, safe and proud above the hot struggles of the poor.

'I can't describe to you how surprised I was to find out I loved her, old sport. I even hoped for a while that she'd throw me over, but she didn't, because she was in love with me too.

She thought I knew a lot because I knew different things from her ... Well, there I was, 'way off my ambitions, getting deeper in love every minute, and all of a sudden I didn't care. What was the use of doing great things if I could have a better time telling her what I was going to do?'

On the last afternoon before he went abroad, he sat with Daisy in his arms for a long, silent time. It was a cold fall day, with fire in the room and her cheeks flushed. Now and then she moved and he changed his arm a little, and once he kissed her dark shining hair. The afternoon had made them tranquil for a while, as if to give them a deep memory for the long parting the next day promised. They had never been closer in their month of love, nor communicated more profoundly one with another, than when she brushed silent lips against his coat's shoulder or when he touched the end of her fingers, gently, as though she were asleep.

He did extraordinarily well in the war. He was a captain before he went to the front, and following the Argonne battles he got his majority and the command of the divisional machine-guns. After the armistice he tried frantically to get home, but some complication or misunderstanding sent him to Oxford instead. He was worried now – there was a quality of nervous despair in Daisy's letters. She didn't see why he couldn't come. She was feeling the pressure of the world outside, and she wanted to see him and feel his presence beside her and be reassured that she was doing the right thing after all.

For Daisy was young and her artificial world was redolent of orchids and pleasant, cheerful snobbery and orchestras which set the rhythm of the year, summing up the sadness and suggestiveness of life in new tunes. All night the saxophones wailed the hopeless comment of the 'Beale Street Blues'[39] while a hundred pairs of golden and silver slippers shuffled the shining dust. At the grey tea hour there were always rooms that throbbed incessantly with this low, sweet fever, while fresh faces drifted here and there like rose petals blown by the sad horns around the floor.

Through this twilight universe Daisy began to move again with the season; suddenly she was again keeping half a dozen dates a day with half a dozen men, and drowsing asleep at dawn with the beads and chiffon of an evening dress tangled among dying orchids on the floor beside her bed. And all the time something within her was crying for a decision. She wanted her life shaped now, immediately – and the decision must be made by some force – of love, of money, of unquestionable practicality – that was close at hand.

That force took shape in the middle of spring with the arrival of Tom Buchanan. There was a wholesome bulkiness about his person and his position, and Daisy was flattered. Doubtless there was a certain struggle and a certain relief. The letter reached Gatsby while he was still at Oxford.

It was dawn now on Long Island and we went about opening the rest of the windows downstairs, filling the house with grey-turning, gold-turning light. The shadow of a tree fell abruptly across the dew and ghostly birds began to sing among the blue leaves. There was a slow, pleasant movement in the air, scarcely a wind, promising a cool, lovely day.

'I don't think she ever loved him.' Gatsby turned around from a window and looked at me challengingly. 'You must remember, old sport, she was very excited this afternoon. He told her those things in a way that frightened her – that made it look as if I was some kind of cheap sharper. And the result was she hardly knew what she was saying.'

He sat down gloomily.

'Of course she might have loved him just for a minute, when they were first married – and loved me more even then, do you see?'

Suddenly he came out with a curious remark.

'In any case,' he said, 'it was just personal.'

What could you make of that, except to suspect some intensity in his conception of the affair that couldn't be measured?

He came back from France when Tom and Daisy were still on their wedding trip, and made a miserable but irresistible journey to Louisville on the last of his army pay. He stayed there a week, walking the streets where their footsteps had clicked together through the November night and revisiting the out-of-the-way places to which they had driven in her white car. Just as Daisy's house had always seemed to him more mysterious and gay than other houses, so his idea of the city itself, even though she was gone from it, was pervaded with a melancholy beauty.

He left feeling that if he had searched harder, he might have found her – that he was leaving her behind. The day-coach – he was penniless now – was hot. He went out to the open vestibule and sat down on a folding-chair, and the station slid away and the backs of unfamiliar buildings moved by. Then out into the spring fields, where a yellow trolley raced them for a minute with people in it who might once have seen the pale magic of her face along the casual street.

The track curved and now it was going away from the sun, which, as it sank lower, seemed to spread itself in benediction over the vanishing city where she had drawn her breath. He stretched out his hand desperately as if to snatch only a wisp of air, to save a fragment of the spot that she had made lovely for him. But it was all going by too fast now for his blurred eyes and he knew that he had lost that part of it, the freshest and the best, forever.

It was nine o'clock when we finished breakfast and went out on the porch. The night had made a sharp difference in the weather and there was an autumn flavour in the air. The gardener, the last one of Gatsby's former servants, came to the foot of the steps.

'I'm going to drain the pool today, Mr Gatsby. Leaves'll start falling pretty soon, and then there's always trouble with the pipes.'

'Don't do it today,' Gatsby answered. He turned to me apologetically. 'You know, old sport, I've never used that pool all summer?'

I looked at my watch and stood up.

'Twelve minutes to my train.'

I didn't want to go to the city. I wasn't worth a decent stroke of work, but it was more than that – I didn't want to leave Gatsby. I missed that train, and then another, before I could get myself away.

'I'll call you up,' I said finally.

'Do, old sport.'

'I'll call you about noon.'

We walked slowly down the steps.

'I suppose Daisy'll call too.' He looked at me anxiously, as if he hoped I'd corroborate this.

'I suppose so.'

'Well, good-bye.'

We shook hands and I started away. Just before I reached the hedge I remembered something and turned around.

'They're a rotten crowd,' I shouted across the lawn. 'You're worth the whole damn bunch put together.'

I've always been glad I said that. It was the only compliment I ever gave him, because I disapproved of him from

146

beginning to end. First he nodded politely, and then his face broke into that radiant and understanding smile, as if we'd been in ecstatic cahoots on that fact all the time. His gorgeous pink rag of a suit made a bright spot of colour against the white steps, and I thought of the night when I first came to his ancestral home, three months before. The lawn and drive had been crowded with the faces of those who guessed at his corruption – and he had stood on those steps, concealing his incorruptible dream, as he waved them good-bye.

I thanked him for his hospitality. We were always thanking him for that – I and the others.

'Good-bye,' I called. 'I enjoyed breakfast, Gatsby.'

Up in the city, I tried for a while to list the quotations on an interminable amount of stock, then I fell asleep in my swivel-chair. Just before noon the phone woke me, and I started up with sweat breaking out on my forehead. It was Jordan Baker; she often called me up at this hour because the uncertainty of her own movements between hotels and clubs and private houses made her hard to find in any other way. Usually her voice came over the wire as something fresh and cool, as if a divot from a green golf-links had come sailing in at the office window, but this morning it seemed harsh and dry.

'I've left Daisy's house,' she said. 'I'm at Hempstead,[40] and I'm going down to Southampton[41] this afternoon.'

Probably it had been tactful to leave Daisy's house, but the act annoyed me, and her next remark made me rigid.

'You weren't so nice to me last night.'

'How could it have mattered then?'

Silence for a moment. Then:

'However – I want to see you.'

'I want to see you, too.'

'Suppose I don't go to Southampton, and come into town this afternoon?'

'No – I don't think this afternoon.'

'Very well.'

'It's impossible this afternoon. Various – '

We talked like that for a while, and then abruptly we weren't talking any longer. I don't know which of us hung up with a sharp click, but I know I didn't care. I couldn't have talked to her across a tea-table that day if I never talked to her again in this world.

I called Gatsby's house a few minutes later, but the line was busy. I tried four times; finally an exasperated central told me the wire was being kept open for long distance from Detroit. Taking out my time-table, I drew a small circle around the three-fifty train. Then I leaned back in my chair and tried to think. It was just noon.

When I passed the ashheaps on the train that morning I had crossed deliberately to the other side of the car. I supposed there'd be a curious crowd around there all day with little boys searching for dark spots in the dust, and some garrulous man telling over and over what had happened, until it became less and less real even to him and he could tell it no longer, and Myrtle Wilson's tragic achievement was forgotten. Now I want to go back a little and tell what happened at the garage after we left there the night before.

They had difficulty in locating the sister, Catherine. She must have broken her rule against drinking that night, for when she arrived she was stupid with liquor and unable to understand that the ambulance had already gone to Flushing. When they convinced her of this, she immediately fainted, as if that was the intolerable part of the affair. Someone, kind or curious, took her in his car and drove her in the wake of her sister's body.

Until long after midnight a changing crowd lapped up against the front of the garage, while George Wilson rocked himself back and forth on the couch inside. For a while the door of the office was open, and everyone who came into the garage glanced irresistibly through it. Finally someone said it was a shame, and closed the door. Michaelis and several other men were with him; first, four or five men, later two or three men. Still later Michaelis had to ask the last stranger to wait there fifteen minutes longer, while he went back to his own place and made a pot of coffee. After that, he stayed there alone with Wilson until dawn.

About three o'clock the quality of Wilson's incoherent muttering changed – he grew quieter and began to talk about the yellow car. He announced that he had a way of finding out whom the yellow car belonged to, and then he blurted out that a couple of months ago his wife had come from the city with her face bruised and her nose swollen.

But when he heard himself say this, he flinched and began to cry 'Oh, my God!' again in his groaning voice. Michaelis made a clumsy attempt to distract him.

'How long have you been married, George? Come on there, try and sit still a minute, and answer my question. How long have you been married?'

'Twelve years.'

'Ever had any children? Come on, George, sit still – I asked you a question. Did you ever have any children?'

The hard brown beetles kept thudding against the dull light, and whenever Michaelis heard a car go tearing along the road outside it sounded to him like the car that hadn't stopped a few hours before. He didn't like to go into the garage, because the work bench was stained where the body had been lying, so he moved uncomfortably around the office – he knew every object

in it before morning – and from time to time sat down beside
Wilson trying to keep him more quiet.

'Have you got a church you go to sometimes, George?
Maybe even if you haven't been there for a long time? Maybe
I could call up the church and get a priest to come over and
he could talk to you, see?'

'Don't belong to any.'

'You ought to have a church, George, for times like this. You
must have gone to church once. Didn't you get married in a
church? Listen, George, listen to me. Didn't you get married
in a church?'

'That was a long time ago.'

The effort of answering broke the rhythm of his rocking –
for a moment he was silent. Then the same half-knowing, half-
bewildered look came back into his faded eyes.

'Look in the drawer there,' he said, pointing at the desk.

'Which drawer?'

'That drawer – that one.'

Michaelis opened the drawer nearest his hand. There was
nothing in it but a small, expensive dog-leash, made of leather
and braided silver. It was apparently new.

'This?' he inquired, holding it up.

Wilson stared and nodded.

'I found it yesterday afternoon. She tried to tell me about
it, but I knew it was something funny.'

'You mean your wife bought it?'

'She had it wrapped in tissue paper on her bureau.'

Michaelis didn't see anything odd in that, and he gave
Wilson a dozen reasons why his wife might have bought the
dog-leash. But conceivably Wilson had heard some of these
same explanations before, from Myrtle, because he began
saying 'Oh, my God!' again in a whisper – his comforter left
several explanations in the air.

'Then he killed her,' said Wilson. His mouth dropped open suddenly.

'Who did?'

'I have a way of finding out.'

'You're morbid, George,' said his friend. 'This has been a strain to you and you don't know what you're saying. You'd better try and sit quiet till morning.'

'He murdered her.'

'It was an accident, George.'

Wilson shook his head. His eyes narrowed and his mouth widened slightly with the ghost of a superior 'Hm!'

'I know,' he said definitely. 'I'm one of these trusting fellas and I don't think any harm to *no*body, but when I get to know a thing I know it. It was the man in that car. She ran out to speak to him and he wouldn't stop.'

Michaelis had seen this too, but it hadn't occurred to him that there was any special significance in it. He believed that Mrs Wilson had been running away from her husband, rather than trying to stop any particular car.

'How could she of been like that?'

'She's a deep one,' said Wilson, as if that answered the question. 'Ah-h-h –'

He began to rock again, and Michaelis stood twisting the leash in his hand.

'Maybe you got some friend that I could telephone for, George?'

This was a forlorn hope – he was almost sure that Wilson had no friend: there was not enough of him for his wife. He was glad a little later when he noticed a change in the room, a blue quickening by the window, and realized that dawn wasn't far off. About five o'clock it was blue enough outside to snap off the light.

Wilson's glazed eyes turned out to the ashheaps, where small grey clouds took on fantastic shapes and scurried here and there in the faint dawn wind.

'I spoke to her,' he muttered, after a long silence. 'I told her she might fool me but she couldn't fool God. I took her to the window' – with an effort he got up and walked to the rear window and leaned with his face pressed against it – 'and I said "God knows what you've been doing, everything you've been doing. You may fool me, but you can't fool God!"'

Standing behind him, Michaelis saw with a shock that he was looking at the eyes of Doctor T. J. Eckleburg, which had just emerged, pale and enormous, from the dissolving night.

'God sees everything,' repeated Wilson.

'That's an advertisement,' Michaelis assured him. Something made him turn away from the window and look back into the room. But Wilson stood there a long time, his face close to the window pane, nodding into the twilight.

By six o'clock Michaelis was worn out, and grateful for the sound of a car stopping outside. It was one of the watchers of the night before who had promised to come back, so he cooked breakfast for three, which he and the other man ate together. Wilson was quieter now, and Michaelis went home to sleep; when he awoke four hours later and hurried back to the garage, Wilson was gone.

His movements – he was on foot all the time – were afterward traced to Port Roosevelt and then to Gad's Hill,[42] where he bought a sandwich that he didn't eat, and a cup of coffee. He must have been tired and walking slowly, for he didn't reach Gad's Hill until noon. Thus far there was no difficulty in accounting for his time – there were boys who had seen a man 'acting sort of crazy', and motorists at whom he stared oddly from the side of the road. Then for three hours he disappeared from view. The police, on the strength of what he said to Michaelis, that he 'had a way of finding out', supposed that he spent that time going from garage to garage thereabout, inquiring for a yellow car. On the other hand, no garage man who had seen him ever came forward, and perhaps he had an easier, surer way of finding out what he wanted to know. By half-past two he was in West Egg, where he asked someone the way to Gatsby's house. So by that time he knew Gatsby's name.

At two o'clock Gatsby put on his bathing-suit and left word with the butler that if anyone phoned word was to be brought to him at the pool. He stopped at the garage for a pneumatic mattress that had amused his guests during the summer, and the chauffeur helped him to pump it up. Then he gave instructions that the open car wasn't to be taken out under any circumstances – and this was strange, because the front right fender needed repair.

Gatsby shouldered the mattress and started for the pool. Once he stopped and shifted it a little, and the chauffeur asked him if he needed help, but he shook his head and in a moment disappeared among the yellowing trees.

No telephone message arrived, but the butler went without his sleep and waited for it until four o'clock – until long after there was anyone to give it to if it came. I have an idea that Gatsby himself didn't believe it would come, and perhaps he no longer cared. If that was true he must have felt that he had lost the old warm world, paid a high price for living too long with a single dream. He must have looked up at an unfamiliar sky through frightening leaves and shivered as he found what a grotesque thing a rose is and how raw the sunlight was upon the scarcely created grass. A new world, material without being real, where poor ghosts, breathing dreams like air, drifted fortuitously about ... like that ashen, fantastic figure gliding toward him through the amorphous trees.

The chauffeur – he was one of Wolfshiem's protégés – heard the shots – afterwards he could only say that he hadn't thought anything much about them. I drove from the station directly to Gatsby's house and my rushing anxiously up the front steps was the first thing that alarmed anyone. But they knew then, I firmly believe. With scarcely a word said, four of us, the chauffeur, butler, gardener, and I hurried down to the pool.

There was a faint, barely perceptible movement of the water as the fresh flow from one end urged its way toward the drain at the other. With little ripples that were hardly the shadows of waves, the laden mattress moved irregularly down the pool. A small gust of wind that scarcely corrugated the surface was enough to disturb its accidental course with its accidental burden. The touch of a cluster of leaves revolved it slowly, tracing, like the leg of transit, a thin red circle in the water.

It was after we started with Gatsby toward the house that the gardener saw Wilson's body a little way off in the grass, and the holocaust was complete.

Chapter IX

AFTER two years I remember the rest of that day, and that night and the next day, only as an endless drill of police and photographers and newspaper men in and out of Gatsby's front door. A rope stretched across the main gate and a policeman by it kept out the curious, but little boys soon discovered that they could enter through my yard, and there were always a few of them clustered open-mouthed about the pool. Someone with a positive manner, perhaps a detective, used the expression 'madman' as he bent over Wilson's body that afternoon, and the adventitious authority of his voice set the key for the newspaper reports next morning.

Most of those reports were a nightmare – grotesque, circumstantial, eager, and untrue. When Michaelis's testimony at the inquest brought to light Wilson's suspicions of his wife I thought the whole tale would shortly be served up in racy pasquinade – but Catherine, who might have said anything, didn't say a word. She showed a surprising amount of character about it too – looked at the corner with determined eyes under that corrected brow of hers, and swore that her sister had never seen Gatsby, that her sister was completely happy with her husband, that her sister had been into no mischief whatever. She convinced herself of it, and cried into her handkerchief, as if the very suggestion was more than she could endure. So Wilson was reduced to a man 'deranged by grief' in order that the case might remain in its simplest form. And it rested there.

But all this part of it seemed remote and unessential. I found myself on Gatsby's side, and alone. From the moment I telephoned news of the catastrophe to West Egg village, every surmise about him, and every practical question, was referred to me. At first I was surprised and confused; then, as he lay in his house and didn't move or breathe or speak, hour upon hour, it grew upon me that I was responsible, because no one else was interested – interested, I mean, with that intense personal interest to which everyone has some vague right at the end.

I called up Daisy half an hour after we found him, called her instinctively and without hesitation. But she and Tom had gone away early that afternoon, and taken baggage with them.

'Left no address?'

'No.'

'Say when they'd be back?'

'No.'

'Any idea where they are? How I could reach them?'

'I don't know. Can't say.'

I wanted to get somebody for him. I wanted to go into the room where he lay and reassure him: 'I'll get somebody for you, Gatsby. Don't worry. Just trust me and I'll get somebody for you –'

Meyer Wolfshiem's name wasn't in the phone book. The butler gave me his office address on Broadway, and I called Information, but by the time I had the number it was long after five, and no one answered the phone.

'Will you ring again?'

'I've rung three times.'

'It's very important.'

'Sorry. I'm afraid no one's there.'

I went back to the drawing-room and thought for an instant that they were chance visitors, all these official people who suddenly filled it. But, though they drew back the sheet and looked at Gatsby with shocked eyes, his protest continued in my brain:

'Look here, old sport, you've got to get somebody for me. You've got to try hard. I can't go through this alone.'

Someone started to ask me questions, but I broke away and going upstairs looked hastily through the unlocked parts of his desk – he'd never told me definitely that his parents were dead. But there was nothing – only the picture of Dan Cody, a token of forgotten violence, staring down from the wall.

Next morning I sent the butler to New York with a letter to Wolfshiem, which asked for information and urged him to come out on the next train. That request seemed superfluous when I wrote it. I was sure he'd start when he saw the newspapers, just as I was sure there'd be a wire from Daisy before noon – but neither a wire nor Mr Wolfshiem arrived; no one arrived except more police and photographers and newspaper men. When the butler brought back Wolfshiem's answer I began to have a feeling of defiance, of scornful solidarity between Gatsby and me against them all.

Dear Mr Carraway. This has been one of the most terrible shocks of my life to me I hardly can believe it that it is true at all. Such a mad act as that man did should make us all think. I cannot come down now as I am tied up in some very important business and cannot get mixed up in this thing now. If there is anything I can do a little later let me know in a letter by Edgar. I hardly know where I am when I hear about a thing like this and am completely knocked down and out.

Yours truly
MEYER WOLFSHIEM

and then hasty addenda beneath:

Let me know about the funeral etc do not know his family at all.

When the phone rang that afternoon and Long Distance

said Chicago was calling I thought this would be Daisy at last. But the connection came through as a man's voice, very thin and far away.

'This is Slagle speaking . . .'

'Yes?' The name was unfamiliar.

'Hell of a note, isn't it? Get my wire?'

'There haven't been any wires.'

'Young Parke's in trouble,' he said rapidly. 'They picked him up when he handed the bonds over the counter.[43] They got a circular from New York giving 'em the numbers just five minutes before. What d'you know about that, hey? You never can tell in these hick towns –'

'Hello!' I interrupted breathlessly. 'Look here – this isn't Mr Gatsby. Mr Gatsby's dead.'

There was a long silence on the other end of the wire, followed by an exclamation . . . then a quick squawk as the connection was broken.

I think it was on the third day that a telegram signed Henry C. Gatz arrived from a town in Minnesota. It said only that the sender was leaving immediately and to postpone the funeral until he came.

It was Gatsby's father, a solemn old man, very helpless and dismayed, bundled up in a long cheap ulster against the warm September day. His eyes leaked continuously with excitement, and when I took the bag and umbrella from his hands he began to pull so incessantly at his sparse grey beard that I had difficulty in getting off his coat. He was on the point of collapse, so I took him into the music-room and made him sit down while I sent for something to eat. But he wouldn't eat, and the glass of milk spilled from his trembling hand.

'I saw it in the Chicago newspaper,' he said. 'It was all in the Chicago newspaper. I started right away.'

'I didn't know how to reach you.'

His eyes, seeing nothing, moved ceaselessly about the room. 'It was a madman,' he said. 'He must have been mad.'

'Wouldn't you like some coffee?' I urged him.

'I don't want anything. I'm all right now, Mr –'

'Carraway.'

'Well, I'm all right now. Where have they got Jimmy?'

I took him into the drawing-room, where his son lay, and left him there. Some little boys had come up on the steps and were looking into the hall; when I told them who had arrived, they went reluctantly away.

After a little while Mr Gatz opened the door and came out, his mouth ajar, his face flushed slightly, his eyes leaking isolated and unpunctual tears. He had reached an age where death no longer has the quality of ghastly surprise, and when he looked around him now for the first time and saw the height and splendour of the hall and the great rooms opening out from it into other rooms, his grief began to be mixed with an awed pride. I helped him to a bedroom upstairs; while he took off his coat and vest I told him that all arrangements had been deferred until he came.

'I didn't know what you'd want, Mr Gatsby –'

'Gatz is my name.'

'– Mr Gatz. I thought you might want to take the body West.'

He shook his head.

'Jimmy always liked it better down East. He rose up to his position in the East. Were you a friend of my boy's, Mr –?'

'We were close friends.'

'He had a big future before him, you know. He was only a young man, but he had a lot of brain power here.'

He touched his head impressively, and I nodded.

'If he'd of lived, he'd of been a great man. A man like James J. Hill.[44] He'd of helped build up the country.'

'That's true.' I said, uncomfortably.

He fumbled at the embroidered coverlet, trying to take it from the bed, and lay down stiffly – was instantly asleep.

That night an obviously frightened person called up, and demanded to know who I was before he would give his name.

'This is Mr Carraway,' I said.

'Oh!' He sounded relieved. 'This is Klipspringer.'

I was relieved too, for that seemed to promise another friend at Gatsby's grave. I didn't want it to be in the papers and draw a sightseeing crowd, so I'd been calling up a few people myself. They were hard to find.

'The funeral's tomorrow,' I said. 'Three o'clock, here at the house. I wish you'd tell anybody who'd be interested.'

'Oh, I will,' he broke out hastily. 'Of course I'm not likely to see anybody, but if I do.'

His tone made me suspicious.

'Of course you'll be there yourself.'

'Well, I'll certainly try. What I called up about is –'

'Wait a minute,' I interrupted. 'How about saying you'll come?'

'Well, the fact is – the truth of the matter is that I'm staying with some people up here in Greenwich,[45] and they rather expect me to be with them tomorrow. In fact, there's a sort of picnic or something. Of course I'll do my best to get away.'

I ejaculated an unrestrained 'Huh!' and he must have heard me, for he went on nervously:

'What I called up about was a pair of shoes I left there. I wonder if it'd be too much trouble to have the butler send them on. You see, they're tennis shoes, and I'm sort of helpless without them. My address is care of B. F. –'

I didn't hear the rest of the name, because I hung up the receiver.

After that I felt a certain shame for Gatsby – one gentleman to whom I telephoned implied that he had got what he deserved. However, that was my fault, for he was one of those who used to sneer most bitterly at Gatsby on the courage of Gatsby's liquor, and I should have known better than to call him.

The morning of the funeral I went up to New York to see Meyer Wolfshiem; I couldn't seem to reach him any other way. The door that I pushed open, on the advice of an elevator boy, was marked 'The Swastika Holding Company',[46] and at first there didn't seem to be anyone inside. But when I'd shouted 'hello' several times in vain, an argument broke out behind a partition, and presently a lovely Jewess appeared at an interior door and scrutinized me with black hostile eyes.

'Nobody's in,' she said. 'Mr Wolfshiem's gone to Chicago.'

The first part of this was obviously untrue, for someone had begun to whistle 'The Rosary', tunelessly, inside.

'Please say that Mr Carraway wants to see him.'

'I can't get him back from Chicago, can I?'

At this moment a voice, unmistakably Wolfshiem's, called 'Stella!' from the other side of the door.

'Leave your name on the desk,' she said quickly. 'I'll give it to him when he gets back.'

'But I know he's there.'

She took a step toward me and began to slide her hands indignantly up and down her hips.

'You young men think you can force your way in here any time,' she scolded. 'We're getting sickantired of it. When I say he's in Chicago, he's in Chicago.'

I mentioned Gatsby.

'Oh-h!' She looked at me over again. 'Will you just – What was your name?'

She vanished. In a moment Meyer Wolfshiem stood solemnly in the doorway, holding out both hands. He drew me into his office, remarking in a reverent voice that it was a sad time for all of us, and offered me a cigar.

'My memory goes back to when first I met him,' he said. 'A young major just out of the army and covered over with medals he got in the war. He was so hard up he had to keep on wearing his uniform because he couldn't buy some regular clothes. First time I saw him was when he came into Winebrenner's poolroom at Forty-third Street and asked for a job. He hadn't eat anything for a couple of days. "Come on have some lunch with me," I said. He ate more than four dollars' worth of food in half an hour.'

'Did you start him in business?' I inquired.

'Start him! I made him.'

'Oh.'

'I raised him up out of nothing, right out of the gutter. I saw right away he was a fine-appearing, gentlemanly young man, and when he told me he was at Oggsford I knew I could use him good. I got him to join the American Legion and he used to stand high there. Right off he did some work for a client of mine up to Albany. We were so thick like that in everything' – he held up two bulbous fingers – 'always together.'

I wondered if this partnership had included the World's Series transaction in 1919.

'Now he's dead,' I said after a moment. 'You were his closest friend, so I know you'll want to come to his funeral this afternoon.'

'I'd like to come.'

'Well, come then.'

The hair in his nostrils quivered slightly, and as he shook his head his eyes filled with tears.

'I can't do it – I can't get mixed up in it,' he said.

'There's nothing to get mixed up in. It's all over now.'

'When a man gets killed I never like to get mixed up in it in any way. I keep out. When I was a young man it was different – if a friend of mine died, no matter how, I stuck with them to the end. You may think that's sentimental, but I mean it – to the bitter end.'

I saw that for some reason of his own he was determined not to come, so I stood up.

'Are you a college man?' he inquired suddenly.

For a moment I thought he was going to suggest a 'gonnegtion', but he only nodded and shook my hand.

'Let us learn to show our friendship for a man when he is alive and not after he is dead,' he suggested. 'After that my own rule is to let everything alone.'

When I left his office the sky had turned dark and I got back to West Egg in a drizzle. After changing my clothes I went next door and found Mr Gatz walking up and down excitedly in the hall. His pride in his son and in his son's possessions was continually increasing and now he had something to show me.

'Jimmy sent me this picture.' He took out his wallet with trembling fingers. 'Look there.'

It was a photograph of the house, cracked in the corners and dirty with many hands. He pointed out every detail to me eagerly. 'Look there!' and then sought admiration from my eyes. He had shown it so often that I think it was more real to him now than the house itself.

'Jimmy sent it to me. I think it's a very pretty picture. It shows up well.'

'Very well. Had you seen him lately?'

'He come out to see me two years ago and bought me the

house I live in now. Of course we was broke up when he run off from home, but I see now there was a reason for it. He knew he had a big future in front of him. And ever since he made a success he was very generous with me.'

He seemed reluctant to put away the picture, held it for another minute, lingeringly, before my eyes. Then he returned the wallet and pulled from his pocket a ragged old copy of a book called *Hopalong Cassidy*.[47]

'Look here, this is a book he had when he was a boy. It just shows you.'

He opened it at the back cover and turned it around for me to see. On the last fly-leaf was printed the word SCHEDULE, and the date September 12, 1906. And underneath:

Rise from bed..	6.00	A.M.
Dumbell exercise and wall-scaling	6.15–6.30	,,
Study electricity, etc..	7.15–8.15	,,
Work	8.30–4.30	P.M.
Baseball and sports	4.30–5.00	,,
Practise elocution, poise and how to attain it..........	5.00–6.00	,,
Study needed inventions..	7.00–9.00	,,

GENERAL RESOLVES

No wasting time at Shafters or [a name, indecipherable]
No more smokeing or chewing.
Bath every other day
Read one improving book or magazine per week
Save $5.00 [crossed out] $3.00 per week
Be better to parents

'I came across this book by accident,' said the old man. 'It just shows you, don't it?'

'It just shows you.'

'Jimmy was bound to get ahead. He always had some resolves like this or something. Do you notice what he's got about improving his mind? He was always great for that. He told me I et like a hog once, and I beat him for it.'

He was reluctant to close the book, reading each item aloud and then looking eagerly at me. I think he rather expected me to copy down the list for my own use.

A little before three the Lutheran minister arrived from Flushing, and I began to look involuntarily out the windows for other cars. So did Gatsby's father. And as the time passed and the servants came in and stood waiting in the hall, his eyes began to blink anxiously, and he spoke of the rain in a worried, uncertain way. The minister glanced several times at his watch, so I took him aside and asked him to wait for half an hour. But it wasn't any use. Nobody came.

About five o'clock our procession of three cars reached the cemetery and stopped in a thick drizzle beside the gate – first a motor hearse, horribly black and wet, then Mr Gatz and the minister and me in the limousine, and a little later four or five servants and the postman from West Egg, in Gatsby's station wagon, all wet to the skin. As we started through the gate into the cemetery I heard a car stop and then the sound of someone splashing after us over the soggy ground. I looked around. It was the man with owl-eyed glasses whom I had found marvelling over Gatsby's books in the library one night three months before.

I'd never seen him since then. I don't know how he knew about the funeral, or even his name. The rain poured down his thick glasses, and he took them off and wiped them to see the protecting canvas unrolled from Gatsby's grave.

I tried to think about Gatsby then for a moment, but he was already too far away, and I could only remember, without resentment, that Daisy hadn't sent a message or a flower.

Dimly I heard someone murmur 'Blessed are the dead that the rain falls on', and then the owl-eyed man said 'Amen to that', in a brave voice.

We straggled down quickly through the rain to the cars. Owl-eyes spoke to me by the gate.

'I couldn't get to the house,' he remarked.

'Neither could anybody else.'

'Go on!' He started. 'Why, my God! they used to go there by the hundreds.'

He took off his glasses and wiped them again, outside and in.

'The poor son-of-a-bitch,' he said.

One of my most vivid memories is of coming back West from prep school and later from college at Christmas time. Those who went farther than Chicago would gather in the old dim Union Station at six o'clock of a December evening, with a few Chicago friends, already caught up into their own holiday gaieties, to bid them a hasty good-bye. I remember the fur coats of the girls returning from Miss This-or-That's and the chatter of frozen breath and the hands waving overhead as we caught sight of old acquaintances, and the matchings of invitations: 'Are you going to the Ordways'? the Herseys'? the Schultzes'?' and the long green tickets clasped tight in our gloved hands. And last the murky yellow cars of the Chicago, Milwaukee and St Paul railroad looking cheerful as Christmas itself on the tracks beside the gate.

When we pulled out into the winter night and the real snow, our snow, began to stretch out beside us and twinkle against the windows, and the dim lights of small Wisconsin stations moved by, a sharp wild brace came suddenly into the air. We drew in deep breaths of it as we walked back from dinner through the cold vestibules, unutterably aware of our identity with this country for one strange hour, before we melted indistinguishably into it again.

That's my Middle West – not the wheat or the prairies or the lost Swede towns, but the thrilling returning trains of my youth, and the street lamps and sleigh bells in the frosty dark and the shadows of holly wreaths thrown by lighted windows on the snow. I am part of that, a little solemn with the feel of those long winters, a little complacent from growing up in the Carraway house in a city where dwellings are still called through decades by a family's name. I see now that this has been a story of the West, after all – Tom and Gatsby, Daisy and Jordan and I, were all Westerners, and perhaps we possessed some deficiency in common which made us subtly unadaptable to Eastern life.

Even when the East excited me most, even when I was most keenly aware of its superiority to the bored, sprawling, swollen towns beyond the Ohio, with their interminable inquisitions which spared only the children and the very old – even then it had always for me a quality of distortion. West Egg, especially, still figures in my more fantastic dreams. I see it as a night scene by El Greco: a hundred houses, at once conventional and grotesque, crouching under a sullen, overhanging sky and a lustreless moon. In the foreground four solemn men in dress suits are walking along the sidewalk with a stretcher on which lies a drunken woman in a white evening dress. Her hand, which dangles over the side, sparkles cold with jewels. Gravely the men turn in at a house – the wrong house. But no one knows the woman's name, and no one cares.

After Gatsby's death the East was haunted for me like that, distorted beyond my eyes' power of correction. So when the blue smoke of brittle leaves was in the air and the wind blew the wet laundry stiff on the line I decided to come back home.

There was one thing to be done before I left, an awkward, unpleasant thing that perhaps had better have been let alone. But I wanted to leave things in order and not just trust that obliging and indifferent sea to sweep my refuse away. I saw Jordan Baker and talked over and around what had happened to us together, and what had happened afterward to me, and she lay perfectly still, listening, in a big chair.

She was dressed to play golf, and I remember thinking she looked like a good illustration, her chin raised a little jauntily, her hair the colour of an autumn leaf, her face the same brown tint as the fingerless glove on her knee. When I had finished she told me without comment that she was engaged to another man. I doubted that, though there were several she could have married at a nod of her head, but I pretended to be surprised. For just a minute I wondered if I wasn't making a mistake, then I thought it all over again quickly and got up to say goodbye.

'Nevertheless you did throw me over,' said Jordan suddenly. 'You threw me over on the telephone. I don't give a damn about you now, but it was a new experience for me, and I felt a little dizzy for a while.'

We shook hands.

'Oh, and do you remember' – she added – 'a conversation we had once about driving a car?'

'Why – not exactly.'

'You said a bad driver was only safe until she met another bad driver? Well, I met another bad driver, didn't I? I mean it was careless of me to make such a wrong guess. I thought you were rather an honest, straightforward person. I thought it was your secret pride.'

'I'm thirty,' I said. 'I'm five years too old to lie to myself and call it honour.'

She didn't answer. Angry, and half in love with her, and tremendously sorry, I turned away.

One afternoon late in October I saw Tom Buchanan. He was walking ahead of me along Fifth Avenue in his alert, aggressive way, his hands out a little from his body as if to fight off interference, his head moving sharply here and there, adapting itself to his restless eyes. Just as I slowed up to avoid overtaking him he stopped and began frowning into the windows of a jewellery store. Suddenly he saw me and walked back, holding out his hand.

'What's the matter, Nick? Do you object to shaking hands with me?'

'Yes. You know what I think of you.'

'You're crazy, Nick,' he said quickly. 'Crazy as hell. I don't know what's the matter with you.'

'Tom,' I inquired, 'what did you say to Wilson that afternoon?'

He stared at me without a word, and I knew I had guessed right about those missing hours. I started to turn away, but he took a step after me and grabbed my arm.

'I told him the truth,' he said. 'He came to the door while we were getting ready to leave, and when I sent down word that we weren't in he tried to force his way upstairs. He was crazy enough to kill me if I hadn't told him who owned the car. His hand was on a revolver in his pocket every minute he was in the house –' He broke off defiantly. 'What if I did tell him? That fellow had it coming to him. He threw dust into your eyes just like he did in Daisy's, but he was a tough one. He ran over Myrtle like you'd run over a dog and never even stopped his car.'

There was nothing I could say, except the one unutterable fact that it wasn't true.

'And if you think I didn't have my share of suffering – look here, when I went to give up that flat and saw that damn box of dog biscuits sitting there on the sideboard, I sat down and cried like a baby. By God it was awful –'

I couldn't forgive him or like him, but I saw that what he had done was, to him, entirely justified. It was all very careless and confused. They were careless people, Tom and Daisy – they smashed up things and creatures and then retreated back into their money or their vast carelessness, or whatever it was that kept them together, and let other people clean up the mess they had made . . .

I shook hands with him; it seemed silly not to, for I felt suddenly as though I were talking to a child. Then he went into the jewellery store to buy a pearl necklace – or perhaps only a pair of cuff buttons – rid of my provincial squeamishness for ever.

Gatsby's house was still empty when I left – the grass on his lawn had grown as long as mine. One of the taxi drivers in the village never took a fare past the entrance gate without stopping for a minute and pointing inside; perhaps it was he who drove Daisy and Gatsby over to East Egg the night of the accident, and perhaps he had made a story about it all his own. I didn't want to hear it and I avoided him when I got off the train.

I spent my Saturday nights in New York because those gleaming, dazzling parties of his were with me so vividly that I could still hear the music and the laughter, faint and incessant, from his garden, and the cars going up and down his drive. One night I did hear a material car there, and saw its lights stop at his front steps. But I didn't investigate. Probably it was some final guest who had been away at the ends of the earth and didn't know that the party was over.

On the last night, with my trunk packed and my car sold to the grocer, I went over and looked at that huge incoherent failure of a house once more. On the white steps an obscene word, scrawled by some boy with a piece of brick, stood out clearly in the moonlight, and I erased it, drawing my shoe raspingly along the stone. Then I wandered down to the beach and sprawled out on the sand.

Most of the big shore places were closed now and there were hardly any lights except the shadowy, moving glow of a ferry-boat across the Sound. And as the moon rose higher the inessential houses began to melt away until gradually I became aware of the old island here that flowered once for Dutch sailors' eyes – a fresh, green breast of the new world. Its vanished trees, the trees that had made way for Gatsby's house, had once pandered in whispers to the last and greatest of all human dreams; for a transitory enchanted moment man must have held his breath in the presence of this continent, compelled into an aesthetic contemplation he neither understood nor desired, face to face for the last time in history with something commensurate to his capacity for wonder.

And as I sat there brooding on the old, unknown world, I thought of Gatsby's wonder when he first picked out the green light at the end of Daisy's dock. He had come a long way to this blue lawn, and his dream must have seemed so close that he could hardly fail to grasp it. He did not know that it was already behind him, somewhere back in that vast obscurity beyond the city, where the dark fields of the republic rolled on under the night.

Gatsby believed in the green light, the orgastic future that year by year recedes before us. It eluded us then, but that's no matter – tomorrow we will run faster, stretch out our arms further ... And one fine morning –

So we beat on, boats against the current, borne back ceaselessly into the past.

Colour – yellow → money, car, gold, Daisy's voice, money.

Green light = future Daisy + Gatsby.

This is possibly the longst lesson ever.

Future + past struggle

Gatsby

Tea party – pathetic fallacy throughout.

CBA

I need a wee so bad! Co!

Notes

Many of these notes draw on *Apparatus for F. Scott Fitzgerald's 'The Great Gatsby'*, by Matthew J. Bruccoli (University of South Carolina Press, 1974). Professor Bruccoli is the great Fitzgerald scholar, and anyone interested in the textual details of this novel should consult his work.

Title (p. 1): Right up to the last moment Fitzgerald preferred *Under the Red, White, and Blue* as the title and, indeed, blamed the novel's initial lack of success on the title it finally carried – one of his few errors of judgement during the inspired revisionary period.

Epigraph by Thomas Park D'Invilliers (p. 5): Written by Fitzgerald. D'Invilliers is a character, based on John Peale Bishop, in *This Side of Paradise*.

1. (p. 8) *Dukes of Buccleuch*: The Duke of Buccleuch also holds the title of Duke of Doncaster. Since Gatsby is snapped with a future Earl of Doncaster in Oxford (p. 65), Fitzgerald may be implying, almost as a private joke, that Nick may be more closely 'related' to Gatsby than he thinks!

2. (p. 9) *graduated from New Haven*: i.e. Yale.

3. (p. 11) *Lake Forest*: An exclusive suburb of Chicago. Ginevra King, an early love of Fitzgerald's, lived there.

4. (p. 13) *the same senior society*: There were six senior (which also meant secret) societies at Yale. Election to one of them was a considerable social achievement.

5. (p. 18) *The Rise of the Coloured Empires*: The allusion is to *The Rising Tide of Color* by Lothrop Stoddard (New York, Scribners, 1920). Bruccoli speculates that Fitzgerald 'did not want to use the correct

title and author'. Also he probably did not want Lothrop Stoddard confused with John L. Stoddard, mentioned on page 47.

6. (p. 23) *Westchester*: A suburb of New York.

7. (p. 23) *Jordan Baker*: The Jordan sports car and the Baker electric here seem to come together. Fitzgerald told Maxwell Perkins that she was based on champion golfer Edith Cummings.

8. (p. 23) *Asheville and Hot Springs and Palm Beach*: Fashionable resorts in North Carolina, Arkansas and Florida.

9. (p. 26) *valley of ashes*: According to Bruccoli, based on Flushing Meadow, a swampland that was being filled in with garbage and ashes and later became the site of the 1939 World's Fair.

10. (p. 31) *Town Tattle*: A scandal magazine of the Twenties.

11. (p. 31) *Simon Called Peter*: A popular novel by Robert Keable (New York, Dutton, 1921), which Fitzgerald disliked and thought immoral.

12. (p. 34) *Montauk Point*: A town at the eastern tip of Long Island.

13. (p. 42) *Frisco*: Joe Frisco, a comedian and eccentric dancer.

14. (p. 42) *Gilda Gray*: A dancing star of the Ziegfield Follies. She introduced a dance called the shimmy.

15. (p. 47) *Stoddard Lectures*: John L. Stoddard wrote fifteen volumes of illustrated travel books under the general title of *John L. Stoddard's Lectures*. ' "Gad's Hill", Dickens's home near Rochester, was illustrated in Volume Nine' (Bruccoli). See note to p. 152.

16. (p. 47) *Belasco*: David Belasco, a Broadway producer known for the realism of his sets.

17. (p. 48) *First Division . . . Twenty-eighth Infantry . . . Sixteenth*: In Fitzgerald's own copy these were revised to 'Third . . . Ninth Machine-Gun Battalion . . . Seventh Infantry'. See also *Argonne Forest* (p. 64). Bruccoli has done the work: 'On June 3, 1918, Nick's Ninth Machine-Gun Battalion was at Château-Thierry and Gatsby's Seventh Infantry was brought up to defend the town on the south riverbank. Both units were in the Third Division . . . *Argonne Forest*: Battle in the Meuse–Argonne offensive (September 25–

November 13, 1918) in which American troops played the key role. Although Gatsby's Third Division fought in the Meuse–Argonne campaign, it was in the Meuse Sector – at the opposite end of the battle line from the Argonne Forest. However, the First Division, Gatsby's and Nick's division in the first printing, was cited by General Pershing for valor in the Argonne.

'Fitzgerald's revision of Nick's and Gatsby's units makes it possible for them to have seen each other at Château-Thierry, but at the same time makes it extremely unlikely for Gatsby to have been in the Argonne Forest. This discrepancy does not necessarily indicate that Gatsby lies about his war record: there is no indication of that in the novel.'

18. (p. 48) *hydroplane*: in the Twenties this word was applied to both motorboats and seaplanes.

19. (p. 58) *Warwick*: A suburb of New York City in Orange County.

20. (p. 60) *bootlegger*: Someone engaged in the illegal sale of alcohol during Prohibition. Said to derive from the fact that dealers in illegal whisky hid the bottles in their boots.

21. (p. 60) *Von Hindenburg*: A German general in World War I and later President of Germany.

22. (p. 65) *Orderi di Danilo*: 'Montenegro has an order called *The Order of Danilo*. Is there any possible way you could find out for me there what it would look like – whether a courtesy decoration given to an American would bear an English inscription – or anything to give verisimilitude to the medal which sounds horribly amateurish?' (Fitzgerald to Perkins, December 1924.) It is absolutely right for Fitzgerald's purposes that he should allow Gatsby to have a medal that *looks* horribly amateurish (fake) but nevertheless has 'verisimilitude'; also that it is this most improbable of medals that Gatsby proffers, while he claims that 'every Allied government gave me a decoration'. Modesty? Humbug? Teasing?

23. (p. 65) *Trinity Quad*: Trinity College, Oxford.

24. (p. 66) *Port Roosevelt*: Bruccoli says this place has not been located or identified with an actual port, though the name is

inevitably suggestive. As he stresses, 'Fitzgerald superimposed a partly mythical geography upon the actual geography of Long Island.'

25. (p. 68) *Meyer Wolfshiem*: Based partly on the famous gambler Arnold Rothstein: 'in *Gatsby* . . . always starting from the *small* focal point that impressed me – my own meeting with Arnold Rothstein, for instance' (Fitzgerald to Corey Ford, July 1937).

26. (p. 71) *the man who fixed the World's Series back in 1919*: The 'Black Sox' affair. In 1919 a group of players in the Chicago White Sox, who were greatly favoured to win the World Series that year, were paid by a gang of professional gamblers to 'throw' the series to the Cincinnati Reds. (The Chicago players were apparently so ham-fisted that, after the second game, the writer Ring Lardner walked through their train compartment singing: 'I'm Forever Throwing Ball Games'.) The agreement among historians seems to be that Arnold Rothstein did not arrange the fix but knew about it and bet accordingly.

27. (p. 73) *Camp Taylor*: Near Louisville, Kentucky, where Fitzgerald himself was once stationed and where he met Zelda Sayre.

28. (p. 79) *Coney Island*: An amusement park in Brooklyn.

29. (p. 82) *The Journal*: A New York newspaper owned by William Randolph Hearst.

30. (p. 82) *Clay's Economics*: *Economics: An Introduction for the General Reader* (New York, Macmillan, 1918).

31. (p. 83) *Castle Rackrent*: A nineteenth-century novel by Maria Edgeworth.

32. (p. 85) *Kant at his church steeple*: Immanuel Kant was reputed to be in the habit of staring at a steeple while he was thinking.

33. (p. 88) *Adam's study*: in the classical style of the Scottish architects and designers Robert and James Adam.

34. (p. 94) *underground pipeline to Canada*: A Prohibition myth that alcohol was being piped into the United States from Canada.

35. (p. 96) *Madame de Maintenon*: Françoise d'Aubigne (1635–1719),

Marquise de Maintenon, second wife of Louis XIV and power behind the throne.

36. (p. 126) *Kapiolani*: A park on the Hawaiian island of Oahu.

37. (p. 126) *Punch Bowl*: A peak on the island of Oahu.

38. (p. 127) *drug-stores*: During Prohibition drugstores were permitted to sell whisky on prescription. Many became fronts for bootlegging.

39. (p. 143) *'Beale Street Blues'*: A famous song written by W. C. Handy in 1917.

40. (p. 147) *Hempstead*: A town on Long Island.

41. (p. 147) *Southampton*: A rich community on the South Shore of Long Island.

42. (p. 152) *Gad's Hill*: According to Bruccoli, no such place can be located on any map of Long Island in the Twenties. So it is part of Fitzgerald's 'mythic geography'. It obviously suggests 'Gatsby' (and *Gat*-sby suggests gun): it is also the site of the mock robbery of Falstaff by Prince Hal in *Henry IV, Part I*.

43. (p. 158) *handed the bonds over the counter*: An indication that Gatsby is involved in handling stolen securities, as Arnold Rothstein probably was.

44. (p. 160) *James J. Hill*: A railroad tycoon who lived in Fitzgerald's home town, St Paul, Minnesota. He built the Great Northern Railroad, which linked the Great Lakes with the Pacific Coast. Fitzgerald alludes to him several times in his work.

45. (p. 160) *Greenwich*: A town in Connecticut.

46. (p. 161) *'The Swastika Holding Company'*: This is not a suggestion that the Jewish Wolfshiem is a fascist! Hitler had adopted the device in 1920, but at the time Fitzgerald was writing this news had not been widely disseminated, and the swastika was simply a decorative device.

47. (p. 164) *Hopalong Cassidy*: A cowboy hero in the novel of that name written by Clarence E. Mulford in 1910 (Chicago, McClurg). Gatsby's inscription of 12 September 1906 is thus a small anachronism.

PENGUIN MODERN CLASSICS

FORTY STORIES
DONALD BARTHELME

'A magical gift of deadpan incongruity' John Updike

In *Forty Stories*, Donald Barthelme invented a random universe in which time, reality, meaning and language are turned exuberantly upside-down. He describes a startling array of occurrences – a lumberjack falls in love with a tree nymph; the poet Goethe becomes a loveable buffoon, spouting such eccentric aphorisms as 'Music is the frozen tapioca in the ice chest of History'; St Anthony's reclusive behaviour causes consternation among his friends and neighbours; and a vast swarm of porcupines, about to descend upon a university to enrol, forces the Dean to turn wrangler to herd them away. Tangling with the ludicrous and challenging the familiar, these small masterpieces provide piercing and hilarious insights into human idiosyncrasies.

'Among the leading innovative writers of modern fiction' *The New York Times*

With an Introduction by Dave Eggers

PENGUIN MODERN CLASSICS

LIGHT YEARS
JAMES SALTER

'An American master of fiction' *Independent*

Negra and Viri are a couple whose enviable life is centred on civilized pleasures, their children, a variety of friends, and days lived to the utmost, be it skating on a frozen river or summers by the sea. It is a world built on matrimony, and its details – the one moment, one hour, one day – recapture everything.

But fine cracks are beginning to spread through the shimmering surface – flaws that will eventually mar the lovely picture beyond repair. Seductive, witty, tender and resonant, *Light Years* is a ravishing novel of lost lives and the elusiveness of happiness.

'Remarkable … a moving ode to beautiful lives frayed by time' *Esquire*

PENGUIN MODERN CLASSICS

THIS SIDE OF PARADISE
F. SCOTT FITZGERALD

With an Introduction and Notes by Patrick O'Donnell

'One of the most wonderful writers of the twentieth century' *Financial Times*

Increasingly disillusioned by the rejection slips that studded the walls of his room and his on/off engagement to Zelda Sayre, Fitzgerald began his third revision of the novel that was to become *This Side of Paradise*. The story of a young man's painful sexual and intellectual awakening that echoes Fitzgerald's own career, it is also a portrait of a lost generation that followed straight on from the First World War, 'grown up to find all Gods dead, all wars fought, all faiths in man shaken' and wanting money and success more than anything else.

read more ●

Penguin Modern Classics

OTHER VOICES, OTHER ROOMS
TRUMAN CAPOTE

'Truman Capote is the most perfect writer of my generation' Norman Mailer

After the death of his mother, thirteen-year-old Joel Knox is summoned to live with a father he has never met in a vast decaying mansion in rural Alabama, its baroque splendour now faded and tarnished. But when he arrives, his father is nowhere to be seen and Joel is greeted instead by his prim, sullen new stepmother Miss Amy and his debauched Cousin Randolph – living like spirits in the fragile decadence of a house full of secrets.

Truman Capote's first novel, *Other Voices, Other Rooms* is a story of hallucinatory power, vividly conjuring up the Gothic landscape of the Deep South and a boy's first glimpse into a mysterious adult world.

With an Introduction by John Berendt

PENGUIN MODERN CLASSICS

THE GREAT GATSBY
F. SCOTT FITZGERALD

With an Introduction and Notes by Tony Tanner

'A classic, perhaps the supreme American novel'
John Carey, *Sunday Times*, Books of the Century

In *The Great Gatsby*, Fitzgerald brilliantly captures both the disillusion of post-war America and the moral failure of a society obsessed with wealth and status. But he does more than render the essence of a particular time and place, for in chronicling Gatsby's tragic pursuit of his dream, Fitzgerald re-creates the universal conflict between illusion and reality.

'Fitzgerald confronts no less a problem than what might be involved, what might be at stake, in trying to see, and *write*, America itself. *The Great Gatsby* is, I believe, the most perfectly crafted work of fiction to come out of America'
Tony Tanner

'It must be one of the most perfect novels ever written. Technique and tact and moral sensibility are as finely tuned as in any of Turgenev's great novels, and yet it is as American as Hollywood' John McGahern, *Irish Times*

PENGUIN MODERN CLASSICS

TENDER IS THE NIGHT
F. SCOTT FITZGERALD

'A tragedy backlit by beauty … captures the glittering hedonism of the South of France in the Twenties' *Express*

The French Riviera in the 1920s was 'discovered' by Dick and Nicole Diver who turned it into the playground of the rich and glamorous. Among their circle is Rosemary Hoyt, the beautiful starlet, who falls in love with Dick and is enraptured by Nicole, unaware of the corruption and dark secrets that haunt their marriage. When Dick becomes entangled with Rosemary, he fractures the delicate structure of his relationship with Nicole and the lustre of their life together begins to tarnish. *Tender is the Night* is an exquisite novel that reflects not only Fitzgerald's own personal tragedy, but also the shattered idealism of the society in which he lived.

Edited by Arnold Goldman

With an Introduction and Notes by Richard Godden

Contemporary ... Provocative ... Outrageous ...
Prophetic ... Groundbreaking ... Funny ... Disturbing ...
Different ... Moving ... Revolutionary ... Inspiring ...
Subversive ... Life-changing ...

What makes a modern classic?

At Penguin Classics our mission has always been to make the best books ever written available to everyone. And that also means constantly redefining and refreshing exactly what makes a 'classic'. That's where Modern Classics come in. Since 1961 they have been an organic, ever-growing and ever-evolving list of books from the last hundred (or so) years that we believe will continue to be read over and over again.

They could be books that have inspired political dissent, such as *Animal Farm*. Some, like *Lolita* or *A Clockwork Orange*, may have caused shock and outrage. Many have led to great films, from *In Cold Blood* to *One Flew Over the Cuckoo's Nest*. They have broken down barriers – whether social, sexual, or, in the case of *Ulysses*, the boundaries of language itself. And they might – like *Goldfinger* or *Scoop* – just be pure classic escapism. Whatever the reason, Penguin Modern Classics continue to inspire, entertain and enlighten millions of readers everywhere.

'No publisher has had more influence on reading habits than Penguin'
Independent

'Penguins provided a crash course in world literature'
Guardian

The best books ever written

PENGUIN CLASSICS

SINCE 1946

Find out more at www.penguinclassics.com